To Be or Not To Be: The Actors

by

Cathrine Goldstein

The New York Artists Series

To Be or Not To Be: The Actors

COPYRIGHT © 2018 by Cathrine Goldstein

Cover Art by *Angela Anderson*

The Wild Rose Press, Inc.
PO Box 708
Adams Basin, NY 14410-0708
Visit us at www.thewildrosepress.com

Publishing History
First Champagne Rose Edition, 2018
Print ISBN 978-1-5092-1710-6
Digital ISBN 978-1-5092-1711-3

The New York Artists Series
Published in the United States of America

"Perchance to dream, Jenna."

She smiled, biting the corner of her lip, exactly where his fingers had been only moments before. He reached up to touch her hair.

"Careful of the wig," she joked.

"And with that sugar addiction of yours, I figured Valentine's Day candy was a given."

"Oh, you know me so well, Mr. Hughes." Jenna fanned herself coquettishly.

He smiled. Trevor tossed the container aside and scooped Jenna into his arms. He held her tight.

"It feels like the nunnery scene." Jenna's voice was soft and breathy.

"Yes, but does this happen in the nunnery scene?" Trevor pulled her closer to him and his lips nearly brushed against hers.

"Maybe it should?"

"Are you telling me…?" Trevor studied her, his gaze locked on hers. "You want me to—?"

The stage manager stuck his head through the door. "Hamlet? Ophelia? Places, please."

Her body ached as he released her.

"Damn it." Trevor shook his head, jumping up and down in place. He stopped and smiled at Jenna, taking her hand and kissing it, before letting go. "Here we go."

"Break a leg, Trevor." She smiled at him, adrenaline rushing through her.

"You too, Jenna."

She made her way to the door and turned back. "Trevor? Here's to not sucking and having to do dinner theatre in the middle of nowhere."

Chuckling, Trevor tossed his head back and Jenna scooted out the door.

Praise for Cathrine Goldstein

"I've enjoyed previous work of Cathrine, but that was within a different genre—lucky me her talent knows no bounds."

~Shawna Shauntia Blog

~*~

"This book was beautiful. It has its funny moments and it has its sad moments... Amazingly written & well portrayed."

~Haddies Haven (5 Stars)

~*~

"A sweet summer romance, perfect for a day at the beach! A Rock Star romance, a whirlwind love affair, an ending that will leave you breathless!"

~Margie's Must Reads

~*~

"Love this... A wonderfully written, touching story."

~Books are Love

~*~

"A sweet romance... Malcolm Angel—The Rock Star bad boy every girl wants..."

~The Phantom Paragrapher (5 Stars)

Dedications

As always, for Jay, Penelope, and Pickle (Sarah)
~*~
And thank you to my parents
who sat through countless productions of *Hamlet*
in an old, decrepit theatre in the middle of Manhattan

A Note from the Author

The author wishes to thank the late William Shakespeare for his writing of the play scenes used within this work:

Hamlet (Act 3, Scene 1; Act 5, Scene 2)
and
Macbeth (Act 1, Scene 7)

Chapter One

Brrrinnnngggg!
Jenna Joyce covered her ears. Maybe, if she avoided it, maybe her phone would just stop ringing. It was too early to be her sister Olivia, so it had to be her mother. There was no doubt. It was time for their weekly argument about Jenna's choice to become an actor.

Jenna craned her neck so she could see directly from her tiny bathroom to the clock on her kitchen wall. Three-thirteen. Damn. Her audition was in just over an hour. She squeezed her eyes shut and mercifully, the ringing stopped.

"Thank God." Jenna exhaled and yanked her hairbrush through her hair. No, she wouldn't be able to dodge her mother much longer, but she was giving herself permission to avoid this particular argument until after her audition. Staring at her reflection, she took a deep breath. Forget fluttering, the butterflies in her stomach raged.

Brrrinnnngggg!
There it was again. Damn. This time she couldn't ignore it. With a shaking hand, Jenna made her way from the bathroom into the main space of her tiny studio apartment. She picked up the black receiver that dwarfed her hand and cheek. "Hel—?"

"Are you wearing makeup? Just wear some

makeup, please."

Jenna exhaled. It was her agent, the lovely but ruthless, Kat Price. "Of course."

"You're not wearing makeup, are you?"

Jenna snickered.

Kat let out an exasperated sigh. "I don't know why you think this is funny. He's picking Ophelia himself. *Himself*, Jenna."

As if Jenna weren't nervous enough. "I know that," she mumbled.

"This isn't still over those damned turtles, is it?"

Kat had many wonderful qualities, however, compassion was not one of them.

"Kat—"

"Jenna, listen to me. I know you think you have a right to a personal grudge against this man, but this is show biz. Get a tougher skin. I'm sure whatever he did, or didn't do, was not personal."

"I was counting on his endorsement."

"And I'm counting on a beach house before I turn seventy."

"But my father had one dying wish. To support that damned charity and Trevor Hughes was the celebrity who was supposed to help. Kat, he pretends to be this great guy—"

"He's a soap star, Jenna. And he's damned good at what he does. And what, or should I say whom, he pretends to be, is Caspian Locke, villain extraordinaire."

"And—"

"And what he did was to give you the chance of a lifetime. Jenna. The man is giving you the opportunity to audition for Ophelia to his Hamlet—in an Off-

Broadway show—and you're not even a year out of acting school." Kat sucked in a deep breath. "Do you know how lucky we are?"

"Yes, I do." Jenna rubbed the bundle of nerves in her belly. "It's just…they're all beautiful soap opera people. There's no use—"

"Oh Lord, save me. Is this going to be another one of those speeches about you not being beautiful so you want to be 'taken seriously'?"

"I'd want to be taken seriously if I was beautiful or—"

"I don't know what your issue is." Kat tapped her acrylic fingernails against her desk. This was what Kat did whenever she was deep in thought, and she did it with equal amounts of enthusiasm, whether she was pondering eyeliner or war. "Damn," she muttered. "I wish I had thought to call in your friend Loretta; that girl could make you a knockout in sixty seconds."

"Mm-hm—"

"Not that you're not already." Kat sighed again. "Listen to me, Jenna. You are incredibly beautiful. And Meryl Streep is the only actor ever to be taken seriously, so schmear some lip gloss on those damned lips, and call me when it's over."

So Jenna did. She slicked on a thin layer of light pink lip gloss, picked up a pile of headshots and résumés from the stack of papers on her desk, and grabbed her worn, light brown, canvas messenger bag. She stuffed the pictures inside and pulled her faded army jacket from her one tiny closet. She made her way to the door just as the phone rang again.

"You need a cell." Kat screamed as Jenna answered the phone.

"I—"

"Don't worry about that now. Are you wearing a dress?"

Jenna looked down at her uniform of old faded jeans, a white t-shirt, and combat boots. "I—"

"You're wearing those boots, aren't you?"

"No…?" Jenna shuffled from foot to foot.

"Wear the one damned dress you own."

Jenna looked over at her clothing rack pushed tightly into a corner. On the rack hung the one dress she did own, a knee-length, dark blue dress covered in tiny flowers, a gift from her mother when Jenna had graduated from the acting academy. It was an incredibly nice gesture, but it came with definite strings attached. Make it big within one year, or move back to upstate New York to help her mother run the family laundry business. Jenna closed her eyes and shook off a wave of terror.

"Kat, it has flowers on—"

"I know. And don't wear your boots with it. Too Nineties."

Jenna hung up the phone, stripped out of her clothes, leaving them in a heap on the floor she mentally labeled as "semi-clean," and pulled the dress off the hanger. She tucked her lips in tight not to get lip gloss on the dress, and pulled it over her head. She looked around. Without combat boots, the only thing she could wear was a pair of previously unworn, black, synthetic ballet flats her mother bought along with the dress.

Jenna slipped on the flats and spun around to take one quick look in the cracked full length mirror that stood near her clothing rack. "Ugh." Jenna rolled her eyes, grabbed her bag, and escaped before her agent could find her again.

****

"Ooo, ow. Ow. Ow." By the time she made her way to the subway, she was already cursing her mother and her agent for forcing her into these shoes. Jenna limped her way up the subway steps and full into New York City cold. She shuddered, pulling her coat closed tightly and wrapping her arms around herself. December in New York meant she was freezing in her flimsy dress and flimsier shoes. Truthfully, if it weren't for the stupid outfit she was wearing, she wouldn't have cared. She took a deep breath and as the frigid air stung her lungs, gazed up and down the avenue. People rushed by. Hotdogs vendors danced in the meager sunlight, trying to stay warm. Young men buzzed past, pushing wheeled wardrobes with the latest top-secret summer fashions. The street was brimming with energy and life. Despite the pain in her heels, she was happy. This crazy, wild, mixed-up city was home. And she was terrified at the idea of ever having to leave.

Jenna pushed on. She walked carefully, trying to keep her heels lifted from her shoes, avoiding direct contact with her blisters. Thankfully, the audition building was nearby.

She hobbled past the statue of the giant button and needle, and crossed the street, finding the old, red brick building. Signing in to the guest book at the front desk, she said hi to a disinterested security guard in a stained and wrinkled white uniform shirt then stepped into the elevator. After a harrowing ride in an elevator that stalled halfway to the seventh floor, she stepped out into a dark hallway.

A small handwritten sign saying, "Hamlet," with a tiny arrow showed the way. She limped down the hallway, stepping around the hazards of the worn frayed areas of the rug and the tiny piles of chipped plaster that had fallen from the broken ceiling and peeling walls. Finally, she found the door to the waiting room.

"Huh." Jenna mumbled to herself. She had been in this building many times before and she was pleasantly surprised Trevor Hughes held auditions in a place like this—a real, honest place—and not some shiny, fake building like Trump Tower. She pushed open the door to find a roomful of other young women, all holding the same sides as she was. She looked at each of them and had to suppress a giggle; one was more beautiful than the next. It was like walking into a casting for a men's magazine. "What am I doing here?" Jenna whispered.

The blonde sitting by the door shifted in her seat. The light floral scent of the girl's perfume wafted by. Good grief. There was no way, no way, someone who looked like Jenna could ever possibly fit into this beautiful cookie-cutter world. But she needed this job. Desperately. Jenna resigned herself, right there and then, to be fabulous. She had no choice. Just like at school, when the beautiful blondes were signing contracts for shampoo commercials and soap operas of their own, Jenna had to shine during her final plays. When she took her curtain call after performing Irina in *Three Sisters*, she got a standing ovation.

Kat Price came right up and gave her business card to Jenna. "Call me. Talent like yours doesn't come along very often. You can be great. You just need some makeup."

Then Kat swooshed her black silk wrap over her shoulders and sauntered away, leaving Jenna to wonder if she had just been complimented or insulted. She didn't ponder it long before Don Oleesa, already her coach, ambled up to Jenna and invited her into his advanced classes. It had been a good day.

This day, however, she wasn't so sure about. As she looked around again, Jenna was certain a few of the girls snickered at her. She thought long and hard about turning and leaving. After all, the audience would have to believe Hamlet was in love with Ophelia—so to star opposite Trevor, they would need someone much more beautiful than she. But to leave meant giving up.

No way. Jenna steeled her nerves, adjusted her army green jacket, and signed herself in. Wincing from the pain of her new blisters, she tip-toed gingerly over to an empty seat and plopped down. She did not put on lip gloss and a dress just to chicken out. Besides, giving up wasn't an option. After forty minutes of running lines in her head, she was finally called into the audition room.

Jenna took one look at Trevor and gasped. For a moment, all her anger dissipated, replaced with a warm flush reminding her she was female. She shook her head, and as her body reflexively fought for its next breath, she discreetly studied him. His head was bowed as he sat on a high stool, clutching a faded acting edition of *Hamlet*. She let her gaze run up him—his boots and jeans, his faded dark gray t-shirt—right up to the scruff on his chin and the dark brown hair that was perfectly wavy and messy, framing his chiseled cheekbones and tanned skin. Like Hamlet himself, Trevor was dark and brooding but good Lord, he was handsome. No wonder millions of women tuned into his show daily to watch him as soap opera villain, Caspian Locke. Really, who could blame them?

Her body leaned forward. She stared at the long strong muscles of his exposed forearms and his large hands grasping a copy of *Hamlet*, and suddenly grew very sad. It was as if he were the unattainable remedy to all her pain. He turned his head slowly and she stepped backward. She smiled a tiny dejected smile at him and he nodded, offering a small smile back. His face seemed to crack with his smile, as if it hadn't held this particular expression in a very long time. His smile seemed honest but she knew better...he was, after all, an actor. And she, more than anyone, knew what an actor's job was—to manufacture emotions for a living.

Jenna shook her head. What the hell just happened? She felt like a ship being tempted toward a rocky shore by the call of this particular siren. Screw that. That smile he just offered was fake, as was everything else about him. He was playing a character, that's all, and she was not about to be sucked in for real. So kudos to him for being a better actor than she anticipated.

Jenna glared at Trevor, sizing him up with a clearer head. No doubt his jeans alone cost more than her month's rent. But still...it was hard not to be lured in. He appeared so pensive and preoccupied, yet when he smiled, a small half-grin, really, it was like he owned her and everything in the room. He wore his darkness like a suit of armor, but underneath, his whole being became the personification of the word "charm."

To see him here, a real person, and not just a character on television, was troubling. He was too good-looking for real life. And frankly, the only way to contain the raw sexuality he oozed was to keep him in a tiny box, locked away in a made-up world. Here…here he was too much. No wonder he was so cheap and slick. What unsuspecting woman could say no to him? Jenna bit her lip, trying to calm her nerves and the feeling of tiny pin pricks surging through her arms and legs. As she inhaled and grounded herself, a searing pain shot up from the raw blisters bulging on the backs of her heels. Just staring at him made her angry; how could he sit there like he was an innocent? Didn't he care at all? He had to know he had let people down, people like her who had counted on his celebrity endorsement to back her charity, the charity she supported to honor her dying father's wish. Jenna shook her head. No. She had to try to be civil, because the ugly truth was, hypocrite or not, she needed this job.

Desperately needing to look at something other than him, she glanced at the script in his hand. "Oh. Is that the edition we're using?" Jenna pointed to the script. "It's my favorite, too. The Royal Shakespeare Company uses that."

There. Poof. The words were gone, and she couldn't take them back. In one moment she had completely made an ass of herself. *We're using? The RSC uses that edition?* There was nothing to do but turn around and leave. She hadn't said hello to him or the casting directors or anyone else at that large table against the far wall. She had simply told him, Trevor Hughes, a man who had been a success in this business since before she was a smart-mouthed, Sartre-reading teenager, that she approved of his edition of *Hamlet*. And that it was used by the most famous acting troupe on the planet. Like he didn't know.

Good God. Why not add he's a fraud? Blood rushed to her cheeks. There was nothing she could do now but set her jaw, try her best to calm her butterflies, and like any good actor, wait for her cue.

Chapter Two

Oh, crap. Trevor looked away and immediately back again. His gaze fell over her shoulder-length black wavy hair and her barely made-up face, settling on the tiny diamond stud on the side of her nose. Her skin color was indescribable—tan, maybe? She had the complexion of a Disney princess hiding in the shadows of a New York City subway station. *Damn, damn, damn.* Trevor ran a hand through his hair, dragging it down across the scruff on his chin. A woman like this could only be trouble to a man like him—a man who was supposed to be engaged to the daughter of the producer of his daytime drama, the same daytime drama that made him a multi-millionaire.

She was stunning but in a raw and honest way, like when you stumble upon the one real, sparkly diamond sitting on a dusty tray at a pawn shop. He never knew women could look like this. He had had spent so much time with Maggie—and she was beautiful, no doubt, with her long blonde hair. If her curves were a racetrack, they would have challenged the most experienced racecar driver in the world's most responsive car. But that's what it came down to. He wasn't responding to Maggie the way he needed to...the way he wanted to. When they started dating four years earlier, Maggie claimed to have no interest in a relationship, just like Trevor. Through the years they had separated a few times—each seeing other people, but both finding their way back to the other when Maggie's father thought it would be good for ratings. And because Maggie's acting talent had definite limits, he was here, staring at the likes of gorgeous Jenna Joyce and feeling pretty freaking guilty about it. *Damn.*

This girl had to be at least ten years his junior. What could someone so young offer? He needed an Ophelia who could make him shine. If only Maggie could handle the role, then everything would be fine. But she couldn't.

Trevor unclenched his jaw. He was sick of being a pawn in someone's game—that's why *Hamlet* was his and his alone. She stared at him, waiting for her cue. He had to audition her. She had asked about the acting edition they were using, something no other actress had picked up on. That was intriguing. She appeared so very different from the overly made-up, sexually overt actresses he had seen that day, and something about this girl made Trevor so very *aware*…of his acting and of himself. He jumped off the stool and stood up taller, fighting for his rightful place but was that on the stage or beside her?

Wait. What the hell was he thinking? This was getting way too complicated, but the good thing was, she would probably be a disappointment, just as everything and everyone else was.

Something stirred deep inside whenever he looked at her. And the way she stared at him, with those giant hazel eyes, really unnerved him. "Yeah," Trevor finally answered. "Glad you recognize the edition." He needed to regain control, so he smiled his most charming smile and watched with satisfaction as her cheeks turned a bright pink. So there, she wasn't so different after all. She was just as easily manipulated by the charms of Caspian Locke as was every other woman out there. "I'm sorry to say you are the only actress we've seen today who knows of this acting edition."

"Actor."

"Excuse me?"

"Nothing."

Trevor took a step closer as this small, ethereal creature put her head down, blushing.

Damn, she wasn't predictable; he liked that. He moved closer still, letting his size intimidate her a bit. "Tell me." Trevor cocked his head, trying to see into her eyes, trying to understand her. He felt like a kid at an aquarium, desperately wanting a turn at the touch tank. Everything was right there, beneath the surface, but his ticket didn't allow him access. She looked so sad and misplaced, Trevor wondered if anyone, anywhere, had ever held that ticket.

She looked up at him. "Actor. Um, nobody really says 'actress' anymore."

"Really?" He waited for her to make eye contact. "Guess I'm showing my age."

She gave a small smile.

It was the segue he needed. "And speaking of age, how old are you?"

"Twenty-two, well, almost twenty-three." Jenna snapped her fingers and cursed. "Damn it. Sorry. I'm only supposed to give you an age range, which my agent tells me is sixteen to twenty-one. Seems ridiculous to me I don't look old enough to play the age I am, but that's the business." She shrugged. "I mean, if I'm twenty-two, then at least one twenty-two year old looks like me, right?"

An uncontrolled grin spread across Trevor's face. It was a feeling he hadn't felt in a very long time. He had no desire to fight her convoluted logic; he was just glad she was over twenty-one and only one tiny decade younger than he. But he shouldn't be glad. Not at all...

She looked over at the casting table and shuffled from foot to foot. They were all waiting on him and it was time to act. Moving across the room and toward her, he could hardly slow himself down. He wasn't walking; he was very nearly pouncing at her. There was something about her...something that made him want to know more. And maybe, was it possible an audience would feel the same way?

In his business, snap decisions were made all the time. As an actor you have only a few moments to make the casting directors like you and today, on the opposite side of the table, he realized how difficult a casting director's job was. Then Jenna walked in and suddenly Trevor's job seemed very, very easy. Something about her, her awkwardness in her simple dress, her petite but strong features, her tiny, perfect shaped nose, and giant hazel eyes, made Trevor want to know more. He was curious and watched, spellbound, as she bit the corner of her full, pouty lower lip. His heart rate increased; he had to get a hold of himself. As nonchalantly as he could, he strolled to the casting table, picked up her résumé, and read it over. "You study with Don Oleesa." He turned to Jenna and raised his eyebrows.

"Yes."

Larry cleared his throat. "Hi Jenna, I'm Larry Mills, the director." He nodded to the three other people sitting beside him. "This is Rachel, the casting director, and this is Megan"—he pointed to a sixty-something woman with gray hair—"and Nolan"—he motioned to a man around Trevor's age—"two of our producers. Don Oleesa is by invitation only. The best in the city. Where'd you make the connection?"

"He saw me perform at school."

"At school?" Larry sounded impressed. "He saw your exam plays?"

"No, my friend's exam plays. I was a first year working with the seniors."

"Excuse me?" Larry peered at Jenna over the top of his glasses. "You began working with Don Oleesa when you were a first year at school?"

"Yes."

"But Don only works with professionals," Larry countered. "I've never heard of anything like that before."

"I'm just lucky, I guess." Jenna shrugged.

"I see." Larry turned Jenna's résumé over, nodding to Trevor.

A zap of electricity shot from Trevor's core, out through his arms. Learning she was a student of Don Oleesa made Trevor want more. Much more. He waited for Jenna to move, but she remained perfectly still. Too still.

"Are you okay?" Trevor's eyebrows knitted.

Jenna nodded. Trevor studied her, amazed, as this odd little creature leaned down and slipped off her shoes, tossing them and that beaten up bag she clutched, aside. Her toenails were painted a bright pink but the paint was chipping. She rolled her toes under, cracking them.

"I'm sorry." Jenna held her arms out to her sides. "My agent made me dress up. I would have been in jeans and a t-shirt too." She tossed her head toward her shoes. "Those stupid things are killing me. Do you mind if I'm barefoot?"

"Uh, n-no." Trevor stumbled on his words, completely caught off guard. He was so used to life being controllable, predictable, and she was throwing everything off—like finding a piece of pink bubble gum in a pack of chocolate candies. He smiled at her, for some reason liking the image of her as pink bubble gum. He looked down at Jenna's bare feet once again. To all six-foot-two-inches of him, Jenna's feet looked no bigger than a doll's. Everything about this girl was unsettling.

Jenna stood back up, clutched her script, and dared him with a raised eyebrow. So she was no fragile doll; she was in this for the fight. It was time to do something.

With his gaze locked on hers, Trevor walked to Jenna and gently pulled the script from her hands. It was damp; her palms were sweating. Was it because of nerves or him? What the hell was he thinking? Trevor inhaled sharply, trying to concentrate.

"I hope you don't mind." He tossed her script onto his stool. It landed smack in the middle. "Let's see what you remember of the scene. We can always improv." He winked. Yes, what he was about to do was amateurish and unorthodox, but he felt compelled to do it, anyway. Besides, fuck it. It was his show and his money, and if anyone didn't like it, they were free to leave, although honestly, no one ever did.

"Okay." She nodded delicately, and her cheeks

turned an even brighter red.

Suddenly all Trevor wanted was to touch her. He lurched forward and slipped his arm around Jenna's tiny waist. She drew a breath.

****

" 'Get thee to a nunnery…' "

Why was he touching her? Jenna exhaled and forced her shoulders from her ears, trying to relax. Maybe this was how they did it in his world, although with every second that passed, as his strong arm muscles tightened around her waist, she was more and more certain she wanted nothing to do with his world.

Jenna closed her eyes. She needed this job. She needed to play this game. Forcing her eyes open, she was caught. His gaze bright and smart, was locked on hers. So she would play. It was only an audition, not a marriage proposal. Jenna rested her weight in his arms, letting the warmth of Trevor's body envelope her. He held her tighter. She closed her eyes and breathed him in. His scent made her nearly giddy; he smelled like the faintest combination of laundry soap and light masculine cologne. She let her Ophelia give over to his Hamlet completely, until her body became nothing more than a warm, malleable ball unsure of its ownership.

Once again she stared into his eyes that were such a light blue, they were the color of her favorite, most worn pair of jeans. The pair she wished she had on right now. Trevor reached out toward her face. His fingernails were rough and jagged, not manicured as she had expected. His hand rested gently on her cheek and her breath raced in and out. She was feeling things: desire, anger, confusion—things she should not have been feeling because he was crossing lines he should not have been crossing. The problem was she wasn't sure she wanted him to stop. And worse, she didn't know if it was her character Ophelia who didn't want him to stop…or her? *Damn it.* Jenna turned her gaze down, away from his. She was too good at living in the moment; she had to remember this was all an act. She was livid with herself for letting him get to her, even for a second.

Trevor leaned down, close enough to kiss her, and whispered, " 'Where's your father?' "

Jenna narrowed her eyes. Yes, this was a completely inappropriate response for Ophelia, but this audition was quickly becoming uncomfortable and unprofessional. " 'At home, my lord.' " Jenna's words were a mere whisper.

" 'Farewell.' " Trevor broke his hold on her. " 'To a nunnery, go.' "

He walked away and Jenna's arms flailed by her sides as she fought to steady herself. She needed to do something to save this audition. How dare he do this to her? How dare he? Ire rose up as a burning sensation, needing a release. Before she could stop them, hot, heavy tears rolled down her cheeks. She tried to speak, her voice weak and muffled. " 'O, what a noble mind is here…' " The words were barely audible through her shaking voice. No. She couldn't blow this. She had to pull it together. Jenna dropped to the floor and sobbed for what felt like minutes—until it was all out of her system—whatever it was.

She looked directly at Trevor whose icy blue gaze was fixed on her. Jenna drew in a breath and did what she did best—act. When she finished Ophelia's monologue, she was a mess of tears and sorrow but she had done it. And it was over.

Trevor rushed to Jenna. She gasped as he grabbed her and lifted her into the air as if she weighed nothing. He swept her legs up into a cradled position and bowed his head. Her breath caught in her throat, and her body tensed. How dare he do this? Who the hell did he think he was? She was right; he was a jerk. Just because he was some stupid soap opera god, he assumed he could do anything to anyone.

Well, screw that. She glowered at him as he set her down and knelt in front of her, placing his head on her tummy. She sucked in a sharp breath and closed her eyes, forcing herself to do what was right. With a shaking hand she reached out and stroked his hair, softly, because that's what Ophelia would do. He looked up, and his eyes changed—they were softer, now. Friendly. He smiled. Unrelenting heat climbed up from Jenna's belly, straight up her torso, settling in her cheeks. Her arms suddenly weighed thousands of pounds. She needed to get out of there and go home.

Trevor stood up. "Nicely done." He held out his hand to shake hers.

Jenna stared at Trevor's hand and crossed her arms in front of her. "Nicely done? Really?" Anger swelled in her chest, churning like a ball of fire. "Listen. I don't know what it's like in your world, but in mine, you don't just go grabbing people and lifting them without asking." She tapped a nervous foot. His swagger, his cockiness, his smell, like the faintest sandalwood—it all read too-much-money-sell-out.

Trevor tilted his head. "We were doing a scene and it was awesome."

"Awesome? Really? How old are you, exactly?"

"Thirty-two."

"And 'awesome' is your choice of word? When you're playing Hamlet?"

"I don't understand." Trevor stuffed his hands into his pockets. "The scene was—"

"Yeah, awesome, I know." Of course she was blowing any slim chance she may have but she didn't care. She didn't want to be involved in anything so unprofessional, and what's more, she refused to be treated like a piece of meat.

"Why are you so angry?" His sparkling eyes clouded over again.

"Because you need boundaries. You can't just grab someone without telling them first. It's amateurish. You should be better than that." Jenna turned to the table. Megan and Nolan stared at her, their mouths open. "I'm sorry for my outburst." Jenna wanted to crumple to the floor but instead met each gaze steadily. "But someone had to tell him."

Jenna stuffed her feet into her shoes and grabbed her messenger bag that was caught up on a leg of a stool. "Damn it." She cursed under her breath, nearly yanking the stool over. Feeling Trevor's gaze on her, she stuffed some loose headshots into her newly freed bag and stormed out the door. She didn't cry until she hit the subway platform.

****

Jenna couldn't go home. Thank goodness her diner was nearby, but not near enough according to her screaming heels. She ducked into a bodega next door, splurging on overpriced bandages for her aching feet. Standing next to the food bar that reeked of yesterday's shepherd's pie, Jenna balanced herself on one foot and then the other as she applied the bandages.

With her oozing blisters finally covered, she hobbled to the Carlton Diner where she worked. Pulling open the door, she was accosted by the smell of homemade matzo ball soup and spanakopita, two smells that really didn't go well together, but at least it was warm inside. Thankfully, she was there at just about the only time of the day the diner was ever empty— ironically, dinnertime. The diner's location in the Theatre District made late nights every bit as packed as breakfasts, but New Yorkers were in too much of a rush to go home to deal with Broadway traffic around six. Jenna limped across the old-fashioned black and white tile floor, past the few patrons sitting on cracked, red plastic chairs tucked tight to white linoleum tables, and plopped herself onto a revolving stool at the nearly empty counter. She buried her head in her hands.

Her best friend, Luis Statesman, was behind the counter. He walked up with a giant sugary-sweet chocolate chip cookie and a covered paper cup filled with milk. "Wow, the dress. Man. You pulled out all the stops for Trevor Hughes."

"Ugh." Jenna rolled her forehead back and forth on the counter.

"That good, huh?" Luis wiped down the counter around her head.

Jenna lifted her head high enough to moan and dropped it back down.

Luis stopped wiping and leaned against the counter. "Oh, come on. You were bad? I don't believe it. Shakespeare's like, your thing. You were incredible as Desdemona. Best I've ever worked with, and I've played Othello more times than I can count, since it's the only role anyone gives a black guy who's freaking good at Shakespeare."

The smell of the over-sugary treat got to Jenna. She lifted her head and picked chocolate chips from the cookie. "Want some?" She held out the cookie to Luis. "It's perfectly stale—a Carlton Diner special."

He put up his hand and shook his head. "C'mon. What happened?"

"He grabbed me during the scene and I lost it. I even told him off. Said he had no boundaries."

Luis chuckled, his dark eyes shining. He threw a rag over his lean shoulder. "Look at it this way, Jen, I'll bet he remembers you."

Jenna dropped her head back down into her hands. "But I had no business doing that. It's his show. And I needed that role."

"You can take a couple of my shifts if you want."

Jenna lifted her head and smiled at Luis. "Thanks, but that wouldn't cut it. And I want out of here, you know? If I keep doing stellar auditions like that, I'll be working here until I'm thirty."

"Hey, working here when you're thirty's not so bad." He lifted his thick black eyebrows and crossed his arms. "Easy on the age stuff, Jen. Thirty's the new twenty you know."

"Sorry. I didn't mean—"

"It's cool. I'm just messing with ya. I get it. Trust me. Acting is transcendent. The acting business sucks. But it sucks less than working in a diner forever so do me a favor. Next time you get an audition, stay on the opposite side of the room from your scene partner."

"Ugh."

Luis handed her a piece of cellophane and she wrapped her cookie then tossed it into her bag. She rubbed the aching blisters on her heels. "And I don't have forever to wait. You know that, Luis."

Luis shook his head and leaned across the counter. "Your plan to make it big one year out of school or else go home is ridiculous. You know that, right?"

"I don't have an option." Jenna looked up at her friend. "That's why the backup plan. If I can't support myself here *and* pay for someone to do my job at the laundry there, Olivia is going to get stuck with the job. And there is no way, no way, I will let her get stuck living her life in that tiny little nothing town." Jenna swallowed hard. "She's so smart, Luis. Really, really smart."

"I know, Jen." He sighed. "She's lucky she's got you for a big sister. She still wanna be a scientist?"

"Yeah. And you and I both know she needs to be able to keep her grades up now, not worry about folding clothes. And she needs to go to a good school, but for that to happen, even with scholarships—"

"I get it." Luis stood up straight. "But donating your eggs is a crap idea, Jenna. Go be a stripper, like every other struggling actress in this city."

Jenna rolled her eyes. "I know you're a fan, Luis, but every stripper out there didn't have a four-point-o grade point average giving them this opportunity. This is a huge lump of money, all at once." Jenna tossed her head back and forth. "Just one donation, and I'll be able to cover a year's salary for someone to help out my mom, I can stay here, and Olivia can just focus on school." Jenna forced away her serious tone. "And this way, I'll be earning money keeping most of my clothes on." She grinned.

"Uh-huh. And what about the fact that your baby is gonna be walking around out there, raised by someone else?"

She sat back and twirled her fork. "I choose not to look at it that way."

"No." He draped the rag over his arm and stared at Jenna. "You choose not to look at it at all. I know you, Jen. Some people would be cool with this—but not you. This is gonna destroy you."

Jenna swallowed hard.

Luis nodded toward her bag. "You drowning your sorrows in stale cookie?"

"Yup."

"That's pathetic...how 'bout we come around with a bottle later? I'm done at ten. Loretta's done at nine. We can stop by."

Jenna smiled, pushing aside her own worries. "No, way. Un-uh. Thanks, though. Drum roll, please..." Jenna used her hands as drumsticks, sounding a drum roll on the counter. "How long's it been?"

"Two years, one month..."

"And?" She leaned forward, keeping the drum roll going. "C'mon, Luis, my hands are hurting."

"...and thirteen days, sober."

Jenna finished her drum roll with a clink of a fork on a nearby salt shaker. "Go you."

Jenna raised her cup of milk, and Luis toasted with his ice water.

"Go home to your girl, Luis. Send her my love. You don't need to babysit me. But thanks."

Jenna squeezed her feet back into the painful shoes, and balancing the cup, hobbled her way home with the intention of drowning her sorrows in stale cookie and milk.

****

Jenna unbolted the four locks on her apartment door and fell inside, trying to ignore the blaring phone. This time she didn't have to guess. It was undoubtedly her agent. Jenna moved to the phone like it was a guillotine; she really didn't want to explain herself, but she knew if she didn't answer, Kat would just call and call until she did.

Jenna lifted the receiver. "Don't ask—"

"I won't." Kat sounded even more chipper than usual. "I'll tell. You got it."

"Got what?"

"The role."

"Which role?"

"Jenna, did you hit your head on the way home?"

"No. What are you talking a—?"

"You got the role. You are going to play Ophelia, opposite Trevor Hughes's Hamlet."

"Oh, crap."

"That's your reaction? Jenna, we're talking a big break for you. Off-Broadway. Paid daytime rehearsals. A month-long run. Opening on Valentine's Day. He's even paying above Equity scale."

"Above scale? Crap." Jenna leaned against the wall and slid down, curling herself into a tight ball.

"I don't understand, Jenna." Kat sounded confused.

"Oh Kat, I wasn't all that good. I was…I was…a mess."

"Well, they loved you. You must have done something right. They're not even asking for a callback. You were that good."

"O-okay." Jenna tripped on her words, trying to make sense of what was happening.

"Jeez…if this is your reaction now, I can't imagine what you'll do when you eventually land a Broadway role."

"Sorry. Thanks, Kat. I'm just confused."

"Well, get unconfused. And some sleep. Rehearsals start tomorrow. Stop by my office on your way, and we'll sign the contracts."

Kat kept talking about schedules and performance dates, and Jenna scribbled down the address of the theatre then hung up the phone, elated and terrified all at the same time. She dragged herself to her feet and plopped down on the futon bed she never bothered to close then wrapped herself up in the crumpled blankets. Could she handle this? Really handle it?

On the one hand, she got it. Elation coursed through her like champagne bubbling through her veins. She got the role and this role would most certainly buy her some additional time. But on the other hand, she got the role. Her smile fell away. Confusion knotted her stomach and she rubbed a burning feeling in her chest. To succeed in this business and help her sister, Jenna would have to betray her father and trust the man who had screwed them both. Sure she could handle Shakespeare but could she handle *him*? The choice really wasn't hers. She was now Ophelia to Trevor's Hamlet. For the next ten weeks or so, Jenna Joyce would belong to Trevor Hughes.

"Oh, crap." Jenna sighed heavily, pulling the broken cookie out of her bag, and stuffed pieces into her mouth.

Chapter Three

Damn it. Now he could *feel* she'd come into rehearsal without even seeing her. Energy coursed through him, settling in his hands. A vein in his temple throbbed. That would have been bad enough, if the vein had remained the only thing throbbing. But it wasn't. Trevor excused himself from a conversation he wasn't really listening to and walked away from his cast mates, to hover near the service table. He pretended deciding between a turkey sandwich and a veggie wrap while he fought to rein in his ridiculous responses to this...this...girl.

Why the hell did he sense she'd come into rehearsal? What was he now, psychic? He sneaked a peek. She drifted by the entrance to the theatre's conference room upstairs where they were having their first read-through. She wore a pair of old faded jeans and a green army jacket. Her hair was loose, grazing her shoulder blades. Her mouth, that damned, luscious, pouty mouth, was slicked with just the right amount of light pink gloss. Perfectly kissable. And the freaking nose ring glimmered when she turned her head. He grabbed a veggie wrap. It was lunchtime but he wasn't hungry, not in the least. Why the hell was she commanding so much space in his brain? She had way too much power and although he didn't know why, he knew he didn't like it.

Sure, it would have been easier not to cast her but that wasn't an option. Her audition was natural and real…she teetered on a cliff, grasping for strength and sanity, but underneath she donned a fragility that was heartbreaking. There was only the slightest allusion to Ophelia's slow descent into madness, and when her Ophelia spoke to his Hamlet, he honestly believed he was the cause of her downfall.

She had, what they referred to in the business, that "X" Factor, that something that makes you unable to take your eyes off a performer. And that's what Jenna had. He wasn't the only one who knew it; Larry spotted it too. Trevor took a deep breath. Larry's insistence they cast her lessened his guilt a tiny bit.

"Hey, Trev…you coming?"

Trevor snapped his head around. He hadn't even noticed Maggie sauntered up. She stood too close to him and batted her fake eyelashes the way she always did when she was trying to control him, that passive-aggressive way that said, "My father signs your paycheck so you'd better do as I say." Trevor's hands balled into fists which he released immediately. How did he get in this position, when he had no interest in a long-term commitment? By being careless, too freaking careless. Who in their right mind dates the producer's daughter thinking he can walk away whenever he wants to? An idiot, that's who. The same idiot who was here, trying to break free of the binds suffocating him, four years later.

All of a sudden Trevor wondered why he ever thought staging *Hamlet* was a good idea. He could have stayed safe, playing Caspian Locke, villain extraordinaire, with millions of adoring fans worldwide.

He could have just been content collecting his impressive paycheck, occasionally showing up at one charity event or another. He could marry Maggie and have a gorgeous wife, with two-point-three beautiful children and live in a cookie cutter McMansion anywhere he wanted in the Tristate area. He could learn to be happy being bored. But no, he had to decide ten years as Caspian was long enough and thirty-two was the age to prove his worth. Because of those decisions, he now had to face villains worse than any he had ever played: the New York theatre critics.

"Trev? You gonna eat that?" Maggie pointed to the sandwich in his hand and smiled. Her polished white teeth gleamed.

"Uh, no." He shook his head, fighting for clarity. "You want it?"

"What?" Maggie stepped back, grimacing. "It has carbs." She shook her head. "Why would you offer me something with carbs?"

"I—" Trevor dropped the untouched sandwich into the trash next to the table, overcome with a desire to go out with a woman who wanted to stuff herself silly with hamburgers and French fries. Do other men have girlfriends who exist on air? Of course he appreciated all the effort Maggie put in to looking good—Pilates three times a week, spin classes twice a week, daily yoga. It took a huge amount of discipline to look like she did. Any man would kill to be with Maggie and that body of hers—large breasts, tiny waist, curvy hips. But the thing was, he and Maggie weren't having any *fun*. Spontaneity wasn't invited into their lives, and all those things he loved to do as a young actor—late night trips to the village, gorging himself on questionable but delicious meals from food trucks, walking the streets of Manhattan at two a.m.—were long gone. Not that he had anything to complain about.

"Let's get started." Trevor clapped his hands together and gestured for Maggie to go before him, but before he could follow, Jenna walked up.

As Jenna stood before him, a warm sensation radiated through Trevor, replacing the agitation of just moments before. He took a deep breath trying to remain calm, wondering what the hell she was going to say. A slight half-smile turned up the corner of his mouth. He liked her unpredictability.

"Hi, Trevor." Jenna extended her hand.

Ah, this must be her peace offering. He nodded, and took her hand in his. It was warm and amazingly strong, despite her diminutive size. "It's okay if I touch your hand then?"

Jenna's cheeks flushed a bright pink. Damn it. He really didn't mean to embarrass her. "I, uh…sorry." He scratched the scruff of his beard, his head pounding.

Jenna squared her shoulders, looking directly at Trevor. "No, I'm sorry…about yesterday. That was unprofessional and well, just dreadful of me. And for that, I apologize. But it doesn't change the fact that you shouldn't have done what you did, and I'm certainly not sorry for telling you to keep your hands to yourself."

"Got it."

"Good." Jenna turned on her heels and then faced him again. "Oh, and thank you for casting me. It was unexpected."

"You're welcome."

She nodded and walked away. Trevor watched her go, wondering what, exactly, was happening.

****

Finding the spot marked "Ophelia" at the table, Jenna slipped into the oversized leather chair, wiping her sweaty palms against the soft, buttery denim of her jeans. Good Lord. If just talking to the man would cause this crazy mixed up reaction in her, how could she possibly play opposite him? No. No way. She was a professional who desperately needed this job; there was no time for schoolgirl nerves or anger.

As everyone else found their seats, Jenna shifted in her chair and fiddled nervously with her hands. She finally rested them on the table then flinched from the shock of the cold glass and chrome. She closed her eyes for a moment, calming herself. She was unused to these swank surroundings; she had never before worked in a theatre of this magnitude or with this much budget. She glanced at the bottle of designer water sitting on the table in front of her and looked at a service table on the opposite side of the room, displaying more food than she could eat in a month. Her stomach grumbled in response.

Trevor cleared his throat. "Uh, everyone, this is Jenna."

The cast members mumbled a "hey," or "hi," most with their noses buried in their scripts. Jenna looked over the group of seasoned professionals. She recognized a few people from Trevor's soap opera: an older woman named Christina, who was playing Hamlet's mother, Gertrude, and another young man playing Hamlet's best friend, Laertes. They were all very welcoming to Jenna. Well, almost all. Jenna glanced down at her script, her shoulders inching toward her ears under the disapproving glare of Maggie

Lourdes, Trevor's girlfriend. Jenna had recognized Maggie immediately because pictures of Trevor and Maggie were all over the gossip papers flanking the registers at the grocery store.

Jenna placed her opened palm on her chest, calming her breathing. Of course Maggie would disapprove of Jenna—Maggie was gorgeous—and it only made sense that she would be playing Ophelia. The audience would believe Hamlet was in love with her, just like they believed Caspian was in love with Maggie's character, Star, on their daytime drama. So why the hell was Jenna playing Ophelia?

Jenna raised her chin, smiling at Maggie. Maggie's perfectly arched eyebrows knitted together and she flinched as if Jenna had tossed hot coals into her eyes. She looked away.

Jenna turned to Trevor and he furrowed his brow. This would be a long ten weeks.

****

Finally, the reading was over and it had been pretty damned successful. After listening to Jenna's performance Trevor felt even better about his decision to cast her, and even a tad less guilty. She was excellent. Trevor sighed, his adrenaline starting to tank. He desperately wanted to work on his lines tonight but he'd need energy to do it. He needed coffee, real coffee, not that muddy swill the caterer had brought in. He made a mental note to switch the caterer to someone who made decent coffee—for God's sake, this was New York City, home to some of the best coffee in the world.

He yawned, raising his arms over his head, before pulling them down forcefully. Yes, coffee was a must.

And maybe…how great would it be to sit with someone at a warm busy coffee shop and talk Shakespeare for hours…? He glanced at his watch. Six-oh-seven. There was no way Maggie would be up for coffee now nor was she really into script analysis, especially when all he'd given her was an understudy role. Besides, she'd complain too much coffee would stain her teeth and she'd want to hit the gym for sure, since he'd made her sit there, bored, for hours.

Trevor leaned back in his chair, his long legs stretching out beneath the conference table. From this vantage point, he saw the actors milling about the room. Jenna hovered near the service table, shoveling in bites of a turkey sandwich while talking to Larry. She polished off the sandwich and grabbed a bunch of grapes. Damn. He chuckled. He'd never before seen a woman eat so fast; it must have been the only meal she had eaten all day…or all week. Huh. The muscles in Trevor's shoulders tightened, and he sat forward, concerned. No one should be hungry, and certainly not one of his actors. He'd make sure he had food brought in to every rehearsal—and better coffee.

Laughing at something Larry said, she popped a grape and covered her mouth with her hand, hiccupping. She laughed harder and hiccupped again; her shoulders rising up and down with each hiccup. Larry offered her water. She drank it back and giggled.

"Trev?"

Trevor peered around Maggie who peeked over her shoulder and turned back to him, cocking her head. "What's got you smiling?"

"Huh?" Trevor glanced up at her standing there in a tight red dress and high boots. Beautiful, beautiful

Maggie.

"What are you so interested in?"

"Nothing." Trevor pushed his chair back and stood to his full six-foot-two inches. Out of the corner of his eye he glimpsed Jenna looking at him.

"I'm gonna head to the gym. You, uh, coming?"

Trevor focused on Maggie. The way she spoke. She really didn't seem to have the slightest interest in whether he went or not. "Do you want me to come?"

Maggie took a step back, her eyes flickering the tiniest bit. "Of course. I mean, I'll be in yoga for an hour and then I'm hitting the steam room and a massage so if you've got some other things to get done..." She shrugged.

Was there ever a time they liked being around each other? "Maggie, it's okay if you don't like working out with me."

"It's just the amount of attention you get from women at the gym, Trevor. I mean, Jesus, it's more than I get from men." She shook her head. "It gets really annoying to be around you sometimes."

He nodded. Truth was, he hated the gym and he hated the attention he got. The only exercise he really liked to do was run. "Tell you what." Trevor placed his hand on Maggie's arm and steered her toward the door. He couldn't get rid of her quickly enough. "You go to the gym, and I'll give you a call in the morning."

Her eyes flashed with relief. "K."

He leaned down to kiss her quickly, while gazing at Jenna. She turned away.

Once Maggie had left, Trevor noticed Jenna was down to two companions, the actors playing Rosencrantz and Guildenstern—the only single male actors in the show. This was work, damn it. Not play time. Those guys didn't need to be hanging around his Ophelia. Not wanting the show to be compromised by some stupid cast romance, Trevor walked over.

"Hey, Trevor." The two remaining men shook his hand.

"Guys." Trevor nodded. There was nothing for him to be worried about; Jenna was too serious to mix business and pleasure. Look at the way she handled her audition, telling him off like that. No, she took it all way too seriously to screw around. He shifted his weight, his shoulders broadening.

"We're going to take off." Rosencrantz smiled at Jenna. "Should we wait for you?"

Trevor held his breath.

"No. Thanks." She shook her delicate head and her hair bounced around her shoulders. "I've got to pack up my stuff. Thanks, though."

As the guys left, an unexpected warmth fell over Trevor, like when the sun hit his shoulders while running in Central Park after that first spring rain. He smiled at Jenna and she cleared her throat, picking at her fingernails nervously. She did a great job during the read-through. What could she be anxious about?

"Nice job, Jenna."

"Oh, uh, thanks."

Jenna moved past him and back to the conference table. She stuffed her script and notes into her old canvas messenger bag. Her movements were rushed, like she couldn't get away fast enough. Was it because he was her boss or was she still pissed about the audition?

"Um, uh, you, too." Jenna closed the flap on her

bag, some of the papers sticking out of the sides.

"Thanks."

She tossed the handle of her bag across her shoulder and a strange feeling of urgency shot through Trevor.

"How are you getting home?" Trevor ran his hand up through his messy hair.

"The train." She shrugged.

"Oh, don't do that. I'll drop you off. I have a car. Want a ride?"

"What?"

He glanced at her sideways, smiling. "It's not a trick question, Jenna. I have a car. I can give you a ride." Trevor leaned in closer.

She shook her head, backing away. "Oh, uh, thanks…but…" Her cheeks reddened as she spoke. She glanced over his shoulder. "Um, thanks, anyway." Jenna wheeled around again and left the room.

I have a car? I can give you a ride? What the hell was he doing? How would he feel if Maggie jumped into the car of some guy she just met…? His chin dropped to his chest. Truthfully, he wouldn't care. Not in the least. As long as she was safe, of course, it wouldn't matter to him if she left him—for good.

He raised his head and looked over the empty conference room. It had been a long time coming, this schism with Maggie. They always had a lukewarm relationship, probably because Trevor never intended to have a relationship at all, but now Trevor itched to get away. Was it because he was finally breaking free of Caspian for a period of time to play Hamlet, or was it because of Jenna Joyce?

It didn't matter. None of it mattered because he

still had years left on his contract as Caspian and walking away would be a disaster. His shoulders weighed heavy as his secret, lifelong dream of producing summer stock in a theatre somewhere upstate slipped even farther from his grasp. There was no way. He was in too deep. Too many people were relying on him. He just couldn't mess it up.

****

Adrenaline coursed through Jenna. She just couldn't go home but she really didn't want to go to the diner. Besides, Luis wasn't working and she had taken an extended leave for rehearsals. She looked at her watch. It was just after six. She knew there was only one place for her to go. Don Oleesa had an acting class starting at seven. Maybe he would let her observe.

Jenna walked down the side street heading to Don's studio, inhaling the cold New York air, longing for the feel of a theatre—a real theatre—a little black box, with some uncomfortable seats in the audience and no props on stage except a few wooden boxes. She lived for the feel of just such a theatre, the magic of working so intimately, the experience of reading what was in the other actors' eyes, the absence of a state-of-the-art sound system. Of course it was good to have money to stage your production, but having so *much* money, like Trevor—well, whose art could survive commercialism?

Don probably hadn't eaten dinner yet so Jenna ducked into a chain health food store on her way. Normally, she liked to cook for him, like she used to cook for her mom and Olivia, but tonight she had no time. Feeding Don Oleesa had become a thing she did a couple of times a week since his last doctor's appointment when he was warned his blood pressure was too high. As Jenna ladled hot chicken noodle soup into a container, she smiled, imagining Don at his doctor's appointment, hunched over, speaking to the doctor who was only a fraction of Don's age, explaining "heightened" blood pressure was an occupational hazard when one worked in the theatre. Jenna knew the doctor's response: that was all fine, but for a man in his nineties, it was give up salt or give up the theatre.

Grabbing a hunk of cornbread, Jenna hurried through the checkout and out onto the street. She pulled her coat around her, and braced herself against the cold as she scurried down the street to Don's studio. She dashed through the front door of the converted industrial building and rushed up the four flights, not bothering to wait for the elevator. She quieted her racing breath as she pulled back the tattered black curtain and stepped inside Don's acting class.

Immediately, she was welcomed with the heart-warming scent of mildew and wood—the smell of an aging, well-used theatre. Jenna slipped in as unobtrusively as she could, and as quietly as possible. She placed her food bag on the small metal riser next to Don's chair. He, never missing a beat, peeked at her out of the corner of his eye.

"Come, come." Don held out his hand for Jenna to sit beside him.

She slunk over and propped herself on the riser next to him. He reached down and took her hand; his hand was warm and gentle. His skin was crepe-like from age and his veins were bulging, easily traceable with her fingertips. He gave a small squeeze, and she squeezed back. It felt so good to be here, with Don, in a real theatre. Her tense shoulders relaxed.

Don scribbled notes ferociously as two actors performed a scene from a new piece opening regionally next month. All too soon they were through and the actors took their place at the center of the tiny stage, waiting for their critique. Both looked haggard and exhausted. Jenna knew this feeling well—acting—real acting, good acting—was nothing short of a possession. You have to leave yourself behind, and become someone else for awhile. It was a hard thing to do, defeating even excellent actors, sometimes.

"Huh." Jenna leaned forward, resting her chin on her hand. She had really never thought of it before but Trevor had been successfully doing this nearly every day of his life for the past ten years.

"Remember Hemingway," Don said and smiled. Coughing, he put up his hand, taking a moment. "Take his brilliant words as advice—be strong in the broken places, my friends."

The actors turned to one another, inhaling sharply. They knew what was coming.

Don began to make his way to his feet. Jenna stood with him, guiding his elbow and offering him his cane. Nodding his appreciation, he shuffled down, and took his place in the center of the stage, the place that had been his home for more than seventy years.

Jenna beamed at Don as he spoke. His critique was poignant and compassionate. Any actor receiving Don Oleesa's evaluation was a lucky actor.

When he was through, Don shuffled back to rejoin Jenna in the audience, and she offered him soup.

"Chicken noodle again?" He didn't bother to look

into the cup.

"You've been fighting this cold for weeks. Chicken noodle's the answer. Besides, it's low salt."

"It's no flavor."

Jenna smiled as he dug into his soup. "Does this help?" Jenna held out a large piece of cornbread.

"Did you bring butter?"

She shook her head.

"Then it doesn't help." Don winked at Jenna and turned his attention back to the stage.

Before she realized it, it was nine o'clock. Don turned his wrist to look at the oversized watchface with the giant numbers. He lifted his glasses to look again. "Does that really say nine?" He turned to Jenna, holding up his wrist.

"Yup."

"Good Lord, time goes faster and faster." Don shuffled back to the center of his stage, facing his adoring students. "And with that, ladies and gentlemen, we part. Until next time."

Jenna smiled. This was the same farewell Don Oleesa had given in every one of his classes, forever. The eight students grabbed their scripts and coats. A couple of actors said, "Hi," to Jenna as they passed by.

Not moving from the stage, Don turned to her. "So rehearsal didn't go well?"

"It went okay, I guess." Jenna bounded onto the stage, joining Don, kicking the theatre floor with the toe of her boot.

"Jenna, you will be an excellent Ophelia. I'm certain of it. Are you having trouble with anything in particular?"

Jenna thought long and hard. What could she say?

She couldn't stand her costar, because he was annoyingly rich and handsome? Because she had personal issues with him? Because he was so incredibly handsome and talented he made her nervous?

She took a deep breath. Trusting Trevor—again— meant betraying the memory of her father. But this job meant securing her future, and her sister's future, as well. At least for the time being. As Jenna went over it in her mind, it was all ludicrous. She knew what Don would tell her: there's no room for personal issues onstage. Find something, anything, in the other actor that's attractive, and use it. Well, there was plenty for her to find physically attractive about Trevor. Jenna shifted her weight from foot to foot. But was there anything about her he could find attractive in return?

"I guess not." Jenna stared at the ground as she spoke.

Don reached out and took her hand. She looked up at him.

"Go get some sleep, Jenna. You have an early call time tomorrow. Come back to me when you're ready to commit to this show."

Jenna began to speak but Don stopped her. "You're not ready. You'll know."

****

Jenna plopped her bag on a chair, pulled on a rehearsal skirt, and slipped her jeans off from underneath. Today was the day to rehearse the nunnery scene, arguably the most important scene in Hamlet and Ophelia's relationship, and the scene that had exploded during Jenna's audition. It would just be Trevor and Jenna onstage, with only Larry and Maggie in the audience. Trevor didn't have an understudy; he was the reason they were selling tickets. Without him, the show would never fly.

Jenna rubbed her temples, trying to soothe her dull, throbbing headache. She took a deep breath, it was now or never. Leaving her script on the chair, Jenna stretched her arms overhead and climbed up onto the stage like a prize fighter entering a ring before a championship bout.

Her heart raced when she spotted him approaching from the wings. As he grew nearer, she turned away. Damn, he was handsome and he had this aura around him. If she didn't know everything she did about him—his lack of a soul, his insincerity, and his worship of money—he would be so, so easy to like. He walked onstage but didn't acknowledge Jenna. Was he avoiding her? Jenna shuffled her feet, and the skirt swayed around her. It didn't matter. She didn't like him and *couldn't* like him but hoped there was maybe some tiny part of him that liked her. That would make their performances more believable. Trevor stood downstage, facing Larry.

"All right, Hamlet, Ophelia. Let's see what you've got."

Jenna's head thumped in response.

Trevor turned to Jenna. " 'Where's your father?' "

" 'At home, my lord.' " Blood rushed to Jenna's cheeks at the disconnect in her bones. He delivered his next lines competently, but where was the passion? The fire?

" 'Heavenly powers, restore him!' " She moved closer as she spoke.

Trevor turned and stepped aside.

Mercifully, Larry stopped them. "All right, guys,

come on over."

As she walked downstage, self-awareness swirled in the base of Jenna's spine, crippling her instincts. She was tight and self-conscious. She was awful, and she knew it.

"It's just not happening for me." Larry plopped his script down and sat back, crossing his arms. "Technically, you're both solid. But emotionally...passionately...the reason we put butts in the seats...it's just not there. Any ideas?"

Trevor sat, hanging one leg off the proscenium stage. The other he bent, resting his elbow on his knee. He looked self-assured and sexy, even though the show was falling apart around them. He turned to Jenna. "I'm not feeling you in the nunnery scene like I did when you auditioned. What's going on?"

Maggie looked up and stopped filing her nails.

"Nothing. I'm sorry." Burning heat rose in Jenna's cheeks. "I—I'll try harder."

"No!" Larry jumped out of his seat, shouting in frustration. "That's the whole thing. You're trying too hard. Both of you are trying too hard."

Jenna's ears burned.

Larry walked over, staring up at the stage. "This can't be fixed by me or Shakespeare. It's something that's too—"

"Glossy." The word sneaked out and there was no way to take it back. Jenna clenched her jaw, facing Larry.

"What?"

"Nothing. Sorry."

"No, tell me." Larry stroked his chin. "What is it?"

Jenna sighed. She would probably get fired, so

what the hell. She was awful anyway. As much as she hated it, she had another plan and it was called a backup plan for a reason. "I think we're too glossy. Too slick. This whole thing"—Jenna turned in a circle, pointing to the theatre space—"is too slick."

"Tell me more." Larry leaned in to listen.

"I think this whole production is too neat and clean and shiny."

"Like a soap opera?" Trevor raised his eyebrows, daring her.

"Your words, not mine." Jenna leveled her gaze on Trevor and then turned back to Larry. "I mean, who rehearses in a theatre like this? A lot of actors work in rehearsal spaces until the week before. This is too much. We're all too comfortable." She shook her head. "Personally, I feel like an overly made-up drag queen. My Ophelia's got so much going on the surface no one would ever guess what's beneath."

Trevor let out a laugh that startled Jenna. She turned to him, spotting the crinkles around his eyes. One corner of her mouth turned up into a smile.

"And you know this from your vast experience in off-off Broadway?" Maggie snapped.

"Maggie…" Trevor admonished.

Trevor glanced at Jenna, and his gorgeous eyes softened. They weren't fake or conniving. They were just concerned. It was too much. She refused to be pitied, and anger surged through her chest. "No, you're right. I don't have the experience you, or anyone else here has. But what I do have is talent. That's why I'm playing Ophelia. So if you don't mind, my director has asked me a question, and I'm going to answer him without your rude interjections." Crap, she hadn't realized she was harboring that much anger. Maggie didn't deserve all of that. Some of it, but not all of it.

Maggie glared at Jenna. She stood purposely and walked down the aisle toward the stage. She stopped in front of Jenna, stretching, highlighting the difference in their bodies. "I'm gonna take off, if that's cool." Maggie batted her big eyes at Larry. She placed her hands on her hips, and posed with one leg out.

"That's fine," Larry dismissed her quickly and turned back to the stage. "Okay guys, tell me—"

"It's not like I'm going to learn anything here," Maggie said in a snippy voice.

Trevor shook his head at her. He walked back upstage, script in hand, as Maggie exited the theatre door.

Jenna watched her go and her booming headache was replaced with a cramp in her belly. She really hadn't meant to be the cause of any strife between Trevor and Maggie.

"Jenna, what, exactly, are you talking about?" asked Larry.

"The truth?"

"Please."

Jenna nodded and sucked in a deep breath. "I think we should be rehearsing in a place a lot less extravagant."

"Go on."

Jenna glanced back to see Trevor. "And I think we should all get our hands a little dirty. Take bigger risks."

"I can't say I disagree." Larry nodded. "Trevor?"

"I think it's worth a try. It can't be any worse."

Jenna swallowed hard, happy he was feeling it, too.

If they both acknowledged the problem, they had a chance at fixing it. Trevor walked downstage, standing close to Jenna. Her body responded to him in an odd way as if he were electrically charged, and she were being shaken by his vibration. She moved a couple of inches away, just to stay focused.

"Jenna, any ideas?"

She glanced at him—at his eyes. Something in them told her he needed this show to be a success just as much as she did and every moment she held onto resentment and anger was another moment wasted. They needed this show to be good. They needed to be good. Together.

"Yeah." Jenna nodded, unease coursing through her veins. "I have an idea." It was a giant risk for Trevor but all theatre was a risk. The best actors took the biggest risks and Trevor was a good actor. Looking up at him, his face strong and determined, she knew he'd be up for it.

Chapter Four

Walking down the broken steps and into a tiny theatre in the basement of the church near Eighth Avenue, Trevor grabbed his nose. "Uh, Jenna? What is that smell?"

"What smell?"

She threw her pert nose into the air and sniffed. Trevor smiled.

"They cook dinner for the homeless upstairs. I think it's…" She repeated the action. "Sauerkraut." She sniffed again. "Yup, sauerkraut."

"Oh, I hate sauerkraut." Trevor covered his nose with his hand.

"Really?" She raised an eyebrow. "Well, now that I know that, I know what to pack for lunch tomorrow," she said in a fun flirty tone as she skipped ahead down a narrow aisle of the audience.

Trevor's mouth turned up into a lopsided grin. This was the first time she ever joked around with him, and he liked it.

She turned back to him. "I rehearsed a show here once. Actually performed it, too."

"How many seats?" Trevor looked around the theatre, taking in the tattered blue cloth seats perched on flimsy risers pushed tight to marred walls which were painted in flat black. The floor was that same flat black, as was the tiny stage before him. Old ripped, black curtains, mended with silver duct tape, lined the stage on three sides. He stubbed his toe against a chair in the audience. "Ow." He rubbed his foot.

"You okay?"

He nodded. "Fine. Thanks. Seats?"

"Ninety-nine. It's a black box."

"Is it Equity code?"

"Yes." She plopped her hands on her hips and tilted her head. "We were all Equity actors performing here. You fancy steady-paycheck-money-making actors don't hold a monopoly on unions you know."

"I'm well aware of that." Trevor's gaze happily followed Jenna as she waltzed around the empty stage. He smiled. She was unquestionably gorgeous but there was more. She was smart and talented but her exuberance and her complete love and respect for the theatre was exciting. He knew that feeling once, but ten years as Caspian Locke killed that enthusiasm. Now, acting was a well-paying craft—not an art. And taking off his shirt was his medium. It was all rather…sad.

"Okay." She smiled, taking him on a tour. "Obviously, you see the audience. The stage area has good wing space. Come on."

Jenna held aside a curtain, and Trevor followed her backstage. He felt an odd warmth around her. The show needed more soul and he was lost as to how to do it but somehow this smart odd young woman seemed to have the answers. She was so happy in the dilapidated theatre, he was beginning to get caught up in her contagious enthusiasm. Stepping backstage, Trevor stopped short. Never, in his life had he seen working conditions so deplorable. "What is this place?"

"Isn't it great?" Jenna walked across a wide plank

that served as a bridge over puddles of water that had collected backstage.

Trevor stared at the puddles. Was she joking? Was he being set up? Would she go so far as to purposely waste his time like this because she disliked him? The sparkle in her eyes told him she was for real.

Jenna looked down beneath her feet. "Oh, the water's just because it rained. It's not always this deep."

"This deep?"

"Yeah. And over here's the dressing area." Jenna pointed to two chairs perched near two broken mirrors. "There's a piano over there." Jenna hopped from board to board, plinking on the piano when she arrived. She sat on a wobbly stool and played a slow sad song.

Trevor watched her, mesmerized. "I didn't know you could play."

She turned back to him. "Yup. My dad taught me."

This was the first time Jenna had given him any insight into her life and he wanted to know more. Trevor balanced himself on one of the boards and walked across, so he could be nearer to Jenna. "Your dad?"

"Yup."

"A musician, huh?"

"Among other things." Jenna popped up and walked across another board. She held her arms out to the sides, flying them up and down like an airplane.

"What other things?"

"Just things. I don't really talk about it." Jenna's expression clouded over.

"Oh. Uh, okay." Trevor stiffened. Why the hell was he hurt she didn't want to share with him? What did he care?

Jenna smiled a small smile at Trevor, as if she understood. "It's not you, Trevor. I just prefer not to talk about certain things."

Trevor nodded, fighting the impulse to go to her and cradle her in his arms—a feeling he had never before experienced. It was an odd sensation, one that made him stand up taller, his muscles tightening. At the very least, he wanted to invite her for coffee. All of a sudden, he fantasized about sitting with Jenna at some small, deserted coffee shop and talking to her late into the night. He wanted to ride a caffeine buzz as they dissected their scripts. And mostly, he wanted to know about her—why she became an actress...uh, actor. Where she lived. What she liked to eat. If she had a pet; if she wanted one. If she was afraid of spiders. If she had any tattoos...and what she would think of his. Everything about this skinny black-haired fireball made him nostalgic and intrigued him, all at once. The most pressing question now, was, why?

"Trevor?"

"Huh?"

"You okay?"

"Yeah, sorry." Trevor shook his head, trying to focus on his surroundings.

"So what do you think? Incredible, right?"

"Uh, yeah. Incredible."

"I made a call before we left the theatre, and I found out it's available." Jenna bounced up and down on her toes, giddy with excitement.

"It's available? Imagine that." He didn't mean to be sarcastic; he genuinely liked the feel of the old theatre.

Jenna's face fell and he was immediately sorry for his tone.

"You hate it." She dropped her arms down to her sides, defeated.

Trevor tried to backpedal. "No. I don't hate it. I just—"

"You hate it." Jenna stuck her hands on her hips, tapping her foot. "Look. We only have five weeks left."

Trevor shuffled uneasily, realizing in just over a month the show would open, and it had to be a success. There was no room for failure so he'd need to step up his game.

Jenna continued. "We need some grit and dirt and reality and this place—"

"Is perfect."

"What?"

"I think it's perfect." Trevor flashed a tentative smile.

"Really?" Jenna's stance softened. She turned her head, eyeing him, waiting for the catch.

Trevor's gaze fell over the ancient stage, torn curtains, and peeling plaster walls. He inhaled the smell of mildew and dampness and his heart raced with possibility for the first time in a very long time. If his usual swank working conditions were nothing more than a façade, well then, this place was a soul. An old, perhaps damaged soul, but definitely a soul. "Really."

Jenna's eyes lit up like she was a little kid asking Santa for a pony.

Trevor saw the vulnerability in her eyes and for a moment, all he wanted to do was to protect her and preserve her enthusiasm. "Yes. I'll cancel the theatre tomorrow and sign the contract on this place."

"Honestly?" Jenna's voice dropped to a sultry tone, and she suddenly didn't seem a hot-headed kid anymore. Right now, in her jeans and t-shirt, she was all woman.

"Yes." Trevor cleared his throat.

"Thank you, Trevor."

Her words were filled with so much sincerity, Trevor looked away. He grappled with his conscience; he wanted to touch her so much, but he knew better.

"Should we go?" Jenna nodded toward the stage area.

He followed her, caught up in the graceful ease of her small body, moving. When they were nearly at the door, Jenna held up her hand to stop him.

"Oh, almost forgot. That's the bathroom. There's only one and there's no sink, so we need to keep a lot of hand sanitizer around."

"What?" Trevor narrowed his eyes. Was she joking? Had she lost her mind?

"But don't worry, the toilet works—most of the time." Jenna flashed Trevor the biggest smile he had ever seen, before disappearing out the theatre door.

On the street, they stood quietly. She pulled on oversized hand-crocheted mittens and a soft, powder-blue hat. He smiled.

"What?"

"Your hat."

"I know. Goofy, right? But it's warm."

"No, not goofy. It's uh, pretty perfect, actually."

Jenna's large hazel eyes widened. "Um, okay then." She turned away and stopped for a moment then looked back at Trevor. "Uh, see you tomorrow—right here." She gazed up at the theatre lovingly.

Trevor raised his hand to wave goodbye and she walked away, leaving him alone on the street corner. His gaze followed her until she turned the corner, out of view. His body tensed, and he had to keep himself from bolting after her to walk her home. He didn't like her disappearing. He didn't like her being unsafe. Walking the streets of Manhattan was difficult for any woman, and for someone who looked so young and attractive...

Trevor dropped his head, grasping the back of his neck with his hand. What the hell was he thinking? She wasn't his responsibility. So he was attracted; it didn't mean anything. He was attracted to his barista too and she was closer to his age and much more his type. And if he avoided sleeping with his obviously interested barista just because he didn't want to risk his morning coffee order, well, he sure as hell wouldn't risk a quickie with his co-star.

Trevor looked down the empty street, after Jenna. This attraction for her was nothing. These feelings he was experiencing were what Hamlet felt for Ophelia, spilling over into real life. That's all. These confusing emotions were the very reason so many theatre romances died before opening night. And he sure as hell couldn't afford any distractions. Sexual tension needed to stay alive onstage...it had no place in real life.

The thing was, it wasn't sexual tension he was fighting. Yes, she looked awesome in her jeans, and her hat was just plain adorable but he was also concerned for her, a feeling he had never felt in all his time with Maggie. Maggie could, and would, take care of herself. But this girl...Trevor looked up at the theatre and then back after Jenna, wondering what, exactly, he'd gotten himself into.

A vibration shook his body; he needed to talk. Not to Maggie, no, he needed a connection to...someone real. He glanced at the time on his phone. Nine-forty. Surely his nephew Toby would be asleep, but maybe his sister Amanda would still be up. He would never burden her with his frivolous thoughts—God knows she had been through enough, monitoring Toby's health alone because her husband took off before Toby's first open heart surgery—but he needed to know Toby was okay since his second open heart surgery a couple of months ago. That would calm his raging thoughts and put everything into some much needed perspective.

His hand shook as he pressed their number on his cell.

"Hello?" Her voice was sleepy.

"Sorry. Did I wake you?"

"Hey, Trevor. Of course not." She paused for a moment. "You okay?"

"Yeah. Of course. Fine. Why?"

"It's just that it's late." She chuckled. "Well, for me, anyway." She yawned. "Sorry, Toby's asleep. He'll be upset he missed you."

"I'll call him in the morning. How are you?" It was such a loaded question, his throat ached as he spoke.

"We're okay." She was much more alert now. "I mean, I'm always nervous. But you know Toby, he's a trooper."

"Yeah." Trevor fought back an ache in his gut. "How's the breathlessness?"

"Comes and goes."

"I'll come visit just as soon as I can."

"Trevor, we're okay. I know you're on a break

from the show, but this play has to be—"

"Amanda, I will be there."

"I know."

Her voice was frail. The last thing he wanted was for her to worry about him, too.

"Do you need anything?"

"No, Trevor. What more could you possibly do for us? We're okay."

"I don't do anything." His voice was soft.

"No? We live in a fully paid-off house you bought for us and you pay all of Toby's exorbitant medical bills because your slacker of a sister can't even afford the co-pays on the medical insurance you got us."

"Hey." Anger riled in his gut. "Don't ever call yourself a slacker. You're in an impossible situation. You banked on the wrong guy."

"But I'm thirty-four. I should be able to take care of myself and my son."

"You work as much as you can so you can be with Toby. We've talked about this, Amanda."

"But Trevor, you're my brother, not my husband."

Damn. He really didn't mean to upset her. "Amanda. I love Toby. You two are the only family I have. I make a lot of money on my show. It makes me happy to help. I promise."

"Speaking of the show, how's Maggie?"

He sighed.

"Things are that good, huh?"

"We have our challenges."

"Trevor. You know I don't butt in on your personal life but you never sound happy anymore. Why do you stay with her?"

He wracked his brain for any possible answer

except the truth.

"Unless…it doesn't have anything to do with us, does it?"

"What are you talking about?"

"I can't believe I never thought of it before but her dad's the producer. Are you afraid to lose your job if you leave her?"

"Of course not." Trevor forced the lie out his teeth. "My contract is iron-clad."

"If you're doing something you don't want to do to support us, I can't let you do that. We'll find another way." The pitch of her voice rose with her angst.

Trevor unclenched his jaw. There was no other way. Even with the best health insurance Trevor could get for them, all in, the out-of-pocket for Toby's care ran hundreds of thousands of dollars. Bare-chested Caspian Locke was the only reason Toby had the help he needed.

"Trevor…you do love your show, right? I mean, you're still having a blast playing Caspian?"

"Of course." He nearly choked on his words.

"Okay. Because if you're not, you need to make a change. And we'll figure something out."

"I know, Amanda."

"Really, Trevor. We'll come up with another way to get the money."

"I know that." What he knew was this was a conversation she needed every few months, when the guilt of being supported by her younger brother became too much. She was quiet. Too quiet. "Amanda. If I ever get tired of playing Caspian, I'll change. And yes, we'll find another way to come up with the money."

"Okay, Trevor. Thank you." She yawned again.

He smiled. "Go back to sleep. Kiss Toby for me, and I'll call him in the morning."

"Thanks, Trevor. 'Night."

Trevor clicked off his phone and sucked in a huge swallow of the icy cold New York air. Fuck.

Chapter Five

Jenna sat on a bench beneath an old payphone near the entrance of Don's studio. She dropped in another quarter, grateful Don insisted the old phone stay in his lobby for use by those few people, like Jenna, who refused to get a cell. She was waiting for Don's seven p.m. class to end—even though it wasn't her class, she had become a regular. Jenna rubbed the throbbing pain in her temple as she spoke to her sister, Olivia.

"When do you have time for homework, then?"

"I get it done." Olivia's voice was strong and confident.

"When? In between folding loads? After you fix a broken machine? I don't want you tied up there forever, Olivia."

"Mom needs help." She didn't mean them in a passive-aggressive way, but when laced with the power of Jenna's own guilt, Olivia's words were like poisonous daggers plunged deep into Jenna's belly.

"I know that." Jenna's voice was soft. "That's why I send her enough money to pay for someone else's salary…"

"But she needs help beyond that. I promise I'm getting my homework done. My grades haven't dropped a bit."

Jenna exhaled. She glanced away from the phone and toward the tattered black curtains leading to Don's rehearsal studio. She loved it here. She loved everything about New York and the acting business. God, how she didn't want to have to go back home.

"Okay." Jenna gripped the receiver tighter, her knuckles whitening. "But if it gets to be too much, please, Olivia. Tell me."

"And risk you walking out on Caspian Locke? No way." Olivia giggled. "It's all anybody at school can talk about."

"His name is Trevor. Trevor Hughes."

"He can call himself anything he wants as long as he keeps his shirt off."

"Olivia." Jenna's word was more of a scold.

"What?"

People were moving behind the curtain. It was time to go.

"He's a person, too." Jenna could practically hear her sister's smirk. "What?"

"You've sure changed your tune from the woman who hated Trevor Hughes, because he no-showed on some charity you were supporting."

"It wasn't just some charity; it was the charity Dad supported." Jenna pressed against her temples, trying to dull the ache. She sighed. "Olivia, please, just please promise me you'll put school first."

"I promise."

An unease swirled through her belly as Jenna hung up the phone.

****

"How'd it go today?" It was after class, and Don had just polished off Jenna's homemade vegetable lasagna.

She smiled, glad to see the nagging cough wasn't

spoiling his appetite.

"Let's see..." Jenna counted on her fingers as she listed things off. "I thought I was going to get fired. Then I told off my understudy, nasty Maggie, who just happens to be Trevor's girlfriend. Then the director told me something was missing in my part, so I told him I thought the whole performance was too slick and lacking substance. Thennnn...I did my best to talk Trevor into moving rehearsals into a decrepit theatre in the hopes of finding the show's soul." Jenna slumped back in her chair, overwhelmed.

"Did he agree?"

"Amazingly so. We rehearse there tomorrow."

"Sounds to me like you had a very productive rehearsal. Are you ready to commit now?"

Jenna sat up, nodding. She handed Don a napkin and grinned at him.

"Good. Let's get to work."

****

Walking into the old theatre the next day, Jenna couldn't think of a time she'd been more nervous. The plate of chocolate chip cookies she carried wobbled in her shaky hands and she said a silent prayer, hoping chocolate would work its magic on these potentially angry actors just as it always did on her. She knew all of them were used to working with real money and here she was, demanding they strip themselves down to the bare minimum and build from there. Who was she to suggest such a thing? It was like she had been drunk the day before, making rash and illogical choices. But the strange thing was, Trevor was right there making them with her.

Still holding the cookies, Jenna ambled down the

audience aisle and toward the stage. She glanced at Larry, sitting front and center, scribbling furiously in his notes. Jenna peered about as actors made their way around the new stage, reading their lines as if nothing had happened. She placed the cookies on a seat in the front row of the audience. Before she could remove her hat and coat and slide on her rehearsal skirt, Christina made her way from behind the curtain.

Christina's gaze locked on Jenna's. "Are you responsible for this?"

Jenna bit the inside corner of her cheek. What could she say except the truth? "Yes, I am."

There were no excuses to be made. She was the most insignificant person here, yet last night, she had wielded the greatest amount of power. This was her doing, and she would have to take the flack for it. Out of the corner of her eye, Jenna spotted Trevor watching them. For a moment she was sorry she had pushed him into making this decision. She could walk away from this show virtually unscathed, but it was his reputation and his friends' reputations on the line here.

"Marvelous," Christina announced, clapping her hands together.

"E-excuse me?"

"It's marvelous." Christina walked to Jenna. "May I take your hands, dear?"

Jenna nodded, certain Trevor must have shared the gory details of her audition, and how she freaked when Trevor touched her. Jenna squeezed her eyes shut for a moment and the other woman reached out and grasped Jenna's hands. Christina's touch was warm and soft, making Jenna long for her mother.

"Excuse the sweaty palms, my dear." Christina

tossed her head gracefully. "I'm afraid it's time for 'the change.'"

Jenna giggled, caught off guard by the candor.

Christina smiled again. "This was the answer we needed. We all"—she turned and faced Maggie as she said this—"*all* of us, need a little more reality in our lives." Christina released Jenna's hands and spun in a large, dramatic circle. "This is *theatre*, people. Let's make some magic."

Trevor applauded and Christina took a tiny bow, smiling. She blew a kiss at Trevor and curtseyed to Jenna.

"Let's go, folks." Larry stood up and walked forward, shoving a cookie into his mouth absentmindedly. "Jenna, these are delicious."

Jenna smiled, her tense shoulders relaxing for the first time all day.

"All right, people. Act three, scene two. Places."

****

Two freaking weeks. Every night after rehearsal, for two solid weeks, Jenna ducked out of the theatre and ran down the street. Where the hell was she heading? Probably running to a boyfriend. Time and again Trevor wanted to ask her for coffee, no big deal, just to bond as cast mates. If they could find some ease and relaxation together in their real life then maybe they could find it onstage too. At least that's what he told himself.

Why was it so difficult to ask her for coffee? It wasn't like he was asking her on a date—there was no way in hell he could do that. He just wanted to take her for coffee at the little diner next door. He wanted to pick her brain, to surround himself with her realness and grit. All his years on the soap wedged a very tall, solid gold wall between his life and reality and he wanted to remember, to know what realness looked like and sounded like…and felt like.

Gazing at her packing up her messenger bag, his body ached with a longing he'd never before experienced. He wanted to pick up their conversation from the night when she showed him the theatre. He wanted to know more about her father, her life, and her. But every night she disappeared as soon as the last words were spoken. Sometimes Trevor was quick enough to catch a glimpse of her running down the street but often she was gone before he'd even collected his script.

Tonight, he decided, would be different. Tonight he would not let anyone or anything get in his way. He was Trevor Hughes, damn it, Prince of Denmark, and he wanted coffee—with Jenna Joyce.

"Jenna?"

She jumped. "Yeah?" She placed her hand on her heart, turning to him.

"Sorry. Didn't mean to make you jump."

"Okay. What's going on?" Jenna peeked at her watch and slid into her army jacket.

"You in a rush?"

"A bit. Can I help you?"

Those words inspired Trevor. "Actually, you can. I would like your insight on our nunnery scene."

"I know, it's flat for me, too."

This would be so much easier than Trevor ever imagined. "So why don't we talk about it. Over coffee."

Jenna shrugged. "Okay." She threw the strap of her messenger bag over her shoulder.

"Okay?" Trevor ran his hand across the scruff on his chin.

Jenna's gaze darted up to him. She cleared her throat. "Yeah. Coffee. Talk. Okay."

"Now good for you?" Trevor's heart raced as he asked the question.

Jenna looked at her watch again. "No. I have to run now."

Trevor nodded, disappointment aching in his gut. He was obviously being turned down because of another man and that just didn't happen to him. He stretched his arms overhead, letting them fall to his sides.

Jenna looked up at him with her giant hazel eyes. "How 'bout later?"

"Later? When?"

"No rehearsals tomorrow, so why don't you come by my place around nine tonight? Is that okay?"

"Uh, sure." Trevor tilted his head. He never expected Jenna to ask him to her apartment.

"Oh, but it's Friday night." Jenna chewed the corner of her lip. She looked away, like she was pondering a complex math equation and then gazed up at him again. "Don't you have a date or something?"

She asked the question with no subtext whatsoever, and Trevor shook his head, perplexed.

"No. Don't you?"

"Yeah, right." Jenna scoffed. "So my place, then?"

He nodded.

"Great. I'm expecting a call. I need to be home." Jenna headed for the theatre door, and Trevor followed after her.

"Should I bring coffee?"

"That'd be great."

"Black?"

Jenna paused and turned back, pulling on those freaking adorable mittens. "Excuse me?"

"Your coffee, black?"

"Oh, yuck, no. Extra cream and four sugars, please."

"Four sugars?"

"You asked." Jenna shrugged, making her way up the steps onto the street.

Trevor followed close behind. Jenna shivered in the cold New York air, and Trevor fought his impulse to give her his jacket to bundle over hers.

"You want to text me your address?"

"Un-uh." She shook her head. "No cell."

"You have no cell phone?" Trevor narrowed his eyes, leaning forward when he asked, his body instinctually wanting to protect her.

"You sound like my agent. Nope."

"What if it's an emergency?"

That wave of misplaced concern washed over Trevor as Jenna shrugged again.

"Look, I really have to go." She pointed at her watch and just then, the first few snowflakes started to fall. "Huh…snow."

Jenna spoke with such girlish enthusiasm, Trevor had to smile.

She turned her soft beautiful face up to the sky and then back to Trevor. "Oh, uh, here."

Just as Trevor reached into his pocket for his cell to input the information, Jenna yanked off her mittens and dug into her bag, fishing out a pen. She took Trevor's hand and he tightened with her touch. Her tiny hand opened his and she lifted her pen, grabbing the cap in her teeth, scrawling her address across his palm. She dropped his hand, pushed the pen back into its cap, and plopped it into her bag.

Trevor cleared his throat as she began to walk away. "See you at nine," he called after her. Despite the strange excitement brewing inside him, he tried to sound relaxed.

"Extra cream, four sugars," she yelled over her shoulder as she sped away.

Chapter Six

Trevor rocked on his heels as he stood on the sidewalk, waiting for Jenna to buzz him up. It was cold—pre-snow in New York cold—that wet bitterness that cuts through even the warmest of coats.

"Come on up." Jenna's voice hummed through the intercom.

Trevor balanced the coffee tray in one hand as he pulled open the door. He stepped inside an old entryway with red paint peeling off the walls. A flight of uneven decrepit stairs lay ahead of him and he glanced around the dark lobby that reeked of cigarettes. He hadn't been in a building this rundown since...well, since this afternoon when they rehearsed in the theatre Jenna recommended. He chuckled.

"Up here."

Jenna's lilting voice called him from above. He looked up, and there she was, hovering above him. An old wall light flickered behind her head.

"Four flights, sorry." She tossed her hair that fell forward again when she looked down. "But you don't want to risk that elevator..." She moved her head vaguely in the opposite direction.

Trevor took the stairs two at a time.

She met him at the door. "Impressive." She smirked. "Two at a time. I tried that once. Nearly killed myself."

"Your legs may not be quite as long as mine." Trevor let his gaze casually run over her outfit of a white t-shirt, and gray sweatpants that gathered beneath her knees. He averted his eyes as quickly as he could, but he was certain he saw the outline of light pink lace beneath her t-shirt.

"And you're not even huffing and puffing. Pretty good. Bet there's an overpriced trainer somewhere we can thank for that, huh?"

Trevor clenched his teeth. "No, actually I run. That's it. And I don't run to stay in shape. I do it to escape."

Jenna's eyes grew soulful. "I get that. Sorry."

Trevor moved the coffee tray from hand to hand. "Can I...can I come in?"

"Oh yeah, sorry."

Jenna stepped aside, and Trevor walked in. Immediately he was surrounded by the slow, sexy sound of a Seventies classic rock band. He liked it.

"So uh, this is it." Jenna spun around.

Trevor glanced about, certain this apartment was smaller than his master bedroom.

"There's the kitchen." Jenna pointed to a dorm-room sized refrigerator and a cook top with a tiny oven. There was a small sink crammed full of dirty dishes. "Over there's the closet." This time Jenna pointed to her clothing rack. "Dining room." She pointed to a tiny table with two chairs near the kitchen area. "And living room-slash-bedroom." She pointed to her opened futon, covered in rumpled blankets and dirty clothes. "That's it." She put her hands on her hips, triumphantly. "Oh wait. Bathroom."

Trevor waited for her to point to a tiny pot in some

corner of the apartment. Thankfully, the bathroom was a separate room with an actual door.

"Relief, right?" She laughed, as if she could read his mind. Her eyes sparkled. "That there's a door to the bathroom? It was for me too, the first time I saw this place."

"It's nice." Trevor lied.

"No, it's not." She dropped her hands to her sides. "It's crap. And it's messy. But it's cheap, and I'm busy."

"I get that." Trevor stood still, holding the coffees.

"For us?" She held out her hand for the tray full of coffees. "Four of them. And oooh, diner coffee. Yum."

"You didn't seem like the gourmet chain type of girl to me."

Jenna's gaze locked on Trevor's. "Thanks."

It was the way she said that one little word, "thanks," that pulled at his heartstrings. Trevor stood up tall as tension crawled across his shoulders like spiders spinning webs. That one small gesture, thinking about what kind of coffee she might like, elicited such a heartfelt response. Didn't anyone else care about her feelings? Then he thought about the boyfriend she disappeared to every night and the spiders turned to giant horror-movie-sized tarantulas, weighing heavily on him. Hell, yeah, someone else cared, so he sure as hell shouldn't—and couldn't.

"Mine?" Jenna pointed to a cup on the tray.

Trying to keep his feelings in check, Trevor nodded.

She took a sip. "This is heaven, thanks."

Trevor didn't budge.

"Oh, I'm sorry. My manners. Sit, please." Jenna

moved a small stack of magazines from one of the kitchen chairs, tossing the magazines onto the bed.

Trevor found his way to the chair and sat awkwardly.

"You look uncomfortable." Jenna tilted her head. "I'm sorry."

"Not uncomfortable—"

"Wait a sec." Jenna bounced the two steps to the kitchen and came back with a cushion. "I used to have cushions on these chairs, and then I washed them and forgot to put them back on. Honestly, I almost always sit in bed when I eat." Jenna handed Trevor a cushion.

He slid the cushion onto the chair, now fantasizing what it would be like to be in Jenna's bed with her, devouring Chinese food as they watched a movie.

Jenna's shoulders slumped forward. "That didn't help, did it?"

"It's fine." Trevor shifted his oversized frame on the tiny chair, feeling uncomfortable for so many reasons. He was so used to being in control and for some reason this tiny person stole the power right out from under him. He ran his hand up through his hair, and he caught Jenna staring at the beads around his wrist. "Mala beads," he offered.

Jenna stood motionless, mesmerized by his wrist. Trevor flexed slightly, sure Jenna was reacting to the size and strength of his arm.

The phone rang.

Jenna jumped. "Oh, shoot. I nearly forgot. Sorry. Do you mind?"

"Of course not."

Trevor tried to make himself comfortable on the chair that was surely built for one of Snow White's dwarfs. He opened his coffee and his script while Jenna answered her phone. He wasn't the slightest bit surprised by the look of her retro phone. He did wonder, however, who this boyfriend was who let Jenna walk around without a cell phone and invite strange men into her apartment. He tried not to eavesdrop, but in an apartment that size, it was impossible not to.

"Yes, okay thanks. Did you get the last letter?"

Jenna's gaze shot over to Trevor; it was obviously the boyfriend and a private conversation. He stood up and made his way to the bathroom, the only place he could go to give her some space.

Trevor stepped into the bathroom and put a fist to his mouth, stifling a laugh. Serious Jenna's shower curtain was decorated with Papa Smurf and Smurfette. He reached his hand out to the Smurfs, desperately wanting to know more about this woman who could recite Shakespeare in perfect iambic pentameter at the drop of a hat but who had Papa Smurf stare at her every morning while she showered. Trevor glared at Papa Smurf. Lucky bastard.

He stepped back from the curtain. Why was he having these thoughts? Why was he even thinking about Jenna in such a way? He couldn't. He absolutely could not think of Jenna as anything more than Ophelia.

Jenna giggled and Trevor turned to the door. Who was this guy who was making her laugh? He would love to hear her giggle again, just as she had that night at the theatre. A twinge of jealousy and anger shot down his arms and he balled his hands into fists, clenching and releasing, over and over. Here he was, Trevor Hughes, aka Caspian Locke, multi-award winning daytime drama star, stuffed into a tiny shoebox bathroom, with Jenna's drugstore brand shampoo and bra she'd left drying over the radiator. His attention drifted to that damned bra. He was thirty-two years old and a complete success…why was he hiding from a little boy on the other end of a phone call and lusting after a girl's bra? Women threw their bras and themselves at him. That's it. Trevor pushed open the bathroom door and rushed out.

Jenna gasped as he entered her tiny room. "Um, Mom? I've got to go. Trevor Hughes just bounded into my kitchen. No, I'm not kidding. Yes, the boy from the soap opera. Yes, Mom, he is very handsome. I have to go now; Trevor looks as if he needs some attention. Bye."

Trevor felt such a relief he wanted nothing more than to hold her. Instead, he grabbed his black coffee and slugged it down.

****

Jenna couldn't explain why the sudden presence of Trevor affected her to her very core. It was the way he entered the room, strong and virile. Something about him standing there made Jenna see him as a man, and not just a pretty boy on television who was also pretty darn good at Shakespeare. But she had to fight that instinct. Despite the fact that underneath it all he was a louse and how bad this would be for the show, she had other pressing reasons she had to remain single.

For one thing, if she thought there would ever be the real possibility of a man in her life, being an egg donor…damn…and for another, she had no time or interest in a relationship. Relationships cloud your judgment and make you lose yourself and your dreams, just as it did for her dad, and there was no way she would let that happen. But despite all that... "Your eyes," she muttered, momentarily transfixed. "They really are incredible."

"Thanks."

He didn't move. Despite everything, Jenna felt so close to Trevor right now, she longed to stand there forever, safe, inside this bubble he created by his masculine, protective aura. She bit her bottom lip.

"Yours, too." He took a step closer, but Jenna stayed still. "Your eye color, I've never seen it before. Hazel, I guess, but they're so light." Trevor took another step and lifted his hand to touch her.

Jenna froze. Oh, hell no. She would not be seduced by Trevor Hughes. She cleared her throat and backed away. "Guess our kids would have some pretty freaky eye color then, huh?"

Trevor dropped his hand and nodded slightly. He knew what she was doing. This guy had been around the block so many times, he had worn out the pavement. He knew women and this was a classic female move. Nothing scares off a guy like talking about kids before you've even been on a date. If he only knew the truth—talking about kids probably terrified her even more than it did him.

Trevor stood up straighter. He was taking control again and in some strange way, she wanted him to. He put down his empty paper cup. "Can we sit on the couch, maybe?"

"We can but it's a futon." She pointed over her shoulder at the pile of dirty clothes she had stacked on her bed. "It's impossible to close."

"Any reason?"

"It's too heavy."

"Maybe I can give it a try?"

"Suit yourself."

Trevor stood over the futon as Jenna made her way to the kitchen area. She stuck her coffee in the microwave and watched it spin around and around. She looked at Trevor. "I warned you, it's too heavy."

"It's not that, but it won't close with all this stuff on top." Trevor turned back to her.

"Oh, right." Jenna's cheeks heated. In a flash she was there, knocking the dirty clothes and blankets off the bed and onto the floor. She left the pink flannel sheets.

"You like pink, huh?" Trevor's eyes made their way to hers.

"I guess. But they're the only pink thing here."

Trevor's gaze dropped down to her t-shirt.

"Oh." Damn, he could probably see her bra through the flimsy t-shirt material. Jenna draped her arm across her shirt, her blush threatening to overtake her entire body.

To his credit, Trevor only smiled at her. He turned back to the futon and closed it with one hand.

"Oh." Jenna was surprised by his strength. She had imagined all those years in a cushy job made him weak. She almost said something to that extent but clamped her mouth shut just in time. "Let me grab our coffees and scripts." Jenna took her coffee out of the microwave and pulled a sugar dish from her cabinet.

Trevor was suddenly there, sending a vibration through her. "Did they forget your sugar? I double-checked with them."

"Un-uh. I like six sugars."

"You said four."

Jenna shrugged. "I wanted to make a good impression."

Trevor laughed and fixed his smile on Jenna.

It made her squirm. She needed to do something. "Hungry?" She tossed her head toward her fridge.

"What do you have?"

"Um..." Jenna stood on her tip-toes to look into her cabinet. "Ramen Noodles and peanut butter."

"That's all the food you have in your house?"

"Well, I only spend money on food to cook for my acting coach. We have a deal; I don't pay for classes and in return I cook for him whenever I can." She pointed to the fridge. "I have cream for coffee. Oh, and I have two kinds of peanut butter. Crunchy too." Jenna grabbed the jars from the cabinet and held them up victoriously. "Oh wait, wait." She stretched up again, and this time her t-shirt pulled up from her sweats. "Seaweed."

Jenna turned just in time to catch Trevor staring at her lower back. She shook the package in her hand.

"What?" Trevor snapped out of his daze.

"Dried seaweed. Want some?"

"No, thanks."

"Okay, but you don't know what you're missing." Jenna tore open the bag and crunched on the seaweed.

"Aren't you ever hungry for more? Like, I don't know, a steak?"

"Sure." She kept crunching on her seaweed. "But being hungry is good. It keeps you real. Even if I make it big someday." She bounced on her toes as she spoke. "I'll still stay as connected to grunge as I can— shopping in my cheap vintage stores; walking down hot dirty streets in late August, choking on the overpowering smell of urine; listening to start-up bands in dive clubs while drinking watered down whiskey; eating lousy but free hors d'oeuvres on opening nights of new gallery shows…" Her eyes were closed as she rattled off her reasons for loving New York, which were almost identical to most people's reasons for hating New York.

Trevor smiled as she shoved in one last piece then wiped her hands on her sweats.

"Okay. Well then, come on. Let's go see what Willy has to say."

"Willy?"

Trevor bristled at the mention of another man's name, and Jenna tilted her head, trying to understand. "Willy? William? Shakespeare?"

"Oh, yeah." Trevor took another big slug of coffee and together they made their way to the couch.

****

What the hell? That was all the food she had in her house? Watching Jenna in her kitchen—if you could call that tiny galley area a kitchen—was incredibly endearing, although Trevor repeatedly fought his impulse to pull out his cell, call his grocery service, and have real food delivered. When she reached up for the bag of seaweed exposing her beautifully toned lower back with two little dimples, placed just so…damn. He fought his every instinct to cross to her and kiss the small of her back, over and over again. He adored those dimples on a woman's lower back—Dimples of Venus—and they were incredibly rare.

Sitting on the futon with her hair draped over one shoulder, legs curled beneath her, script in one hand, coffee in the other, Trevor couldn't remember a time he had ever seen a more beautiful woman. She blew on the steaming cup of coffee, rolling her neck, and her nose ring sparkled. Trevor was transfixed. He dropped his head, shaking it. Damn it. No. He had no business being attracted to her. His feelings were an occupational hazard. Period. He was supposed to have them; they were only natural. Hamlet needed to fall in love with Ophelia, and sometimes, those feelings transferred offstage and into real life.

Still balancing her coffee, Jenna moved to stretch her back and Trevor felt an unexpected urge. Quickly he sat down next to her and opened his script. Great. The nunnery scene. This wouldn't help. Something on the wall caught his attention—a poster with a picture of a rainbow, and one single word: "Dream." He took a moment to process this. Aside from a few photos, this was the only piece of artwork hanging in Jenna's entire apartment.

"Nice poster."

Jenna looked at her wall. "Oh, thanks." She blushed. "My dad gave me that."

"He's a dreamer?" Trevor pushed more than he should, thrilled to discover anything about her.

"He was."

"Oh." Crap. "Uh, Jenna, I'm sorry."

Her eyes glassed over and Trevor shifted in his seat uncomfortably. He wasn't equipped to fix this. He wracked his brain, thinking of any advice he had heard. "Sometimes talking helps. Do you want to talk a—?"

Jenna shook her head, and the conversation was over. His jaw clenched. He was angry with himself for pressing her but he also felt like he missed a real opportunity to know Jenna better. How could an actor of her caliber be so disconnected in real life? He glanced at the poster again. Something else was attached to it...Trevor stood and walked over for a closer look. A tiny sticker read: "Save the Turtles."

"You have to be kidding me."

"What?" Jenna's eyes followed him.

"This 'Save the Turtles' sticker. Why do you have it?"

He ran his finger across the sticker then turned to see Jenna's face redden and her eyes narrow. She got up from the couch and walked to him.

"Really?" Jenna crossed her arms in front of her chest. Her nostrils flared as she spoke. "You really want to know?"

"Yes." Trevor nodded.

"Well, this was a cause my dad cared about—*greatly*."

"Okay..."

"And we took a trip once. Just us. The two of us. When we first found out he was sick. We couldn't afford it and I don't know how he did it but we did. We flew down to Florida to watch the loggerhead sea turtles hatch. And while we stood there, witnessing life begin, my father told me about his love for these little creatures and how they were nearly endangered and how he wished he could have done something for them."

A tear slipped down Jenna's cheek, and Trevor desperately wanted to wipe it away. Instead, he backed up, giving her space.

She lifted the corner of her t-shirt, dabbing at her eye. "It was all a metaphor, of course. That wasn't lost on me. I knew it wasn't just the turtles, I knew he wished he could have done more with his life. So I stood near a man with a death sentence, witnessing new life and it changed me. I swore then and there I would do something for those stupid little turtles and honor his dying wish."

"So you support the cause?"

Jenna glared at him, fury dancing in her eyes. "I did more than hang a dumb little sign, if that's what you're referring to." She turned away, anger shaking her tiny body.

Trevor moved toward her, wanting to reach for her, wanting to fix this. "I don't understand why you're mad at me."

"Really? Really, Trevor?"

"Jenna, you've been angry at me since the day you met me. Just tell me."

"When my father passed my mom was a wreck, as, I guess, she should have been. So it was my job to take care of the finances." Jenna shrugged. "It wasn't difficult; he left just a tiny bit of money, barely enough to pay for his small funeral with just a little left over."

"I'm sorry."

"Anywayyyyy..." Jenna exaggerated her words, obviously wanting to regain control of the conversation. "I took that little bit of money he left and instead of investing back into the family business or tucking it away for my sister's education, I thought of him and what I could do to make a difference in his name and to make his memory live on. So I donated it to the Sea Turtle Fund."

"That was incredibly—"

"Stupid?" Jenna raised her eyebrows at him. "Oh

yes, I know. My mother has informed me of this countless times."

"I was going to say generous."

"Well, stupid would have been right because in doing that I put my faith in someone who let me down." Jenna was close to him now, her tiny body moving up and down in time with her seething breath. "I trusted you. You, you asshole."

Trevor started at her word as Jenna turned her back and walked away.

"Jenna, what are you talking about?" If any other woman had called him an asshole, Trevor would have left. For sure. But Jenna's pain and anger, misdirected as it was, kept him there.

She stood at the window. "You were supposed to believe in this cause too."

"Jenna, I'm sorry, I just don't understand what I have to do with any of this."

"I donated the money right at the time when the Sea Turtle Fund said they were getting a huge endorsement from a celebrity who was about to do a series of public service announcements for them. And when he did, they would be able to do significant research, not just on the turtles, but on all types of sea life. And that would have made my small donation and my dad's desire, have some…purpose."

"Ohhhh…" Trevor walked toward her. "The PSAs. I'm sorry Jenna. I never knew what happened to those. One day I got a call from my agent telling me they were canceled. They never gave a reason why. I assumed they went with someone more high profile. Sometimes my character is such a bad guy, causes are afraid to side with me. Or sometimes they just cancel. I wasn't happy they were canceled either. I had my own reasons for doing them."

"Really?"

"Yes."

Jenna's eyes softened. For the first time ever, he saw hope in them. She bowed her head.

"I—I had no idea. I thought you just didn't care." Her words were quiet.

"No." Tentatively, he took a step closer. "The truth is I, uh…" He dropped his head and latched his hand to the back of his neck. "I care a lot more than anyone realizes." He lifted his head, facing Jenna.

She glanced up at him. "I'm so sorry. I called you an asshole. I don't usually do that."

"It's okay. I've been called worse." Trevor smiled, lost in her gorgeous eyes, wishing he could alleviate even some of the angst she was feeling. He would gladly stand there, letting her curse and scream if that's what it took. He understood the pain of loss. He moved closer, and she looked up at him. She didn't step away.

"I understand if you want to leave." Her voice was weak.

"I don't want to leave."

Trevor fixed his gaze on Jenna and she gave him a small sad smile. She seemed different now—still Jenna, but at least one layer of protection had been stripped away.

"Jenna…" He very nearly whispered, making his voice soft and calming. "I want to show you something."

"Yes?"

There was need in her, no doubt. Every cell in his body wanted so badly to fill that space, that emptiness, in her…and he wished to God she could fill that void in him. Without a word, Trevor reached up behind his head, and with one hand, yanked off his t-shirt. She gasped, and he smiled.

It was a natural effortless action for him—one he repeated time after time on the soap—but this time it meant more. This time he was invested. Jenna's eyes widened, focusing on his chest—not on his perfectly toned abdomen or the width of his upper body, but on what he wanted her to see: the sea turtle, tattooed just over his heart.

"How? Why?" Jenna stepped forward.

"I've got a nephew. He's five but he's loved turtles, forever. Obsessed with them." Trevor smiled, thinking of Toby. "I got the tattoo a couple of years ago, when Toby and I were…" He stalled for a moment, careful with his words. "Doing some research on turtles, and I learned about their cause."

Jenna looked up at him, soaking in his every word.

"Toby thinks it's great. Makes him smile every time I take him to the beach." He shrugged. "And I figured I spend so much time with my shirt off anyway, it might as well do some good."

Jenna giggled. The sound warmed Trevor's heart. He shifted, and her body moved with his.

"No one knows about the tattoo because the soap covers it. It doesn't fit Caspian's bad boy image but I was going to do the PSAs shirtless, making fun of myself."

Jenna smiled again.

"The turtle fund had contacted me to do the PSAs because of my connection to them. I honestly don't know why they were canceled. I'm sorry if I let you down." The ache in his gut told Trevor he really was sorry he had disappointed her. "Not that it matches what the PSAs would have brought in, but I make a sizable donation to the turtles every year. I understand your father's affinity toward them, Jen."

Her eyes danced across his as she raised her hand to his chest, placing her warm fingers on the tattoo.

Trevor inhaled sharply.

"Sorry." Jenna pulled her hand away and looked up at him, her eyes wide with wonder. "I never should have—you and Maggie...ugh." Jenna put her head in her hands. "That was so tacky of me. I'm sorry."

Trevor wasn't sorry. He took her hand and placed it back on his chest. She tried to pull away, but he held her fast.

"Don't pull away. Please."

Her shoulders moved in time with her hurried breath.

Good God, what was he doing? Whatever it was, her hand was so warm, and her touch so gentle...and it felt so...freaking...good.

She swallowed, hard. "I'm not getting between you and Maggie. And I'm not interested in being some part-time tramp, sneaking—"

"Shh..." He shook his head, closing his eyes. He flattened Jenna's palm and held it against his heart, feeling...complete. "Of course not, Jenna."

Slowly, her fingers moving beneath his grasp, she traced the outline of the turtle. His breath quickened and his nipples hardened. He opened his eyes and she glanced up at him, her hurried breathing sounding like a growl...passion flickering in her eyes. He grabbed both of her hands and drew them to him. She closed her eyes, and Trevor felt the power was all his...

But he needed to be careful of how he used it.

He let go of her hands just to reach out and stroke her soft, beautiful cheek, and in that instant he knew his feelings were not an occupational hazard and this was not some casual theatre romance.

****

Jenna never wanted to move. Ever. The feeling of Trevor's hand on her face was so intimate and comforting...and now, damn it, her first line of defense was down. That seed of resentment she had toward him was obliterated, and now she wasn't sure she could trust herself. Correction, she *knew* she couldn't trust herself.

Trevor made her feel warm and safe and so incredibly excited—she desperately wanted him to overpower her and protect her all at once. Her stomach clenched as her breathing grew shallower. She allowed herself a moment, just a moment, and she nuzzled against his hand. He cupped her cheek. She loved the feel of his hand on her; she wanted to step forward, closer to him, burying herself in his chest. She wanted to feel his strong hands wrap around her waist. She wanted to feel his kiss.

But she couldn't. No way. Thank goodness Maggie was in the picture; she was the insurance Jenna needed. Jenna would never do anything with Trevor as long as he was with Maggie—and frankly, she'd never respect him if he did. But standing before her without his shirt...how much willpower could she be expected to have? As her body warmed with his touch, her mind wandered. If Maggie were gone...and if his kiss led to more...and if they jumped into a relationship...no, no, no. This was the reason the psychologist recommended it was best to stay single until the process was over. There were no "ifs" here—there were only cold, hard facts.

She had to do something to lighten the moment before they got carried away. "I was thinking…" Jenna muttered, stepping back from Trevor. His hand dropped, and she shuddered without his touch.

He threw his shirt back on, and she shivered in the void he left behind.

"It's not that I'm great or anything but Shakespeare just makes sense to me. The show's coming up fast, so uh, if there's anything you want to go over…" Jenna shrugged and sipped her drink, hoping steaming hot coffee might cool her off.

Trevor's face changed as he processed her words, no doubt trying to understand why she was shutting down. He bristled. "Do you think there's something I should be working on?"

"No, no." Jenna lifted her gaze to him. "I didn't mean that at all. But sometimes I like to run lines with someone else. It brings a fresh perspective."

"You run lines with someone else?" He stepped closer to her.

The depth of his voice, the way he focused on her then…all of it made Jenna think he might be jealous.

"I don't mean someone other than you."

His gaze was heavy on her, and she squirmed.

"I mean when I practice with my coach. In class, you know?"

Trevor raised his eyebrows at her, and she stumbled forward.

"I mean, you could run them with me instead of rehearsing alone." She was tripping over her words, but she couldn't stop herself. "Not that I think you're ever alone." Jenna's cheeks burned. She looked up at Trevor, desperate, and the side of his mouth turned up slightly, putting her somewhat at ease. Her shoulders slumped and she had a strange, heavy sensation in her core. She felt like she was cheating on him…it was all too bizarre.

"Okay." Trevor scratched the scruff on his chin.

"What's okay?" She fought for coherent thought.

"I'd love to work on a soliloquy with you. Anything in particular?"

Jenna pulled herself together, making her way back to the couch. She sat, picking up her pencil and script. She shrugged, playing with the pencil, twirling it then bit down on the eraser end and noticed Trevor staring. He looked away and cleared his throat.

"Maybe your, 'To be or not to be'?" She looked at him sideways, gauging his reaction.

"You do get right to it, don't you?"

"Stupid idea." Jenna waved off the idea with her hand. "Sorry. Let's just plow through the nunnery scene."

Suddenly the words fell effortlessly from his mouth. " 'To be, or not to be: that is the question. Whether 'tis nobler in the mind to suffer the slings and arrows of outrageous fortune, or to take arms against a sea of troubles, and by opposing end them? To die: to sleep; no more…' "

Jenna was lost in his words. He spoke with ease, and compassion, and grace. He was as good as any Hamlet had ever been…no…better.

When he reached, " 'And lose the name of action,' " Jenna jumped from her seat and threw her arms around

Trevor's neck. She pushed herself against him tightly, and Trevor wrapped his arms around her.

He pulled back, smiling. "C'mon kid, let's get to work."

She nodded, her heart racing.

Chapter Seven

For hours, Jenna and Trevor sat side by side on Jenna's tiny couch. They ripped apart every scene Jenna had and dissected his soliloquies. For the first time in a very long time, Trevor had shrugged off Caspian, leaving him behind like footprints in the snow, and he felt freer and happier because of it. By one in the morning, he was elated and exhausted. He looked over to see Jenna had fallen asleep. She leaned back against the futon cushion, but she didn't look at all comfortable—what she did look was beautiful. Too beautiful.

He needed to leave.

Trevor stood and stretched to his full height. He grabbed his script and glanced at the door with the four deadbolts. If he left—which he should—it would mean she would be here, asleep, with an unlocked door and no doorman downstairs. Crap. Energy coursed through him, and now he was fully awake. He shoved his hand into his pocket, fishing out his phone. He scrolled through his texts. No message from Maggie. Not that he really expected one, it wasn't like they checked in with each other, but...shouldn't they check in with each other? Shouldn't two people who were planning to, someday in the future, spend their lives together, check in with each other? Tell the other person they were okay? That they left the gym and made it home unscathed? Or…that they were going to spend the night in the apartment of their very sexy costar…?

Trevor looked at the deadbolts again. As a man, it was his job to protect those who needed protecting, so there was no way he could go and leave her with an unlocked door. Of course, he could wake Jenna and she could lock up behind him but it was late and his driver was certainly asleep and getting a cab in this neighborhood at this hour—oh, fuck it. Who was he fooling? The God's honest truth was he didn't want to go.

His fingers stalled over his phone screen—he should text Maggie to let her know where he was—but it was late. Too late. He stuffed his phone back into his pocket and glanced around the apartment. Sure, Jenna would be pissed if she woke to find him there, but there was no way he was going to slip out and leave her door unlocked. Let her be angry. Let Maggie be pissed. He wouldn't do anything inappropriate and this was the logical, reasonable, mature decision. Leaving was just too unsafe. If the boyfriend showed up, Trevor would explain his reasons for staying. Any man worth his weight would agree with Trevor's actions. Yes. He would stay. Trevor nodded to himself. His impulse was right; it was his motive he doubted.

As carefully as he could, he slid Jenna down on the couch. He pulled a blanket from the pile on the floor and covered her. She murmured and smiled in her sleep and Trevor could have stayed there forever, watching over her. But what he needed was sleep and distance. He pulled another blanket and pillow from the pile and made himself a bed on the floor, as far away from Jenna as possible. As he pulled the blanket around himself, he caught a whiff of her—she smelled like clean, fresh herbs. It was the aroma he had tried to ignore while they sat side by side on the futon.

"Her shampoo," Trevor mumbled, pulling the blanket higher. With thoughts of her bright eyes and coy smile, Trevor drifted to sleep.

****

Trevor woke to find Jenna on the couch, looking at him. He sat up quickly, expecting holy hell. Instead, she smiled.

"Well, I guess we've answered that age-old question: did Hamlet and Ophelia ever spend the night together…?" She stretched, uncrossed her legs, and stood. "Coffee?" She pulled at her t-shirt as she asked.

"Sure."

"Black, I know." She crinkled up her nose.

Trevor could barely contain the excitement he felt waking up after spending the night with Jenna. He liked it. Actually, he liked it way, way too much, which could be rather evident if she noticed. He waited for her to look away before he pushed the blanket off his body. He drew his leg up, resting his arm on it casually, hoping the change of position would offer some camouflage.

Jenna walked to her window and opened the shade. "Huh, snow." She turned to him. "We haven't had much yet this year. I love the snow. You?"

Trevor thought about how much he hated trudging through the filthy New York snow, slipping on the sidewalks, and being splashed as cars rushed through the slushy puddles. There was only one thing he could say… "Yeah, I love it too."

Damn. How easily those words slipped out. He had

never said he loved anything, or anyone, ever before. Not even Maggie.

Jenna nodded along, enthusiastically. She stood there by that window, the bright light reflecting off her hair. Trevor thought about her father. Was she lonely? No, look at her, she could be with anyone she wanted, whenever she wanted. But yet she wasn't. She was living here. Alone. Without even a cat. He ached for her loneliness. He understood it.

"How about we go play in the snow?"

Jenna turned to him, smiling. "Really?"

"Really."

Her exuberant mood suddenly darkened. "I don't know." She gazed back out the window.

"You want to play alone?"

She shook her head.

"So then, let's go."

Now under control, Trevor stood up and crossed to Jenna. He leaned on the opposite side of the window. She looked so beautiful in the soft light, he began to lose his battle with restraint, once again. For a moment, all he could imagine was turning her to face that wall she was resting against, his body pressed up hard against hers—one of his hands flattened against the wall, the other stroking her beautiful face and hair as she leaned back toward him. He imagined turning her around, tucking her into a sultry cocoon he created with his forearms pressed up against the wall, her body willingly trapped by him...her giant eyes, hiding nothing, telling him it was all up to him.

"Trevor?" Jenna eyed him curiously.

Trevor shoved his hands into his jeans quickly and adapted his best carefree demeanor. "Yeah?" He

91

smiled, mentally counting to a thousand, wondering if he would need to make a quick exit. He took a deep breath, fighting his desire, not wanting to go anywhere.

She cocked her head, squinting.

"Look, Jenna, I'm not talking about what color our children's eyes will be."

She winced at his words. He lifted his hand, brushing back a piece of her hair that had fallen across her face. She closed her eyes.

"But Maggie…"

Trevor chuckled. "I promise, Maggie has no interest in playing in the snow."

She looked away.

"Jenna. I'm just talking about having some fun. Snowmen and snowball fights." And that was the truth. Because no matter how much he enjoyed being with her, nothing could happen between them.

"Snowball fights?" Jenna's mood changed again and her eyes flew open, wide. She raised an eyebrow in a dare.

"Scared?"

"I come from upstate. We have snow in August."

"Doesn't mean you can hold your own in a snowball fight."

"I had a nasty boy living next door." Jenna placed her hands on her hips. "You know the Christmas movie where the elf has a snowball fight? I'm just saying I think I can hold my own."

"Never saw it. But I'll take that as a challenge."

"Wait, you never saw it?"

"Nope."

"It's a Christmas classic. That's un-American. We need to rectify this, stat."

"Okay. I'll make you a deal. After the snowball fight, if you win, we watch the movie together."

"When?"

"Tonight." Trevor's pulse quickened, his heartbeat in his throat.

Jenna chewed her lip as she processed his suggestion. "Okay." She crossed her arms in front of her.

"Really?"

"It'll probably be good for us to build a friendship offstage. It'll carry onstage too."

A searing pain shot through Trevor's gut. Why did he feel so defeated when he got what he wanted?

"Wait. It'll never happen, but what happens if you win?"

Trevor smiled at her. "We watch the movie then, too."

Jenna grinned.

****

While Trevor ran home to change, Jenna took longer than she meant preparing to go play in the snow. She threw on her favorite jeans and t-shirt, and piled on a warm fuzzy white sweater. She tied up her boots, and although she didn't want to admit it, even to herself, she added just a touch of lip gloss.

At eleven, her door buzzed. "I'll come down," Jenna said into the intercom. She made one final pass of her apartment, grabbed her coat, stuffed her wallet and lip gloss into her pocket and then headed out. It took a good three minutes for her to lock her door, because she double-checked each lock as she went. She turned and nearly bumped into Trevor.

"Oh." Jenna stood back, her heart pounding.

"How'd you get in?"

"Someone was leaving. I grabbed the door."

She nodded. "You didn't have to meet me at the door."

"Of course I did."

Jenna moved back one more step and landed flat up against her door. Trevor stood too close, unnerving her. She bit her bottom lip, looking down at her boots. The air between them was charged and Jenna took a moment to calm her breathing. They were just two co-workers, spending some time together. Playing in the snow. That was all.

"My car's waiting."

And just like that, the fuse blew on the electric current running between them. "Your car?"

"Yes."

He spoke with such cockiness, Jenna wanted to throw something at him. Here she was, preparing to sell her eggs so she could make enough money to stay in the city, and more importantly, keep her sister from working at the laundry business, and he was trying to impress her with a car. Were the rich really that out of touch with the rest of the world?

Jenna shook her head. Maybe she should pretend to be sick? No way. He'd offer to get her soup or something and make his way back into her apartment. Sighing heavily, she turned and clumped down the stairs, muttering as she went. He held the apartment building door open for her, and she walked out onto the street.

As soon as she saw the freshly fallen snow, her mood brightened. "It's beautiful."

"Yes," Trevor answered, smiling at her.

Jenna fidgeted in her boots. Was this all a big seduction game? Did he really think she would be the next girl to throw herself at Trevor Hughes? Was he that guy who kept a girlfriend but had fun on the side? Was he looking for one of those lame theatre romances that lasts until opening night when everyone gets drunk and hooks up and gets pissed off for the remainder of the run? Jenna set her jaw. That would not happen to her. And as far as anything that might last longer, that wasn't on the table. Not even with a normal guy, let alone someone who no doubt disposed of women with more frequency than the average person flushed the toilet. And it probably meant about the same. She sighed.

Since she wouldn't fall for his seduction game, she acquiesced and climbed into the back of his black luxury Town car. The driver closed her door, and Trevor slid in.

Jenna leaned back against the heated seats. "This feels nice," she murmured.

Trevor smiled. "Maybe cars aren't all bad, huh?"

Jenna shrugged.

"Where to, Mr. Hughes?"

"Central Park, please. Fifth Avenue entrance."

Jenna had an odd reaction to the sound of the name "Mr. Hughes." She had worked so hard to consider Trevor just an average guy, she'd nearly forgotten he commanded respect in the world. She sneaked a peek at him out of the corner of her eye.

"Concerned?"

"What?" Jenna sat up straight and pulled off her mittens. The car was too warm.

"About the snowball fight."

"Oh." She tossed her head back and smiled, despite…everything that was crowding her brain. "Not the slightest bit. You?"

"Nope."

They drove in silence for another fifteen minutes, and Jenna stared out the window at the city. "It's so beautiful, it looks like it's dusted in powdered sugar."

Trevor laughed. "That is one insatiable sugar jones you have."

"Here we are, Mr. Hughes. Central Park."

Trevor slid forward in his seat to talk to the driver. "Thanks." He looked at Jenna as he spoke. "It shouldn't be long until I destroy Ms. Joyce, so hang tight. We have a lunch reservation at twelve-thirty."

She looked down at her clothes. "I'm not really dressed for lunch."

"Not to worry. This place is cool. Besides, I think you look terrific."

Jenna's face flushed. "Uh, thanks." Were snowballs in the park followed by lunch regular stops along his path to seduction? She shook her head. Look at him. Wavy messy brown hair, the slightest scruff covering a really strong jaw, bright, smart eyes…he didn't need to seduce anyone—women threw themselves at him. And he certainly wouldn't work to seduce the likes of her. Maybe he just wanted to take her to lunch. Jenna's heart lurched a bit. "Where are we going? For lunch?"

"Sushi." When he smiled, slight wrinkles formed around his eyes.

"Sushi?"

"Yeah. The way you tore into that seaweed yesterday, I thought it was a safe bet. And based on your phone and your vintage jacket"—Trevor touched the collar of her jacket as he spoke—"you seem into retro. I thought you'd find this place cool."

"Oh, uh, thanks. That was very…thoughtful." Jenna fought the urge to take his hand. Instead, she smiled.

Trevor smiled back.

****

It didn't take long for Jenna to have a pile of snowballs waist high. Problem was, so did he. Trevor looked at Jenna, caught in a dilemma. Of course he would let her win, but how to do it without her knowing was the catch. A woman like Jenna would hate to be babied and yet he had an incredibly strong desire to baby her.

"All right," she sang out, the happiest Trevor had ever seen her. "Prepare for your quick demise."

She picked up a snowball and tossed it at Trevor. It hit him square in the chest. Okay, she had pretty good aim. This could be a fairer fight than he anticipated.

Trevor returned a shot that hit her on the back when she turned to run.

"Not good enough," she called out, tossing two snowballs simultaneously.

"You're ambidextrous," he shouted. "That's not fair."

"Not ambidextrous, it's a perk of playing piano. Both hands do what I ask."

Trevor shrugged off his very inappropriate thought as she tossed another snowball and another, each hitting him again in the chest. Then she threw another, clocking Trevor on the jaw. He dusted the snow off his scruff.

"All right," he warned, picking up an armful of snowballs and walking toward her.

"No," Jenna shrieked, running away and trying to hide behind her fort.

"Oh no, there's no hiding. This is war." Trevor bounded across the snow.

She shrieked again and ran toward his fort, with Trevor close behind. She looked so happy and carefree, Trevor couldn't get enough. She picked up an armful of snowballs and tossed them at Trevor just as he threw a few at her. They walked closer and closer until they were within arms' distance, both pelting the other with snowballs. Jenna was laughing so hard she looked like she could barely catch her breath. Trevor threw one final snowball, and it snuck into the collar of her coat.

"Oh, cold..." Jenna wiggled about, trying to remove the snow.

Trevor frowned. Damn, he never should have let it go this far. He moved to help, but just as he did—bam! Jenna threw a whole armful of snowballs at him, pelting him on the chest, arms, and face.

"Oh, you little brat."

Jenna ran and Trevor chased after her. It took only a moment for him to catch her. He grabbed her hand and swung her around. Momentum pushed her against his chest, and Trevor seized the moment. There, in the middle of Central Park, he wrapped his arms around her. He pulled her higher until she balanced on her tippy-toes and he moved her closer still, covering nearly her entire back with his one hand. Overcome, he let his other hand drop to the small of her back...inching its way down.

He kept his hands still when she tensed, but then

she gave over and her small hands wrapped around his waist, warming his back. It was so right to have Jenna in his arms—he was himself for the first time, ever. Here, with Jenna, he didn't have to manufacture sex appeal; she wasn't expecting him to be anything but himself. He didn't have to walk a certain way, or smile a certain way. He could just be, and it was an incredibly freeing experience. He was finally with a woman who understood the difference between reality and fiction, and especially, between Trevor Hughes and Caspian Locke. No, he couldn't and shouldn't do this...he had never and would never cheat on Maggie, but still...this was a moment that couldn't be denied. He knew, first hand, everything could end today, and if it did, he would be eternally sorry he hadn't shared this minute with Jenna Joyce in the middle of Central Park.

But then again, everything could end today.

He dropped his hands, backing away from her. "I uh, I'm sorry."

Jenna turned her eyes down toward the snow. Her cheeks flushed a deep red color.

"Jenna..." Oh, damn it. The last thing he wanted was for her to be embarrassed or feel bad. "I'm sorry, I should never have—"

She put up her hand, stopping him. "No. I should never have come. It was a really, really bad idea. I'm sorry." She began to walk off.

"Jenna, wait." Trevor called after her. "Let me take you to lunch. Please."

She turned to face him. "Thanks, Trevor; I appreciate it, but no." She cleared her throat. "I'll uh, I'll see you in rehearsal."

She put up her hand, waving goodbye.

"Jenna…"

Trevor rubbed a searing pain in his gut as he watched her walk off.

Chapter Eight

Missing the opportunity to watch a movie with Trevor hurt way more than it should have. The only answer for Jenna was to drown herself in work; it was the healthiest and safest option she had. Thankfully, Don said they could meet for a Saturday night emergency session.

Jenna arrived at Don's theatre early, carrying a pan of homemade, low-cholesterol, salt-free, blonde brownies. Standing outside the black curtain leading to the theatre, she cocked her head, surprised to hear voices inside. It was odd for Don to coach on a Saturday night; most of his actors were performing on Broadway at that time.

Clutching the brownies tightly, Jenna hesitated. She didn't want to walk in on someone's coaching session but as she stood there listening, her tummy clenched. She recognized the voice inside. With anger annihilating manners, Jenna pulled back the curtain and barged in. "Trevor?" Jenna blurted. "Why are you here?"

Don turned to Jenna. "You're early, Jenna. We will be finishing up in a few moments." He held up his hand to her, leaning forward as he coughed.

Damn it. Don's cough was deeper. She peered at Trevor to see if he noticed it, too. His brow was furrowed; of course he noticed. She shook her head.

No, Don was strong. He would be fine as long as she dragged him to the doctor first thing on Monday. But tonight...Jenna's face scrunched into a scowl...tonight, she had to deal with Trevor.

Still carrying her brownies and with all the grace of a petulant child throwing a temper tantrum, Jenna ignored Don's words and marched onstage to confront Trevor. "Why? Why are you here? Are you following me?"

Trevor turned to her, his gaze heavy on hers. "No, Jenna. I'm not following you. I study with Don, too."

"What? Why didn't you tell me?" Jenna turned to Don. "Why didn't either of you tell me?" Hurt ricocheted through her like a ball bearing in a pinball game.

"Because it wasn't your business." Don answered flatly.

"What do you mean it wasn't my business? This is my show, too."

"Yes. And Trevor is Hamlet. Trevor's been my student for a very long time."

"Why didn't you tell me?" Jenna turned to Trevor.

"You didn't ask."

"That's convenient." Jenna tossed the brownies onto a chair and threw her bag down. She stormed over to Trevor. "You, you...*liar*."

"Okay." Trevor turned to Jenna, his chest heaving. His voice was sharp, echoing through the theatre.

She took a tiny step backward.

"Before you get so self-righteous, why don't you tell me why you stormed off from the park this morning?"

She glanced at Don then focused on Trevor, lifting

her eyebrows. "You know why…" There was no way she wanted to get into this in front of Don.

"Is it the boyfriend?"

"What?"

"Your boyfriend."

She squeezed her eyes shut, trying to make sense of what he was saying, and then opened them, glaring at Trevor. "You think I would have been spending my Saturday playing in the park with you if I had a boyfriend?"

"I just assumed."

"No. I don't have a boyfriend." She clenched her jaw. "You think because you have a girlfriend, I have to have a boyfriend? Does it lessen your guilt?"

"No. It's not about guilt. Maggie and I, there are things you don't know—situations you don't understand."

"Oh please." She stepped back, rolling her eyes. "What, now you're going to give me some lame story about how Maggie doesn't understand you?"

"Of course not. I take full responsibility for everything I do, but I never meant for Maggie and I to last as long as we have. I don't love her, Jenna."

Butterflies raced around her stomach, and Jenna put a hand to her abdomen, trying to calm them. "Does she know that?"

"I don't know. But the fact is, you were there, too. With me, in the park. And if I hadn't stopped us—"

Jenna narrowed her eyes. "Nothing would have happened. I can promise you that."

"That's not what I think."

"So maybe I had a momentary lapse in judgment. But nothing's going to happen between us, I can promise you that." She cocked her head, searching his eyes. "You should have told me you study with Don. I was right about you from the beginning. You—with this façade like you're such a great guy but the truth is you're a liar. You're lying to Maggie and you've been lying to me."

Trevor stepped forward, grabbing her forearm. Her eyes widened.

"I am not a liar. Maggie and I are in a complicated situation which you know nothing about. You want to know the real reason I didn't tell you about Don? The real reason is because the only thing you have in your sad little life is your talent. And I know you hate me, and soap operas, and everything we stand for—commercialism, greed, lack of talent, no soul—so I tried to spare you the bitter truth. I study with Don because I have talent, too. And whatever this is you have"—Trevor ran his hand up and down the air—"This hatred for money and success, I think it's because you don't have either. And let me tell you something, Jenna; you think poverty proves you have a soul? Grow up and stop romanticizing failure. You think money makes me a sell-out? I have survived off my art, my craft, for a long time. You've only been at this for a year. One year. I've been at it for over a decade. Take it from me, eating Ramen noodles and peanut butter three times a day gets old fast. So forgive me for wanting more."

Jenna broke her arm free and took a large step back. "How dare you?" More than anything she wanted to quit the play. But she couldn't. She needed the money desperately and she needed to prove she could be a success, just like she promised her father on his deathbed. "I understand if you want to fire me." Jenna stood up tall as she addressed Trevor. "But I'd prefer you didn't." She turned to Don. "I'm sorry I interrupted. It was rude and unprofessional."

Don nodded.

Jenna grabbed her bag and made her way to the curtain. Tears ached in her eyes. Good God, what had Trevor done to her? She fought back the tears, refusing to let them fall.

"Jenna?" Trevor stood there with his hands out. "You don't have to run away again."

"I'm not running away." Jenna spoke through her teeth. Oh, screw this. She threw her bag down onto the floor and stormed back to Trevor. "I have never, ever run away, Trevor. Not from anything. You have no idea what you're talking about."

"Then tell me."

Jenna wiped her nose with her sleeve, fighting to calm her breathing. "I follow through on every promise I make. But I didn't promise you anything, except to be a damned good Ophelia. Just stay clear of me."

"Why?"

"How about because of Maggie?"

"Oh, screw Maggie."

"You do. That's the problem."

Trevor turned away and back again. "I mean, pretend Maggie wasn't in the picture. Tell me why you wouldn't be with me."

"I can't."

"You can't, or you don't want to?" Trevor crossed his arms over his wide chest. "Tell me you don't get some kind of thrill out of Caspian Locke chasing after you while you hide your deep, dark secret?"

He shook his head, walking away, and Jenna went after him.

"Hey!"

Trevor spun around to face her.

Jenna's head throbbed, and her heart raced. "Who the hell do you think you are?" Her voice was louder than she meant it to be. "I am a fully functioning person, and if I say something then that's the way it is, whether you like it or not. I'm not a child, and I'm not playing games here. And as far as being thrilled Caspian Locke is chasing after me...one, I don't think you're chasing after me and two, I don't give a damn about some made-up television character." Jenna stepped closer; a wall of energy wedged between them. She lowered her voice. "I've never once thought of you as anyone except Trevor Hughes, and when we're rehearsing, Hamlet. That's it." Jenna drew in a deep breath, hurt radiating through her. "This is your own insecurity you're dumping on me. And as far as the rest of it, you don't have to like the way I live, or the way I eat, or anything about me. I'm not here for you to fix, Trevor. I just am. And screw you if you don't like me."

Jenna was interrupted by the sound of Don clapping. She turned to him, startled.

"Oh, Jenna, Jenna, Jenna."

She stood on the stage, staring at Don, trying to slow her panting. Her heart sprinted. She could feel Trevor's gaze burrowing into the side of her head, but she didn't care. She bit the inside of her cheek, fighting to calm down.

"I'm happy to see this fire exists in you. Finally." Don held his cane in one hand and lifted it up toward the heavens. "I guess all it took to unlock it was this handsome young man."

Jenna's cheeks burned, her feet glued to the floor.

Don smiled at her. "For God's sake, Jenna, now find this passion in your work."

"But that's the only place I have passion."

"No, that's the only place you let yourself feel feelings. But this is the first time I've seen genuine *passion* in you." Don turned to Trevor. "In *either* of you." Don shifted so he could speak to both of them at once. "Trevor, Jenna…you are both excellent young actors. And Trevor, you'll take any risk thrown at you but you've spent so many years playing one particular character, you've forgotten what reality is. Until now."

Don smiled and went on. "And Jenna. Sweet Jenna." Don motioned for her to walk to the center of the stage, next to Trevor. She did. "You are such a good actor, with such a guarded heart, except when it comes to me. You have done so much for me—cooking, straightening my apartment, transcribing my notes, worrying about me through this blasted cold." He shook his fist to heaven, doing his classic King Lear.

"I like to do it."

"Yes, and you do a wonderful job of taking care of me. But don't you think it's time all that exceptional love you have locked away in your heart was given to someone else?"

Jenna opened her mouth to speak, but Don put up his hand.

"Not me, Jenna. I'm an old, old, man. And we have been there for each other—each helping the other in those times we've missed the great loves of our lives. But your great love was filial love, Jenna. And now it's time for you to find your real love. You need to let go.

You're terrified to go too far, in your work and your life."

Jenna gasped.

"Am I wrong?"

She shook her head.

It took some time but Don pulled a wallet from his hip pocket. "Come, come." He opened the faded brown leather wallet and turned to a picture, equally faded. "My Evelyn."

Jenna had seen the picture many times before but she was happy to see it again.

"She was my reason for living."

"But all those years you lived for your art."

"No, Jenna. I lived for her. And she lived for me. Yes, I had passion in my art, but only because of her." Don slid his finger down the picture gently, as if he were caressing her cheek. "When she passed, I thought I had lost my reason for living. Then I turned to Trevor, and you, and a few more of my favorite students, and I figured I could teach you, not how to act—you know that—but how to feel."

Jenna shifted her weight from foot to foot and glanced at Trevor. He stood perfectly still, hanging on Don's every word.

"But I was wrong. You can't teach someone to feel, you can only tell them it's okay to do so." Don turned his still brilliantly sharp blue eyes to Trevor and Jenna, and then he whistled. "Evelyn and I, we loved each other passionately and completely. Some days she drove me crazy, and sometimes I drove her nuts, but at the end of the day, we always came home to each other. It wasn't always easy—no, not by any means. I think one of the most trying times of our lives was early on when I played Hamlet and she played Ophelia. What I saw tonight were two people who care more about each other than they want to admit. Whether you explore this in your real lives or only on the stage is up to you. But I saw passion in both of you tonight—passion for your art, and passion for each other."

Don rearranged himself and coughed louder and longer.

Jenna grabbed his water and offered it to him.

He shook his head while his eyes smiled at her. "I will give you both a word or two of unsolicited advice…be nice to each other. When it comes down to it, you need each other on that stage. You support one another and feed off each other. Be someone the other person can rely on onstage, and in real life, too. And one more thing." Don took them each by the hand. "I am giving you permission to feel. Be passionate. Fight, love, live your lives. Believe me, it goes so much faster than you could ever imagine." He smiled. "Ernest Hemingway…" He shook his head. "He understood. Trust each other."

Trevor shifted toward Jenna, but she looked away.

Don dropped their hands and continued. "It's Saturday night, for God's sake. Go make love. And if you're not making love then at the very least, take a break."

Jenna's cheeks flushed, and she glanced at Trevor who stared at the theatre floor. His gaze found hers and she looked away.

Don shook his head at them, smiling. "Head over to the coffee shop. Have a bite. Hamlet and Ophelia have been around for hundreds of years. They'll still be here tomorrow."

****

"What do you think?" Trevor asked as they stood on the street corner. All he wanted to do was to hold Jenna and make everything right but he couldn't. He was incredibly sorry for the rude things he said, and if she gave him the chance, he was certain he could make it up to her. As she stood there shivering on the sidewalk, he knew he had been a bully. He had berated her to prove his own worth and because of his own insecurities. She really never said a bad word about his soap opera; it was all in his head, and he had no idea she imagined he was trying to change her. That was the very opposite of the truth. He liked her exactly as she was.

"I think it's late."

"Jenna." He reached out and took her hand, thrilled she didn't pull away. "Let's go get some coffee. Please. Let me get you something to eat." He was certain she was about to say yes, when some tourists spotted him.

"Caspian!" A woman shouted to him as a group of six middle-aged women approached Trevor. They were dressed similarly, in brightly colored car-length coats, with dress pants and sensible boots. One was blonder than the next, and each had sprayed her hair into a perfectly coiffed shoulder-length bob. Not a single hair on any one head moved when the women did.

"It's Caspian Locke!" shouted another.

They surrounded Trevor, nudging Jenna out of the way as they pulled their cell phones from their designer bags. They linked arms with him, one on each side, and he forced smile after smile as they snapped selfies with him.

Jenna backed away slowly.

"Jenna," he mouthed.
But Jenna just put up her hand and walked away.

Chapter Nine

"Trevor?"

Amanda stood in the doorway of her kitchen, rubbing sleep from her eyes. She yawned as she spoke, glancing at the clock on the kitchen wall. "It's six in the morning. You must have left at five to get out here to the Island. You okay?"

"Yeah, yeah. Sure." Trevor pulled off his skullcap and dark gray parka, hanging them on a chair at the kitchen table. Leaving at five was no big deal, considering he'd been up all night, and had already gone on a five-mile run that morning. "I'm sorry to come by so early."

Amanda stood on her tiptoes and gave him a kiss on the cheek. She patted his arm, and made her way straight to the coffeepot. She poured ground coffee beans into a filter in the pot, and added water. "You don't have to be sorry. You're always welcome; you know that."

Trevor plopped onto a chair.

Amanda turned from the coffeepot and leaned against the counter, waiting for the coffee to drip. "Are those donuts?" She nodded to the box on the table.

"Yeah." Trevor smiled. "Don't be mad. It's Sunday."

"He shouldn't be eating junk, Trevor."

"Neither should I." Trevor patted his gut as he

spoke.

Amanda chuckled, tossing her head.

She was so beautiful, with long honey brown hair and eyes a similar color to his, but under those eyes were dark circles from many sleepless nights, and worry was permanently etched on her forehead. Yes, she was beautiful, but exhausted. She certainly wasn't heavy, but she was much sturdier than the female actors he encountered every day. Amanda had to be. She had no option but to be strong.

"I'm sure all those adoring fans you have around the world wouldn't care if you were carrying a few extra pounds."

He chuckled, looking around the kitchen. It was a nice house he had bought her, not small, but not huge, just the right size for her to handle, with plenty of room for the two of them. It was in a great suburban neighborhood with kids for Toby to play with when he was feeling well enough to do so. She had added lots of homey touches—decorative kitchen towels, a never-filled cow-shaped cookie jar, soft, flowing curtains on the bay window that overlooked the nicely landscaped backyard.

Smiling, Trevor turned to the fridge. Absolutely his favorite parts of the décor were Toby's drawings Amanda had taped to the cabinets and sides of the fridge. Trevor nodded to one. "He's into pirates, now, huh?"

Amanda glanced at the sketch and turned back to the coffeepot. She took two heavy red, oversized mugs from the cabinet and poured coffee. "Oh, yes. Started a few days ago. One of the nurses at his checkup was dressed like one. Complete with a parrot on his shoulder."

"Huh." Trevor looked off.

"Trevor." Amanda placed a mug full of steaming coffee in front of him and sat down across the table from him. "We don't need a troupe of actors dressed like pirates showing up this afternoon for a play date. I know how you think." She winked, adding sugar and cream to her coffee.

Trevor smiled.

"What?" She blew on her coffee.

"Nothing. It's just the cream and sugar."

"Yeah? I've been drinking my coffee like this forever, and you drink yours black. What's the big deal?"

"It just reminded me of someone."

"Someone, huh?" Amanda put down her mug and rested her arms on the table. "Trevor. What's going on?"

"Nothing, why?" He took a sip of the strong coffee. Why was he here, exactly?

"Why? Because you're out here at six in the morning."

"I was wondering how Toby was doing. I just wanted to check up on you two."

She sat back, crossing her arms. "And it couldn't wait until dinner tonight? You know, through the years, you may have fallen into the role of caretaker in our relationship but you're still my baby brother, and I know when something is on your mind." She sat forward. "What is it, Trevor?"

Trevor looked at his sister, wanting to spill his guts—desperate to tell her everything. He wanted to explain he didn't like being with Maggie anymore and he would love to know what life would be like with Jenna Joyce. He needed to be challenged as an actor again, and he was so damned sick and tired of being Caspian Locke. But how could he tell her all this when Caspian was the reason she could afford medical care for Toby? He lifted his mug to his lips, draining his coffee. The sharp bitter taste was just what he needed to shake him from this freaking ridiculous fantasy world he lived in.

"Trevor?"

"I just had a craving for donuts."

She sighed, twirling her coffee mug in her hands. "Cravings can be really powerful things. All I hope, Trevor, is that you explore this craving you're having and don't miss out on life because of fear and obligation." She raised her eyebrows.

"It's not that simple."

"Sure it is. Until you take a leap, you'll never know what else there is for you." She smiled. "Who is she?"

Trevor's gaze dashed up to his sister's. "No one. I don't know what you're talking about."

Amanda cocked her head and repeated her question.

"My Ophelia." Trevor dropped his head into his hand. He raised it again. "Her name's Jenna. Jenna Joyce. She's a fucking incredible actor."

Amanda's eyes flickered with understanding.

"She's young."

"How young?"

"Twenty-two." He shook his head. "And she's impossible and petulant sometimes but she's smart, and deep, and thoughtful. She dragged me to this decrepit theatre to rehearse the show, and I...I fucking love it.

She reminds me of what real life is like—that it's not all a shiny soap opera."

"Trevor." Amanda reached out and took his hand, giving it a small squeeze. "You, of all people, know life is not a shiny soap opera." She let go of his hand, wrapping hers around her mug.

He nodded. "We got into a huge fight last night, and I was this mega jerk—an overpowering bully."

"So apologize."

"It's not that easy."

"Of course it is." Amanda sighed. "She look like Maggie?"

"No." He shook his head. "Nothing like her. She's dark and exotic looking—black hair, mesmerizing light hazel eyes, skinny."

"Let me guess, nose ring?"

"Yeah." Trevor's mouth turned up into a lopsided grin.

"Trevor." Amanda dropped the tone of her voice. "You need to figure out what's right for you here. Not what's right for us, or Maggie. Just you."

"But it's not realistic."

"The best things usually aren't." She stood up and took her coffee mug to the sink. "So go talk to her. Get lost. I'll tell Toby you'll be back for dinner?"

"Yeah." Trevor stood, pulling on his coat and hat, an uncontrolled grin spreading across his face. Yes, it was true Amanda didn't understand all the gory details—that leaving Maggie could potentially mean being fired as Caspian—but her encouragement made him feel better than he had in weeks. No, he would never do anything with Jenna, but he also didn't have to leave it the awkward way it was now.

Trevor's hands and arms tingled as he thought about getting to Jenna. His gaze fell to the chairs around the kitchen table—four. Four chairs. There were just enough for Amanda and Toby and he and Jenna. His heart raced as he considered bringing her back with him to have dinner with his sister and his nephew—something he never did with Maggie. Maggie had met them once at a daytime drama picnic he was hosting but she had no interest in pursuing a relationship beyond that one encounter.

"Good." Amanda smiled. "We're making healthy baked ziti." She glanced at the clock. "You've got twelve hours. Go."

She laughed, grabbing his empty mug from the table as Trevor sprinted out of the house.

****

Jenna woke to pounding on her door. "Trevor?" She rubbed the sleep from her eyes, got up and peered through the peephole. Her heart fell when she saw Luis standing there, dancing back and forth to his own beat.

"Yo, Jen." Luis pounded again. "Jenna."

Jenna yanked open the door. "Shh, I gave you a key so you wouldn't wake up my neighbors."

"Correction, you gave us keys so Loretta and I could check up on you from time to time to make sure you're not dead. I didn't want to barge in, you know, in case you weren't a-lone." Luis peered around Jenna and into the apartment.

"Slim chance of that." Jenna scratched her elbow.

"Girl, you look like hell."

"Thanks." Jenna stepped aside. "You coming in?"

"Just for a second."

As Luis stepped past her, Jenna glanced at his long

navy dress coat over a deep blue suit with a white shirt, unbuttoned at the collar. "Wow. You look great. Nice suit."

"Thanks. Loretta just got it for me, says blue's my color."

"I would say."

"So you'd better get some clothes on and wash that pretty face of yours so you can try to keep up with me." Luis grinned.

"Oh Luis, I'm not in the mood to go anywhere."

"Too bad for you because this has nothing to do with you."

"What?"

"Loretta and I are getting hitched. Today. Now." Luis looked at his watch. "Well, in forty-five minutes, so move."

"She finally said yes?"

"She didn't have a choice."

Jenna dropped her chin, trying to understand. "Luis, are you going to be a father?"

"Good Lord, no. I just mean she got so sick of me begging and whining for her to marry me, she finally said yes. Last night."

Jenna jumped up and down, clapping. She hugged Luis tightly.

"All right, all right." Luis untangled Jenna's arms from around his neck. "So get your skinny ass moving so you can be my best person. And Loretta's bridesmaid and all that shit."

"Yes." Jenna ran for the bathroom. On the way she grabbed her one dress. She held it for a moment. The last time she wore this dress was when she met Trevor. One look at the dress made her angry and sad and melancholic…why was she having these complicated feelings?

Luis narrowed his eyes. "Don't tell me you're getting all girly on me?"

"What? No." Jenna squashed her thoughts and entered the bathroom. She splashed water on her face, threw on some lip gloss, and yanked a brush through her hair. She tugged on her dress, and was done in seconds flat.

"Wow." Luis whistled when she emerged from the bathroom.

Jenna took a small bow. "Thank you, but where's Loretta?"

"With her sister, in the car."

"Bebe? Cool. Haven't seen her in awhile. Where are we going?" Jenna stuffed things into her bag, trying to hurry. "City Hall at this hour?" Jenna looked at her watch.

"Nope. Bebe's now an online ordained minister."

"Really? Will the marriage be legal?"

"Legal enough."

"Well, all right then." Jenna grabbed her coat and stuffed her horribly uncomfortable flats into her bag. She laced her boots and threw on her hat and mittens.

"Girl, no one can kill an outfit faster than you."

Jenna grinned at Luis and he held the door for her. They bounded down the stairs and onto the street.

Jenna peered in the window of Luis's black classic GT Fastback. With her hair pinned up, a beautifully dressed Loretta, wearing a simple fitted white lace dress, huddled next to Bebe, who was wearing a long black robe. Both had dress coats bunched on their laps. Jenna waved at them.

"Isn't Loretta sitting up front?" Jenna asked.

"Don't want to risk seeing the bride."

"Got it."

Luis opened the door for Jenna and in her peripheral vision, she spotted... "Trevor?" She turned to him.

"Jenna." His voice was low and strong as he approached Luis's car.

Jenna's breath began to race and she stood there, paralyzed.

"Heading somewhere?"

"It's my wedding, man." Luis walked over to Trevor and clasped his hand. "I'm Luis. You must be Trevor."

"Yes, I am. Congratulations." Trevor smiled at Luis.

"Thanks."

"And nice car."

"Thank you very much. This is my baby."

Loretta glared at Luis from the backseat.

"Woman hears everything." Luis shook his head. "It's eerie." Luis looked back and forth from Jenna to Trevor and back again.

Trevor pulled his gaze off Jenna for a moment to speak to Luis. "I know you from somewhere..."

"Yeah? See a lot of Shakespeare? I play Othello...constantly."

"Yes, but not that." Trevor snapped his fingers, remembering something. "Downtown. You were in that amazing Brecht retrospective."

"You saw that?" Luis's eyes widened.

Jenna rolled hers. "Guys, it's cold."

"Yeah, yeah." Luis waved her off as he stared at

Trevor. "I can't believe you saw that. It wasn't exactly a commercial success. Hence the reason I'm back working at the diner."

"That's a shame. I would have loved to produce that. Or something like it. Who knows? Maybe someday." Trevor glanced past Luis with a faraway look in his eyes.

"That's awesome, man." Luis shook Trevor's hand, again.

Trevor turned to Jenna. "Did you hear that, Jenna?" Trevor had a huge grin plastered on his face. "He said it was, 'awesome.' "

Jenna rolled her eyes again and clicked her tongue.

"Hey, man, want to come to a wedding?"

"Luis…" Jenna shook her head.

"Don't be silly, Jen. It's a wedding. A time to celebrate love."

Jenna forced a smile, refusing to ruin Luis's moment.

"Should I follow you?" Trevor stepped closer to Jenna as he spoke.

"Sure."

"How about Jenna rides with me?" Trevor's voice was deep and in control. "We have some things to talk—"

"No we don't," Jenna interrupted. "And I have a better idea. How about the girls and I take the warm, swanky car, and you guys ride in this 'awesome' automobile we just don't seem to appreciate."

"Done!" Every single person spoke in unison.

As Loretta and Bebe climbed out of the backseat and onto the cold street, they noticed Trevor. "Good Lord." Bebe slapped her knee. "Aren't you Caspian

Locke?"

"Yes, I am." Trevor smiled. Standing there in an unzipped dark gray parka over his fitted black sweater and dark jeans, he looked every bit the soap opera star.

"I'm Bebe, sister of the bride and completely unattached, unless you count my husband, Sam, whom I don't." She held out her hand, delicately.

"Sam is a very lucky man," Trevor added, bending down and kissing Bebe's hand.

Despite the swirling anger in her core, Jenna smirked at Trevor's actions. She looked away, immediately. She would never forgive him for the horrid things he said last night, no matter how sweet his actions, or how incredibly masculine he looked in his coat and jeans.

"Ooo-wee, Caspian Locke just kissed me." Bebe fanned herself despite the cold.

"His name is Trevor," Loretta corrected.

"Not to me, it's not."

Jenna stole a glance at Trevor who set his jaw, forcing a smile. Until this moment, she never considered how hard it must be to be loved as someone you're not. He glanced at her and Jenna looked away.

"Come on, Bebe." Loretta yanked her sister toward Trevor's car. "You can't have him, but you can have his car."

"I guess that's something," Bebe mumbled, following after her sister.

Jenna stared at Trevor before getting into his car.

****

As she stood near Trevor on the rooftop of a brownstone on the Lower East Side, Jenna shuddered. Yes, she understood the romance of it all, but it was still freaking cooooold to get married in the early morning on a rooftop, in Manhattan in January. Despite the frigid temperatures and the fact that Trevor was there and Jenna was still angry and embarrassed about yesterday, she giggled, giddy with happiness for her friends. Only Luis and Loretta would do something this impulsive and this beautiful. The bride and groom faced one another and Loretta held a tiny bouquet of bodega red roses with a long white ribbon. With the icy morning dawning behind them, they looked like they were caught in a photograph. Jenna shoved her mitten-covered hands into her coat pockets, wishing, maybe for the first time ever, she had a cell phone to snap a picture for her friends.

Bebe led them through a short, nontraditional service, filled with personal stories and lots of laughter and then Luis and Loretta recited the vows they had written. The groom's eyes lit up as he proclaimed his love for his bride, and Jenna's eyes welled as Loretta shed a single tear that Luis reached out to wipe away. It had been a long, long time for them; thank heavens they had made it. Who knows, maybe once in awhile, love really does win.

Jenna peeked at Trevor out of the corner of her eye. He turned to her; his expression sad and serious, but sweet and tender all at once. It sent a shiver up her spine and down her fingers. She hugged herself, trying to stay warm in her coat, bouncing on her toes as Bebe spoke.

"I now pronounce you husband and wife!" Bebe squealed as she applauded.

Jenna and Trevor clapped along as Luis and Loretta shared their first kiss as a married couple.

Loretta pointed at Jenna, waving her bouquet. "You going to take this, or are you going to make me throw it at you?"

Jenna's gut ached as she forced a laugh. Catching the bouquet wasn't just a waste; it was a reminder of all those things she could never and would never have.

"No, no..." Jenna waved the bouquet away. "You keep it, for memories."

Luis took the bouquet from Loretta's hand and marched up to Jenna. He placed it in her hands, gently pushing it against her. He raised his eyebrows, nodding. "You deserve happiness too, Jen." He turned and ran back to Loretta, lifting her into the air, spinning her around.

The bouquet stung Jenna's hands, as if the roses had never been dethorned.

Trevor eyed her quizzically as Luis and Loretta made their way over. Bebe followed.

"Congratulations!" Jenna hugged Loretta and Luis.

Trevor hugged Loretta and held out his hand to Luis. "Congratulations. It was beautiful. Really. I have no freaking idea why you got married on a rooftop in January, but..."

"We met here." Loretta smiled as she spoke, her beautiful white teeth gleaming. "I was the makeup artist on one of his first movies."

"Some low-budget piece of crap that barely covered rent for a month." Luis shook his head, pulling Loretta in for a hug and releasing her. "Loretta was the best thing about it. And about everything else in my life."

Jenna smiled, blowing warm air into her mittens. "Uh, guys, want to hit the diner for breakfast? I'm sure the Carlton can fit our wedding party."

"Yes." Loretta rubbed her hands together. "I'm freezing."

"Absolutely." Luis held out his hand. "After you, Mrs. Statesman."

Giggling, Loretta sauntered past Luis. Jenna followed. Despite her smile, her teeth chattered from the freezing temperature.

"Here." Trevor came up behind her, slipping off his coat and draping it around her shoulders.

The coat hung to her mid-thigh, and good lord it was warm and smelled so incredibly good. "Trevor, I can't take your coat." She shimmied around, trying to shrug out of his coat, but he pulled it back onto her.

"Please. Consider it a peace offering for me being such an asshole yesterday." He opened his mouth to speak again, but his cell rang. "I'm sorry." Trevor excused himself and made his way to the opposite side of the rooftop. "Go ahead with Luis and Loretta, I'll catch up."

"It's cool man, we can wait." Luis embraced Loretta's face, kissing her over and over. Jenna smiled, turning away.

Within a minute or two, Trevor stuffed his phone into his pocket and jogged back to meet the wedding party. He stood before Jenna. Pain clouded his gorgeous face.

"Trevor, what is it?"

"We have to go. Right now."

The ground rushed upward as she steadied herself. "It's Don, isn't it?" She knew it in her core. That hot unease that swirled through her gut was the same sensation she had when her dad had come into her bedroom that night he told her he was sick. "It is, isn't it?"

"Yes."

Luis stepped up. "Trevor? What's going on?"

"I'm sorry to have to tell you this on your wedding day, but Don's not doing well."

"What's happening?" Jenna's voice was a hoarse whisper.

Trevor took Jenna's hand, holding it protectively. He spoke to each of them. "He's at Lenox Hill. They don't know how much time he has."

"Christ." Luis ran a hand through his hair.

Trevor turned to Luis. "Come on. My car is downstairs."

Still holding Jenna's hand tightly, the five of them rushed down the staircase and into Trevor's waiting car.

****

At the hospital, the bad news came quickly. The five of them huddled together in the hallway outside Don's room as the doctor spoke.

"I'm afraid he doesn't have much longer."

Trevor shrugged off his chill, turning to the doctor. "What does he need? Whatever it is—do it. Spare no expense."

"We're giving him medication for any discomfort he may have but you need to understand, Mr. Hughes, he's over ninety years old with an advanced case of pneumonia…" The doctor sighed, looking over the small group of Don's friends. "I'm really sorry to have to say this but you'll all need to prepare yourselves for the worst. You should all say your goodbyes."

Trevor's hands dangled at his sides. The scariest part of death is that it doesn't give a damn whom you are and how much money you can throw at it. It's an insatiable, wild dog, and once it picks its victim, hope is the first thing it devours. He shuddered.

Jenna reached out and took Trevor's hand and suddenly warmth replaced the horrible cold ache swirling throughout him. She squeezed his hand and nodded. With her cheeks still pink from the cold, she practically radiated warmth and strength and he knew she was with him in a way no one had ever been before. Through all the years of being strong for Amanda and Toby, he had always been completely alone. But right now, here, in the hallway next to Don's hospital room waiting for the unthinkable, he felt surrounded by friends—real friends—maybe for the first time ever.

"Well." The doctor cleared his throat. "You can go in two at a time if you'd like."

Jenna let go of his hand and sadness enveloped Trevor once more.

He stood up taller, fighting his way through his haze of pain. "Luis, Loretta, why don't you go first? Maybe you can still salvage some of your wedding afternoon this way."

"Thanks, man. There won't be any way to salvage today but I'd like to go home with Loretta and drop Bebe off at the airport." Luis shook Trevor's hand and escorted a teary Loretta into Don's room.

"I'm going to wait downstairs." Bebe hugged Jenna and Trevor.

"Bye, Bebe." Jenna kissed her on the cheek.

Trevor walked her to the elevator, pressing the button. "Would you like me to take you to the lobby?"

She gave a pained smile, patting him on the hand. "I would love it, Trevor, but no, thank you."

Bebe stepped onto the elevator and the door closed. Trevor turned to Jenna, fighting an overpowering desire to run to her and hold her. She held out her hand to him, and he walked to her, taking her hand in his.

"Should you call Maggie?" Her words were soft, and she stared at the door to Don's room as she spoke.

Trevor shook his head. The very last thing he wanted now was Maggie. "No. She's not a student of Don's. They don't have a relationship."

"I uh, meant, for you. To have her here with you." She glanced up at Trevor.

"No." He held her hand tighter. "I'd rather be here with you."

****

After saying goodbye to Luis and Loretta, Trevor and Jenna walked into Don's hospital room, hand in hand. He lay there, his eyes closed, looking jaundiced and weak. He had a battery of tubes and machines hooked up to him, including a respirator.

"It's always the same thing," Jenna mumbled.

"What's that?" Trevor turned to her.

"It always comes to this. And you know what the strangest thing is?"

"What?"

"The smell. It always smells the same at the end. Like recycled air and warm cafeteria trays and medicine and astringent. It doesn't matter that he breathed New York City air for his entire life. It doesn't matter that once, while performing in Italy, his wife smelled the warm, salty air of the Mediterranean nestled in his beard; it doesn't matter that his winter coat always reeked of mothballs—"

Jenna choked on her words and turned to Trevor.

She hesitated but he caught her in his arms, pulling her tightly to his chest. Her small body relaxed, and he wanted to keep her there, forever, forgetting everything bad that surrounded them. She dragged in a deep breath and pulled away.

"I'm so selfish."

"How's that?" Trevor looked into her eyes.

"I went to him last night because I was mad at you." Jenna's words were choppy. "He was *dying* and I wanted him to coach me in acting and in life."

"I was there, too. That's what he would have wanted, Jen. That's all he ever wanted—to work, and to help other actors be their best."

She glanced at Don. "This is what my father looked like at the end," Jenna confided. "Only he was much younger. Fifty-two. Cancer."

"I'm sorry."

Jenna looked up at him. "I'm sorry, too. For…for the way I've been treating you." She glanced at the floor. "I'm so sorry for what I said to you last night."

"We both said things we didn't mean. I'm sorry, too. It was passion talking."

"All that…crap, it just seems so unimportant now, doesn't it? Everything seems unimportant compared."

"Not everything."

She gave him a small smile and they both walked to Don, one on each side. They held his hands.

Jenna stroked Don's hand with her thumb as she spoke. "It's like losing my father all over again."

"I know."

"You lost your father, too?"

Trevor nodded, a lump forming in his throat. "When I was a teenager. September 11. He worked in the North Tower."

"Oh, Trevor." Jenna covered her mouth with her hand.

"He..." Trevor cleared his throat. "He never saw me become a success."

"I'm so, so sorry," Jenna whispered. "That has to be one of the worst ways ever to lose someone you love. I can't imagine I thought I had the monopoly on pain."

"All death hurts. Whether you're prepared for it or not."

The doctor walked in, and Trevor and Jenna stepped away from Don's bedside. "It's time, you two. His vitals are bad. He's not breathing on his own. He'll be gone at any moment." The doctor took a clipboard from the end of Don's bed and wedged it under his arm. "I saw him perform when I was just a boy. He's had a long run. Let's let him rest now with his Evelyn."

Trevor nodded. "It's amazing how many lives he's affected, isn't it?"

The doctor sighed as a nurse entered, shutting down his IV drips.

Jenna's gaze followed the nurse. "Wait— I...shouldn't we give him some more time?"

Trevor stepped to her and took her hand again. "There is no more time, Jenna. I'm sorry."

She turned away as the nurse clicked off the ventilator. Jenna squeezed his hand so tightly, it ached. When the doctor and nurse left, Trevor said, "Want to say goodbye?" He pulled her gently to Don's bed, and she lightened her grip.

"Yes." Jenna turned to Don. "Goodbye, Don. Thank you, for everything. We will miss you. I love you." Jenna's voice cracked but she fought back her tears. "And with that, ladies and gentlemen, we part. Until next time."

Trevor moved closer to Don. " 'Now cracks a noble heart. Good night, sweet prince; and flights of angels sing thee to thy rest.' "

****

"I…I don't want to be alone today." Jenna moved slowly, whispering to Trevor as he escorted her out of the hospital room. She felt light-headed and entirely aimless.

"Neither do I," he whispered back.

As they made their way out of the sliding front doors of the hospital and out onto Seventy-Seventh Street, Jenna stopped and turned to Trevor. It was still so cold, she shivered. He unzipped his coat, ready to wrap her up in it, once more. She held up her hand to stop him; she couldn't let him freeze again.

"No." She sighed. "Come on. Let's get in your car. It's warm."

Trevor nodded and texted his driver to pull up the car. They stood side by side on the street, waiting. She was freezing but too numb to care. After a few minutes, the car pulled up alongside them, and they climbed in.

"Where to?" Trevor asked, warming his hands against the heating vents.

Jenna shrugged, completely lost. "I don't want to see anyone. And I don't want to go to my apartment. I still have dishes from the last meal I cooked for him." Her voice cracked and Trevor took her hand, gently.

"We'll go to my place."

His voice was definitive and Jenna's heart raced.

"But Trevor we can't…I can't…"

"Jenna. We both just lost someone we loved. Let's just go grieve together."

Jenna nodded, feeling such a surge of thankfulness she leaned over and kissed Trevor on the cheek. He smiled as the car rolled forward.

Chapter Ten

As the car pulled up to a townhouse on the Lower West Side, Jenna's shaking knees stopped trembling. She slid her sweaty palm from his hand and wiped it on her dress, pretending she needed to scratch an itchy knee.

Trevor turned to her. "We're here."

Jenna nodded, completely unsure as to why she was here. She was so lost at this moment; she certainly did not want to be alone but she wasn't sure she wanted to be here, either. What she was sure of was she wanted to be with Trevor. And that was a real problem.

The driver opened the door, and Trevor exited first. He held out his hand for Jenna and she placed her hand in his as he helped her from the car. She stood on the sidewalk staring up at a modest brick apartment building, with a designer clothing store at ground level, and seven more stories of apartments above. It had a definite retro industrial feel, and the apartments were connected by ladders and fire escapes.

"You live here?"

"Yes." Trevor gave her a tiny smile. "You like it?"

"Yes." Despite her melancholy, Jenna's heart raced from excitement. She loved this neighborhood with its dive bars, small bistros, and trendy galleries, and she loved that he lived here and not in some uber-fancy high-rise somewhere.

"It's freezing out here. Let's go in."

Jenna nodded, shivering, still unsure of what to do, but yet deep inside, a strange contentment brewed. Trevor walked to a well-worn green door next to the entrance to the boutique and unlocked three separate locks. Holding the door open with his foot he nodded to her. "Come on."

Jenna stepped inside to a beautifully finished hallway of dark cherry wood floors and white walls. They walked the hallway to an elevator bank. The door of an industrial elevator was opened, waiting for them.

"Is this a converted warehouse?"

"Yes." He smiled as they stepped onto the elevator. Trevor dropped the gate and pressed a button marked "PH."

Steadying herself, Jenna grasped the metal grate on the side of the elevator cage as they took a shaky ride to the penthouse.

"It's safe." Trevor smiled. "I promise. They're just trying to maintain somewhat of an authentic feel."

The elevator came to a rough halt and Trevor opened the gate. They stepped out into a small red-brick lined hallway and Trevor inserted a key into a large, black metal door, unlocking it and sliding it open like a barn door.

"Cool door." Jenna stepped inside to the small foyer of her dream apartment. "Oh my goodness." She spun around taking in the brick walls, dark hardwood floors, exposed steel columns, and industrial piping. "This is incredible."

To her left was a living area with a low black leather couch and two matching chairs, and to the right, a long, hand-carved wooden table, with two long benches on either side, and chrome chairs flanking the ends. It had an espresso cup and opened paper left on top. Large, silver, pendulum lamps hung down over the table. Trevor moved to the side and dropped his keys into a leather bowl on a long dark wood table in the entrance area. In the far back corner, a staircase of wire and suspended wood led to a loft. The loft hung out into the room and was partitioned by picture windows. Tall green plants lined the window, blocking their view into the bedroom. Past the staircase was a wall of waist-to-ceiling high windows, overlooking the avenue.

"Make yourself at home."

Jenna walked into the middle of the apartment, catching a glimpse of the white-and-chrome kitchen with silver high-end appliances, but she didn't stop. Instead, she went straight for the windows. She stood before the glass and stared out at Manhattan below her. "The view..." she muttered. "It's..." She shook her head. "We're not that high, yet I can see down Broadway, and so many buildings...I...I don't feel like I'm looking at it. I feel like I'm part of it. I can't even imagine what this must be like at night."

Suddenly Trevor was at her side. "Stay."

Jenna didn't dare turn to him. His breath was warm on her neck, and her heart raced in response.

Gently, he pushed her hair back behind her ear, and whispered once more. "Stay and find out. Just for a while. Just until we...get through today."

He choked on his words. His bright blue eyes were glassy and his face looked drawn. He appeared as sad and lost as she was feeling. Her heart ached to see him like this. She reached out and stroked his cheek, gently. He placed his hand on hers, closing his eyes. Every fiber of her being wanted to melt into him, against him, just to make his hurting stop. "Do you...should I call Maggie?" There was no subtext in her words. She truly didn't want him to be hurting, and if Maggie could help, then she was the answer.

"What?" His body stiffened in response. "No, no." He stepped back, clearing his throat. "Can I, uh, get you something? Coffee?"

"Coffee would be great, thanks."

"Kitchen's over here. Make yourself comfortable." Trevor walked into the kitchen as he spoke. He stood behind a large breakfast bar, dropping beans into a coffee grinder.

Jenna followed him into the kitchen, walking past a display wall with at least twenty awards and trophies balanced on three shelves made of reclaimed wood and industrial pipes, suspended from the wall. Jenna pointed to them and Trevor shrugged. She walked closer to inspect them. "Daytime Emmy, Daytime Emmy, People's Choice..." She rattled off award after award. "Huh, Kids' Choice." She smiled and made her way into the kitchen. She plopped down on a high leather stool, still eyeing the view of Manhattan.

"That view's something, huh?" He smiled as he waited for the coffee to brew.

"I'll say." Jenna clasped her hands together, leaning against the counter. "The whole place is amazing. Looks just like my place." She grinned, trying anything to keep the mood light and as pain free as possible.

"Glad you like it." He placed a mug of coffee in front of her. "Extra cream, six sugars."

"Thanks." She blew on the coffee, taking a sip.

"Good grief. This is fabulous."

"Good." He took a swallow of his coffee and placed his mug on the counter. "C'mere. I want to show you something."

Trevor took her hand. When he touched her, excitement radiated from her belly, out through her hands, tingling her fingertips. Gently leading her away from the kitchen, he pulled her down a hallway—running adjacent to the kitchen—she hadn't noticed before. He pushed open a door revealing a slightly messy room filled with music. There were framed albums on the wall, four or five guitars in a corner, an LP player, and stacks of vinyl. Jenna spied an electric piano in the corner and walked to it. She ran her fingers gently and silently down the keys.

"You can play if you'd like."

Jenna jumped.

"Sorry. I didn't mean to frighten you."

"It's okay. You just surprised me…"

Jenna squeezed her eyes shut. He was directly behind her, and he reached his arms around her to the keyboard…his body just barely brushing up against hers. He was strong, and powerful, and the feel of him this close made her light-headed.

Trevor plinked a few notes and then, taking her hands in his, led them back to the keys. He was so close now…she leaned back into the swell of his body—not touching—but still, her body vibrated from his proximity. She longed to lift her hands from the keys and wrap them around his neck. She wanted him to reach out and place his hands on her hips to turn her to him. She wanted him to…no. She needed to stop this. This—this place and whatever she was feeling, it was only a dream. And worse, it was a dream brought on by a nightmare. She opened her eyes and wiggled away. She was cold and empty as soon as she left the safety of Trevor's aura.

He ran his hand through his hair. "I uh, want to show you this."

He led her to a door that opened to a rooftop terrace. The terrace was about the size of the music room, with shoulder-high brick walls on two sides and a finished dark wood floor. The wall overlooking the city was waist-high glass with a metal guard rail, flanked by low shrubs in a long wooden box. A few more plants were tucked in the corners of the terrace. Two simple, light gray wooden chairs sat next to a small matching table.

Jenna ambled forward to gaze at the view. She turned to Trevor, giddy despite their day. "It's breathtaking." She looked back out over the city, thinking of Don, her mood changing as quickly as the pedestrians rushing by on the street below. Now, she wasn't giddy. Now, she was just sad. The warmth of the sun did little to battle the freezing temperature. "This is so New York."

"What's that?" Trevor met her at the guardrail.

She stared out over the city. "The penthouse, and this terrace, the view, they are all stunning. But this day. This day is New York—it's bright and sunny, but it's bitter cold. There can never be the good without the bad."

"Isn't that balance?" Trevor moved closer to her. "Isn't that what life is? The yin and yang? Life balancing death?"

"I just don't understand why there has to be so

much bad." She wiped away a tear, turning to Trevor.

He moved closer to her. "I want to hold you so much, right now."

"Trevor..."

Her body ached for him, and she gripped the guardrail. He moved closer until they were nearly touching, standing side by side, looking out over Manhattan.

****

Jenna was so beautiful standing on his terrace and it felt so right to have her there. In all his years with Maggie, she only ventured onto the patio a handful of times, always complaining about New York weather. But the patio was his favorite place in the world—and today, with Don's passing, it was the only place that felt okay. Problem was, it may be that it felt okay because of Jenna.

"So uh." Trevor really wasn't sure what to do next. They stood on his balcony, both of them sad and lonely, and he wanted to fix it. But the only times he had women to his place was with the intention of seducing them. And truth be told, he never really had to seduce a single one. They were always ready to throw themselves at him. And if his looks and his celebrity didn't do it then his apartment and view of Manhattan certainly did.

But Jenna...Jenna was different. She was serious, and smart, and beautiful—she was so intriguing, but so distant. He inhaled, deeply, floating in uncharted waters, unsure if he'd be able to swim. Yeah, his attraction to her ran deeper than a casual theatre relationship. He didn't want her because she was his Ophelia. He wanted her, because she was Jenna. "Do you want to go inside?"

Jenna continued to gaze out over Manhattan. "Not really. Can we stay just a little longer?"

"You must be freezing." He looked at her thin coat.

"I don't really feel anything. I'm kind of numb…"

"Yeah."

"Trevor…?" She turned to him, sighing. "I…I'm sorry for the way I've been acting toward you."

His body swayed toward her. He wanted to tell her it was all okay. That none of it mattered, but there was more she wanted to say.

"We had no money, my parents, my sister, and me. And whatever we did have went to my dad's doctor bills early on. So we had nothing left at the end to prolong his life in any way. At that moment, the moment when I watched him slip away, I got so angry at rich people. I felt they had everything, including the ability to keep their loved ones alive."

He inhaled deeply.

"That's at least part of the reason I've been so awful to you. I've been angry you have money and success, and I don't. You could have kept my father alive, but I couldn't."

"Jenna." Trevor's heart ached for her. "You heard what the doctor said. When it's time, it's time. You are not the reason he died. Cancer is."

"Yes, but my father gave it all up for me. All of it. His dreams, his plans, *all* of it. He died a slow, horrible death while cancer ate away at him, and you know why? Because it had already eaten away at his dreams. Failure devoured his very soul, and after that, it's easy for something to destroy a body. I mean, who cares at that point?"

"Jenna, you are not to blame."

"It's so easy to say that but so difficult to believe."

"I know." He clasped his hands tightly, leaning against the guardrail. "I told you my father worked in the North Tower, so everyone just assumed he was in finance."

"He wasn't?" She turned to him, her brow furrowed.

"No." Trevor stood up taller, facing Jenna. "He worked at the restaurant at the top of the tower. My entire life. He started off in the kitchen, and worked his way up to a waiter. It was hard work and a tough way to support a family. He gave my sister and me everything he could; we were never hungry but we never had luxuries like extra clothes or toys or electronics. This city is a crazy expensive place to raise a family, even in the boroughs."

"Which borough?"

"Queens."

"I never knew."

"No one does."

"Your mom?"

"She passed when I was twelve. Breast cancer."

"Good grief, Trevor. I'm so sorry." Her eyes welled with tears.

"My sister is older than me; she was already eighteen when my father died. My sister and I lived in that house until I went to college, and well, soon after, I became Caspian."

"Where is your sister?"

"On Long Island. With her son."

Jenna beamed. "Your nephew, Toby. Are you close?"

"Yeah. I was supposed to head there for dinner tonight, but…"

She crinkled her brow. "No, you should go. When you lose someone you love, it's important to be around someone who makes you feel better."

He reached out and caressed her cheek, gently. "I am."

****

Fuck, fuck, fuck. What the hell he doing? There was no way he could start something with Jenna—it was unfair to Maggie, and most of all, to Jenna. So what if she was the most beautiful woman he'd ever seen? Who cared that she was real and honest, and gritty…? He was all turned around because of Don's passing. That's all.

A gust of wind blew past, and Jenna shivered.

"Come on." Trevor's voice was a whisper as he led her back inside to the music room. He grabbed the shoulders of her coat to help her ease out of it, but she clutched it tightly around her, turning to him.

She dropped her chin and gazed up at him. "Should I go?"

He read her like they were playing a scene. They were actors and her three little words were sitting out there, loaded with subtext. He knew what she was asking: Was it okay with Maggie that she was there? And could she trust him to keep their relationship platonic…? Well, who the hell knew? All he knew for sure was that he didn't want her to leave. Not now—not ever.

"No. You shouldn't go. Stay. Please."

She slid out of her coat, and he tossed it onto a chair in the corner of the room.

"This is nice." Jenna smiled as she curled up on the oversized couch. "It's comfortable here. The whole penthouse is beautiful, but this room…it's just special."

"I decorated this room."

"Really?" Jenna raised her eyebrows. "I love it. The vintage LPs on the wall, the artwork, the huge cushions on the floor. The couch and chairs. It's perfect."

Trevor smiled, thinking the exact same thing about her. "Do you want something else to drink? More coffee?"

"No, thanks."

Jenna looked up at him in a way that confused him. He furrowed his brow, trying to make sense of it. If that look were on any other woman at any other time, he would have taken her straight to his bedroom. But Jenna meant something more. He was sure she wanted him to share himself with her, but she didn't want his body—not yet anyway. She wanted his soul…and the problem was, for the first time ever, he might just be willing to give it.

"Will you sit with me?" She pulled her feet up tighter, making room for him on the couch.

Trevor didn't need to be asked twice. He made his way to the couch and sat down next to her. They sat side by side, awkwardly, like pre-pubescent 'tweens at their first dance.

"What do we do now? For Don, I mean?" She yawned, her eyelids heavy.

"I'm the executor, so I have to plan the funeral. I know what he wanted; it's pretty straight-forward."

She nodded, placing her arm on the back of the couch, resting her head against it. With her black hair draped across her shoulder, she looked peaceful and beautiful. She yawned again, covering her mouth. "Sorry." She stretched her arms overhead, resuming her position. "I didn't sleep very well last night."

"No. Me either." He forced his arms to stay at his sides. "You can take a nap if you'd like."

"I don't want to be in the way." As sleep overtook her, her words were becoming a murmur.

"Jenna, please."

Within minutes, Jenna's body relaxed and her breathing deepened. He smiled. This was technically the second time they had slept together and he'd never even kissed her. Come to think of it, this was the first woman he'd ever had to his apartment whom he hadn't kissed—not that he didn't want to. As he watched her sleep, he fought hard against the fantasies racing through his mind. He imagined he and Jenna lying together on the couch after Thai takeout and a long night of listening to his LPs. He would lie still, mesmerized by her soft voice reciting Shakespeare, running his hand up and down the worn cotton of one of his vintage rock t-shirts she'd be wearing. After a few minutes, he'd free his hand beneath the t-shirt, caressing the soft skin of her back, unhooking her lacy pink bra with one hand, while his other hand lifted her chin so he could kiss her softly, over and over again.

Damn. Now he was uncomfortable. He sat up straight, trying to alleviate both the ache in his jeans and the guilt he was feeling. He was with Maggie—planning to propose to Maggie—how dare he have fantasies about another woman? But that's all they were, just fantasies—and men did it all the time. Lots of married men watch porn or visit strip clubs, they weren't technically cheating. So why'd he feel so awful? He stretched in his seat, trying to make room in his jeans. Because he wasn't that guy—he was a guy who wanted to be with only one woman. Problem was, it was the wrong woman.

But what if...? Trevor gazed at Jenna lying there, sleeping on his couch, and his body ached to pull her near. What if he were to end it with Maggie, then what? So what if her father was angry and canceled his contract? He was so damned sick and tired of playing Caspian Locke. It was time to move on. Amanda's house was paid for, Toby was much better—they were just monitoring him now after his last open heart surgery a few months back, so maybe, just maybe, Trevor could break away from his obligations...? Why the hell not? He had plenty of money in the bank to hold them all over until he found work again. But what kind of work? Theatre? Who would hire a washed up soap villain? Trevor took a deep breath, rubbing the dull ache in his temples. Could this be his time to fulfill his lifelong dream of opening a theatre upstate...? But opening a theatre was a huge, expensive risk, and how would he ever make ends meet if, God forbid, Toby had a relapse? Even if his theatre company did well, theatre didn't pay close to what he made as Caspian now. And even seven figures in the double digits that he had stashed away in the bank would be easily annihilated if Toby needed additional medical treatments that insurance wouldn't cover...

Sadness settled on Trevor like a suffocating blanket. Sometimes, sometimes it would be freaking great to be just a fraction of the bad guy Caspian was. How awesome to go through life not giving a damn about anyone but yourself—and the next woman you're going to bed. He stood up quickly, jostling the couch. Jenna murmured.

The walls were closing in on him, so Trevor ducked out of the music room and onto the patio. He took a deep breath of the freezing New York air. He needed to call Amanda and cancel on dinner. He hated to disappoint Toby, but she would certainly understand and smooth things over for him. Trevor dug his phone from his pocket and scrolled through the texts. The last one was from Maggie who had been on a shopping day with her mother. She texted she was exhausted and was turning in early. Complete with a yawning emoticon. Maggie's incessant use of emoticons was never fun, but it used to be a hell of a lot less annoying than it was now. He held the phone tightly in his grasp, debating texting Maggie to tell her about Don. No. No way. He just wasn't ready to share this with her, yet. Besides, she barely knew Don. Trevor scrolled away from Maggie's text and found Amanda's number, calling her.

"Uncle Trevor?"

"Hey, Toby. What are you doing answering Mom's phone?" The suffocating feeling lessened as he spoke to Toby. No matter how unhappy Trevor was, his nephew could always make him feel better.

"I beat her to the phone and recognized your number."

Trevor chuckled.

"What's wrong?"

"What?" Trevor was caught off-guard. "Why do you think something's wrong?"

"Your voice sounds funny. And because if you're calling it probably means you're not coming. So why not?"

"You're a pretty smart kid, you know that?"

"Why aren't you coming, Uncle Trevor?"

Trevor looked out over Manhattan, debating what to tell Toby. He didn't want to just no-show like Toby's useless father, or offer some lame excuse. But what could he tell him?

"A friend of mine…he uh…" Trevor choked on his words, clearing his voice. Why was he so torn up? Don was a ninety-three-year-old man. This was bound to happen sooner rather than later.

"Did he go to heaven?" Toby's voice was low and serious.

Toby had so much concern for Trevor, Trevor's heart ached. But he owed him the truth. "Yes, Toby, my friend went to heaven."

"Oh."

The line was quiet for whole moments.

"It's nice you know. Heaven. That's what Mommy tells me."

"Yeah?"

"Yeah. It has video games and ponies and all the donuts you want. Plus, you never have to brush your teeth."

"Sounds pretty awesome."

"It is. So Mommy says I don't ever have to be afraid if I have to go there."

Trevor shoved the side of his fist to his mouth, choking back a sob.

"Uncle Trevor?"

Trevor cleared his throat. "Yeah, Toby. I'm here." He wiped a tear that fell down his cheek. "But let me tell you something. You're not going to heaven for a very long, long time. Okay? I'll be there way before you. And I'll be waiting with all the donuts you want."

"Promise?"

Trevor turned, peering into the music room at beautiful, smart, talented Jenna curled up on his couch—exactly where she should be, and yet should never be, all at once. Maybe she felt him staring, because she woke, sitting up lazily, looking around. She turned to him and held up her hand, offering a single wave. She took her coat off the chair and pulled it on, wrapping her arms around herself, making her way to the door of the patio. She stepped out onto the patio, and the wind blew her hair back from her face—and in her eyes he saw…everything.

"Uncle Trevor? Do you promise you'll be in heaven before me?"

Trevor swallowed hard. "Yes, Toby, I promise I'll be in heaven before you."

"Trevor?" Amanda had taken the phone away from Toby. "What's going on?"

"Don Oleesa passed this morning." His shoulders slumped with grief.

"Oh, Trevor, I'm so sorry."

"Thanks." He fought to steady his voice. "Would you tell Toby I'm sorry about tonight, but I will be there next week, no matter what?"

"Of course, Trevor. Do you need anything? Is there anything I can do?"

"Nah. Thanks, Amanda. 'Night."

Trevor clicked off the phone, and Jenna turned to him, her eyes glassy from sleep and unexpressed tears.

"Was that your nephew?"

Trevor just nodded.

"Is there a reason he believes he could be in heaven before you?"

"Yes." His throat ached, and his gut wrenched as he spoke.

"How sick is he?"

"He was born with a congenital heart condition, truncus arteriosus. It's pretty rare. Something like one in every ten thousand kids has it. He uh, he had an abnormal truncal valve—not an aortic and pulmonary like we have. They performed a surgery when he was only a couple months old." Trevor's voice cracked, and he cleared his throat. "Excuse me. That's why I got the tattoo—he's got a scar on his chest, and my tattoo is a way to match him. Anyway, a couple of months ago he had another open heart surgery, because his conduit pipe was too narrow. Blood couldn't flow through. Well, about a week ago he started feeling breathless. Amanda's not worried. At least, she says she's not. They're playing around with his medications, blood thinners and such. Everyone's hoping they don't need to operate again. If they do, it'll be his third open heart surgery. But this time they may not need to. It looks good—there's no reason to think..." Trevor's words fell away.

"Oh, Trevor..." Jenna stepped up and put her arms around Trevor, holding him tightly.

She felt so freaking good...he wrapped his arms around her waist and dropped his head, burying his nose in her hair, holding back the sobs that wanted to be set free. But no, he couldn't do this, no matter how good it felt. He stiffened, dropping his hands and standing up tall.

She stepped back, her eyes wide with surprise. "I

should probably go." She moved toward the apartment door.

"Wait."

She turned back.

"I like you, Jenna. Way more than I should. And the reason I can't be with you…Maggie…"

"I understand." She forced a small smile.

"No, you don't. Maggie and I never had anything real, but the soap likes us together—"

"Well you're the two most beautiful people I've ever seen." She shrugged.

"Hardly." He stepped closer. "Her father is my boss. The producer. Of all the cliché, stupid situations to get into…" He shook his head. "I never expected it to go this far. And now she wants more."

"To get married?"

"Yes."

Jenna's tanned skin whitened.

"It's not what I want, but I may not have a choice. My nephew, my sister, they rely on my income, and if I were to leave Maggie…"

"You may have to leave Caspian."

"Yes. They'll keep Caspian, but they can replace me. It happens all the time. They'll find a way around my contracts, and then what would I do? Truthfully, I'd love to leave Caspian, but I just can't."

"I understand, Trevor." She stepped up and placed a warm hand on his forearm. "Believe me. I—"

Suddenly, Jenna pulled her hand away, snapping her head around as a clap of thunder echoed overhead.

"A winter rainstorm." She tugged her jacket closed tighter around her tiny waist, turning to Trevor. Her movements were clipped, like a startled baby bird that had fallen from its nest. "I should leave. It's going to get nasty, and it'll be hard to get home and—"

"Wait." He moved, blocking her way.

She caught her breath.

He reached out and took her hand, intertwining it in his. "Just stay a few more minutes. Just until the storm passes."

"Trevor." She pulled her hand from his. "We both know this storm isn't going to pass."

She smiled sadly, and turning on her heels, left.

Chapter Eleven

Each smack of a raindrop on her head felt like a knife to her heart. She hated leaving Trevor, but she had no choice, not only for her own reasons, which felt so selfish and silly right now, but especially for his. For his sake and the sake of his family, she needed to stay clear of the incredibly handsome, sexy, talented Trevor Hughes. When she first met him and thought he was an asshole for abandoning a charity that meant so much to her…damn. She never would have guessed Trevor was supporting his sister, or that his nephew was so very ill. She never knew he was sick and tired of being Caspian, but he stayed for them. And she, of all people, understood doing something you hated to help someone you love.

Jenna pounded up West Broadway, making her way to her train. Thump, thump, thump, the rain hit harder and harder, each drop a slap against her skin. Why was walking away from Trevor so painful? It's not that there could ever be anything between them— not with his situation and hers. But…she jumped a puddle as she trudged on. They had so much in common: the desire to take care of their families, their mutual love for theatre, the loss of their fathers, the loss of their beloved acting coach…and beneath it all, a crazy attraction for one another.

Dodging fellow New Yorkers, she ran faster as the

rain came down harder. Drenched, Jenna thought of his warm penthouse and the complicated elevator she had fought against to make her escape—could it have been a sign she was supposed to stay? No. She couldn't afford to think like that. There was way too much at stake—the health and well-being of a child. Besides, even if his situation were different, she was alone, and thanks to her circumstances, she would remain that way.

But their situations weren't different. They were very straightforward. She would continue on her path to be an egg donor so she could help support her sister, and he would stay with Maggie to support his. It was the way things were supposed to be. Jenna looked up and rain pummeled her face. But what if? She snapped her head down and marched on. There was no "what-if" for them. She had no time for these thoughts—it wasn't as if she chose this life.

****

Trevor stood frozen on his balcony, watching Jenna. From his vantage point on the eighth floor he could see her on the street, making her way through the busy city and the rain. He stared, transfixed, as she traveled farther and farther from him.

He was paralyzed. Why the hell was he being such a fucking wimp? He was a man, damn it. A tall, strong, successful, wealthy man. He wanted her, and she wanted him—but there was no feasible way...

Forget his crazy attraction to her—her incredibly bright eyes, her small, toned body, that fucking nose ring, the tiny little stud that glistened against her tanned skin—there was so much he wanted to say to her. He wanted to understand her problems, and talk about his.

He wanted them to lounge together on his couch, drinking gallons of coffee while they laughed, or cried, or just sat quietly together. When they had talked through every detail of their lives from their deepest fears to their most outlandish dreams, he wanted to lift her up into his arms and carry her up the stairs to his bedroom, making love to her for hours. Trevor sighed. Despite having a life most people would kill for, he had become quite the expert in wanting what he couldn't have, and what could never happen.

With his stomach in knots and his head pounding, Trevor made the necessary phone calls for Don Oleesa's funeral. Although it pained him to do so, he also canceled rehearsals for the next two days. He wanted to—*needed* to—see Jenna. At least he was sure she would be at the funeral, even if they couldn't be there together as he had hoped. Sad and confused, Trevor made his way to the music room to lose himself.

****

Don's funeral service was held at St. Malachy's Church in Manhattan. The church was mobbed with actors and various people the acting coach had known throughout his life. It was standing room only for many latecomers, and Jenna sat wedged between Luis and Loretta on one side of her, and her agent, Kat Price on the other. Jenna wore her same blue dress, having given it a quick wash in her bathroom sink, and letting it line dry in her kitchen. She didn't have the time or the desire to trudge to the laundry fourteen blocks away. Despite her efforts, it was still damp in places.

Trevor sat three rows up, next to Maggie. He was wearing a gorgeous charcoal suit, tailored perfectly to his body. Before he took his seat, Jenna caught how the suit accented his wide shoulders and nipped in at his toned abdomen. Normally, she really didn't like the suit and tie look, but good grief, he could make even that look sexy and dangerous. Jenna's gaze burned into his back.

"Why don't you just sleep with him already?" Kat's voice was too loud.

Jenna's jaw dropped, and she turned to Kat. Heat radiated from her core and stung her cheeks. "Kat...? We're at a funeral. How could you—?"

"Oh please. It's Don Oleesa's funeral. He would want us all to be celebrating life and love, and not mourning his death. You know that as well as anyone, Jenna."

Jenna fidgeted, uncomfortably.

"It's clear you want to..." Kat leaned in and whispered now, "have relations with him."

Jenna buried her face in her hands.

Kat spoke in her regular voice again. "And from the number of times he's turned around—"

"Eleven," Luis leaned over and whispered.

"You, too?" Jenna spoke in a hurried hush.

"Jen, the man showed up at your door at eight on a Sunday morning to see you and came to our freaking cold wedding on a rooftop in January. Then he whooshed us all into his waiting car to rush us to the hospital."

"That is true," Loretta chimed in, fanning herself with a prayer book. The growing crowd made the church stifling.

"Really?" Kat leaned across Jenna to Loretta.

"Oh, yeah." Loretta nodded enthusiastically.

Luis chimed in. "That's kickass testosterone stuff

155

you bring out in him, Jen. It was like a scene out of a romance novel or some shit."

"Luis," Loretta reprimanded, slapping Luis on the shoulder with her prayer book. "Language. We're in church."

Luis rubbed his arm.

"Really?" Kat repeated. She turned to Jenna, her eyes bright, eyebrows raised.

"Yes." Jenna mumbled her answer as Trevor turned around again.

"Twelve," Luis interjected.

Jenna sighed. "But it wasn't a big deal. I was confused and sad, he took control. That was all."

"I'm confused all the time," Kat said, "and I sure as hell don't have the likes of *him*"—she lifted her oversized clutch to point at Trevor—"taking control for me."

"Guys," Jenna snapped.

A man next to them shushed her.

Jenna continued in a whisper. "We are at a funeral. Don Oleesa's funeral. And no matter how much he would have wanted us all to go on, let's please show some respect."

"Amen to that," Loretta agreed.

Luis and Kat mumbled and sat forward in their seats as the priest motioned to Jenna.

"Young lady, would you like to speak?"

Jenna's cheeks flushed.

"You got caught talking." Luis chuckled quietly, smiling at Jenna.

"I can't do this." Jenna turned to Luis and Loretta. The one thing Jenna feared the most, aside from letting down her sister or falling for Trevor, was being unprepared to speak in front of people. She moaned. "Uh..." Jenna looked around, panicked. A sea of faces stared back at her, and suddenly it was a year ago, and Jenna was at her father's funeral, with Don at her side. Don had traveled by train for hours, wading through crowds of people at Penn Station, getting jostled as he waited for a cab, just to be there for Jenna. The least she could do was to be here for him, now.

Maggie snickered.

Jenna took a deep breath and stood. She smoothed her dress and walked forward slowly. She stepped up next to the priest and said a polite "thank you." Facing the crowd, she inhaled sharply, gripping the sides of the podium. She surveyed the packed church and nodded. These people were here because they loved Don.

"I didn't plan to speak today..." Jenna turned her face away from the crowd and cleared her throat before going on. "Excuse me."

Luis caught her gaze, and he motioned for her to speak. Loretta gave her a thumbs up, and Kat mimed for her to stand up taller. She turned to Trevor and he smiled at her.

"When I think of Don," Jenna spoke softly but with confidence into the mic at the podium, "I think of his eyes. How they lit up when he was directing, or when one of his students had a break-through, and especially, when he talked about his Evelyn." Jenna gave a small smile to Trevor who nodded back. She continued. "Anyone who's been around Don for more than a minute knows of his love of Ernest Hemingway's writing."

Most of the congregation chuckled.

"So I think it's only fitting for Mr. Hemingway to

say our final words about Don." Jenna swallowed hard, thinking of Don's smiling face before her. As she quoted her favorite passage from *The Old Man and the Sea*—the one that told of the old man's eyes—a tear escaped, running down her cheek. She didn't bother to wipe it away. She stepped down from the podium, feeling Trevor's gaze on her as she walked past many sorrowful parishioners and back to her seat.

****

When the service ended, Jenna sat tight in her seat. Maybe if she didn't move, she wouldn't have to face Trevor and Maggie—or admit that Don was really gone.

Luis leaned over. "You have to eventually move you know."

She shook her head.

"Come on." Luis stood, offering Jenna his hand. "We're gonna head to the diner. You need to eat."

Jenna didn't speak.

Luis cocked his head. "Want to tell me what happened?"

Jenna stood with Luis as the crowd filed out of the pews and into the aisles. Trevor and Maggie stood near their seats in the front of the church talking to people as they walked by. Trevor glanced toward Jenna and smiled.

"Nothing." Jenna made eye contact with Luis. "Nothing can happen, Luis."

"Because of your dumb ass plan or because of Baywatch Barbie over there?" He nodded to Maggie.

"Both."

"Yeah?" Luis crossed his arms. "Let me tell you something, Jen, you're a smart girl but you don't know shit about men. He's about as attracted to her as I am to Kat."

Jenna giggled. "I doubt that."

"I don't. You all think you're so intuitive but you're clueless. He hasn't touched her once. Not once. The man's in pain, and all he can do is look to you. He wants you, not her."

"Even if you're right, there's nothing we can do about it."

Luis held up his left hand, flashing his gold wedding band. "That's exactly what I used to think—there was no fucking way I could ever get Loretta to marry me. And now—" Luis grinned. "Come on."

Jenna followed Luis out into the aisle. Out of the corner of her eye she caught sight of Trevor moving toward them. They stopped, allowing people to pass, as Trevor stepped up, extending his hand to Luis. The men shook.

"Luis, Jenna. I thought I'd miss you. Where's Loretta?"

Luis pointed to the front door. "Over there with Kat."

Trevor nodded, his gaze settling on Jenna's face. She turned away.

Luis shook his head. "Trev, we're heading to our diner to grab a bite. The Carlton on Eighth. How 'bout you join us, and you can buy us that wedding meal you promised?"

"I'd love to." Trevor's face brightened.

"Great." Luis stepped back to let someone pass. "Grab your girl, and we'll meet you there. We're planning a good-memories-only tribute to Don with all his favorite foods. Bacon and greasy eggs, home fries, and lots of cornbread smeared in butter."

Trevor hesitated. "Well uh, Maggie isn't much into diner food. She's macro or vegan or something…" He looked over his shoulder at Maggie who was talking to a small group of people and back again.

"Ask her. She can sip sparkling water or whatever women like that do."

"Uh, thanks." Trevor shifted closer to Jenna.

"Come on, Jen." Luis tossed his head to the door. "I wanna remember Don with a freaking huge chocolate milkshake. See ya there, Trev."

"Yeah. Uh, Jenna?" Trevor grabbed her arm.

She wheeled around, and he let go.

"Can I talk to you for a moment?"

She turned to Luis. "I'll meet you guys at the diner, okay?"

Luis winked at Jenna. "See ya."

Trevor and Jenna stood in the aisle of the still busy church.

"Jenna. I want to—"

"Wait, Trevor. Please. I don't think I can get into anything heavy right now. I know you're here with Maggie and I know why. And even if you weren't, I'd still have my reasons for having to remain single. There's nothing between us, so there's nothing to feel bad about." She pointed her thumb behind her. "It's a sad day today, and I want to be with my friends to remember Don. I'm going to go to the diner. I hope to see you there." With her head aching, Jenna turned and left the church.

****

Trevor's heart pounded as he walked into the diner. Of course he wanted to come to mourn Don with his new friends but he also wanted to understand what Jenna was saying to him. She very clearly told him that even if he left Maggie, she still couldn't be with him. But why?

He honestly had asked Maggie to come but she had no interest in sitting with a bunch of "nobodies" eating diner food. Thank God. Sometimes things really do work out. He stepped into the retro diner, and the smell of matzoh ball soup warmed him immediately. He missed eating in diners like this with real everyday people. Sure, fancy dinners out were great but sometimes he just wanted to be a regular person again. A woman in a nearby banquette noticed him and smiled. He waved to her politely then spotted Jenna sitting at a large table, her back to the wall. Loretta was on one side of her and an empty chair on the other. Three other people were standing near the table, talking. Three people that needed seats. Trevor's pace quickened like he were in a high-stakes game of musical chairs. He pushed forward toward that seat next to Jenna, but the woman jumped up from her booth, blocking his way.

"Are you Caspian Locke?" She dropped her gaze and smiled, blushing.

Trevor peered around the woman to that empty seat next to Jenna. One of the men talking to Larry moved toward Jenna. Damn it. "Uh, yes. Yes, I am. Would you like an autograph?" His gaze was still on that seat, agitation forming in his esophagus. He rubbed away the pain.

"Let me just grab something…"

The woman headed back toward her booth—could she move any slower? Energy coursed up and down

Trevor's arms. His legs ached as he forced himself to stay still. He glanced at the woman who was digging through her bag while she giggled with the two others at the table. He turned back to Jenna. Crap. The man talking to Larry turned in profile. It was Guildenstern and he was making a move toward Jenna.

Trevor bounded to the woman's table, startling her with his sudden presence. He smiled, yanking his tie loose from his neck and pulling it over his head. He felt his pockets for a pen. Damn it. Luckily a waitress was at the next table. "May I?" He pointed to her marker pen, and she handed it over, her jaw slack with surprise. He laid his tie flat on the table and scrolled "Love, Caspian" down the front. Winking, he handed the tie to the woman and her two friends smiled at him.

He checked the progress of Guildenstern but he was stalled, talking to Christina. Quickly, Trevor scrolled the same "Love, Caspian" message on their paper placemats and without taking a breath, gave the waitress back her pen, finally making his way toward Jenna.

The large group of Don's friends took up the entire back of the diner. There were so many people who had joined the party, they had several tables pushed together to accommodate all of them. Trevor scanned the table, seeing Larry and some other actors from the show. He smiled. That's one of the things he loved about the New York theatre; there's only a few degrees of separation between actors—and nearly all are welcoming to each other. Despite the sorrow that covered the group, there was a happy, peaceful feel about them. Larry spotted him.

"Trevor." He pushed his glasses up higher onto his

nose. "Come on. There's a seat over there next to Jenna. We're just about to take turns toasting Don."

Oh, yes, at moments like this, Trevor was so very glad he hired Larry for their director. Trevor slid in next to Jenna, the sparks between them nearly painful. She took a deep breath, shifting in her seat. He sat as still as he could, forcing himself to keep his hands to himself as person after person toasted Don, mentioning how wonderful Don was, and what they had learned from him.

Finally, it was Trevor's turn. He stood, smoothing his jacket, and Jenna's gaze followed him. "I'd love to raise a glass, but"—Trevor looked down at the empty spot before him—"the waiter hasn't been by yet."

People chuckled as Jenna handed him her coffee.

He smiled at her, and raising the mug, he spoke. "I've known Don for many, many years. Like most of you here, he was more than my acting coach; he was my dear friend. And what I know about Don is that he was a fabulous teacher who believed every minute of every day is an opportunity to learn. What I learned from him was that I want to be more like Don—to honor truth in work and in life." Trevor let his gaze fall on Jenna, and her cheeks flushed. "And what I was reminded of today is that life is uncertain. Many of us know that first hand. So let's not waste the time we have." He raised the mug again as he sat.

"Here, here." Luis raised his juice and everyone followed. "To Don, the greatest teacher and friend. May we all learn from him and find truth in our work and in our lives."

"Here, here."

People sipped their drinks, as conversation ensued.

Trevor took a slug of Jenna's coffee and grimaced. "How do you drink that?"

She smiled. "I'll get you some black coffee." She put her hand up to signal the waiter's attention.

"Wait."

She dropped her hand. The warmth of her coffee felt great as he cradled her mug between his hands. He spoke in a low murmur. "The coffee can wait."

He let go of the mug to place his hand on hers, and her eyes dashed up to his. She peeked at her cast mates at the opposite end of the table and slipped her hand from his, fidgeting with her spoon. It was clear their relationship—or whatever it was—made her uncomfortable. Crap. That was the last thing he wanted to make her feel.

"Can I talk to you?"

"Of course." She kept her gaze turned down to the table.

"What did you mean at the church? That even if I weren't involved with someone, you couldn't be with me?"

"I meant exactly what I said." She glanced up at him.

"Why not?"

She turned to him, leaning closer. Although the restaurant was busy, it was like they were the only two people there, huddled together in their own little world.

"Jenna? Why couldn't you be with me?"

"What does it matter? You are with someone." She tilted her head, speaking quietly. "And we both know it's for the best."

"That doesn't answer my question."

"Why can't I be with you? Well, for one thing,

there is no reason to choose to be with another person, because in the end, we are all alone." She stared down at the spotted spoon before her.

Trevor flinched at her words. They were so sad, and so finite. They were words that came from someone who had experienced too much pain. Thank goodness he was smart enough to know what this was—grief. And everyone deals with grief in his or her own way. "Don wasn't alone at the end," Trevor countered, spinning the cup in his hand. "We were with him."

She shrugged.

"And when Evelyn passed, Don was there."

"You know that?" She looked up at him.

"Of course. I was there, too."

Jenna gave a tiny smile, taking the mug from him, and sipping her coffee.

"And what if you're completely wrong?" Hell, yeah, it was time to dare her. Jenna was always up for a challenge. "What if the only thing that matters in life is being with someone else, because you never know when your end will come?"

"Excuse me?"

"What about all of those poor souls, like my dad, on September 11? What about those people who wait to take their vacations, because they're too busy with work, just to find out they have a terminal disease? What if I walk out of here and get hit by a bus?"

Jenna gripped the table with both hands. "Trevor, stop."

"But what if, Jenna? Isn't that all the more reason to live life now?"

"So what are you saying?" Jenna's voice was raspy and low.

"Tell me why you can't be with me."

"I can't."

Her gaze searched his. They sat, staring at each other. There was nothing more he could say, or do.

"Trevor. I know what's going on here. Death. It—it changes your perspective." Her gaze dropped to the table and back to him. "At least, it does until we once again get completely caught up in the ridiculous minutia of life." She twirled her fork absentmindedly, and leaned forward in her seat. "You were reminded you don't want to waste the time you have? So don't waste it wondering about me. It shouldn't matter to you why I couldn't be with you in some fictitious world. You shouldn't be here, Trevor."

He inhaled sharply.

"Look, I'm not trying to be mean. I'm trying to save us both from something we're going to regret. You can't risk everything on a relationship that could be over at any moment."

Trevor adjusted in his seat. "What makes you think it would be over at any moment?"

"Because if it isn't—that's even worse."

"Jenna. I'm sorry. I'm a pretty smart guy but I'm lost."

Jenna lifted her thumb to her mouth and bit at the nail. "I really like you, Trevor."

"I really like you too, Jenna."

"But I'm not dumping my problems on you. The only thing there is for us is the show. Let's act the hell out of it—as we both can. Let's be there for each other just like Don told us to be."

"He also told us to make love." Trevor raised his eyebrows, smirking.

Jenna blushed that soft pink color Trevor loved. "Trevor…"

"Jenna, look. I'm a grown man, and I know what's at stake here. At least for me. And no, I would never mess that up. And in case you didn't notice, I have pretty wide shoulders. I promise I can handle whatever you dump on me." He grinned. "But what I'm feeling toward you…"

Her gaze leveled on his. "It doesn't matter. Whatever this is…" She waved her hand back and forth between them. "It doesn't matter. Not in comparison to everything else." She sighed. "We have less than two weeks until we open, then a month-long run. And then that's it, Trevor. It has to be it."

"I don't want that to be it, Jenna. Can't we at least be friends?"

"Friends?"

"Yeah. Go to a movie together. Work on our lines. Talk when we need to."

"That sounds an awful lot like dating to me."

"You're telling me you don't do those things with Luis?"

"Of course I do."

"Even without Loretta around?"

"Sure. But that's different."

"Why?"

"Because I don't want Luis to kiss me…"

Trevor grunted his exhale, shifting in his seat. Her soft voice telling him she wanted to be kissed went straight to his groin. Damn it.

She bit the corner of her lip, looking away and back again. "Does Maggie like to run with you?"

"What?"

"Run. Do you go running together?"

"No."

"Well, we're sure as hell not going to sit in a dark movie theatre together, but maybe, if it's okay with her, maybe we could run together some mornings."

"I'll come by tomorrow at seven."

She pursed her lips together, fighting her smile. "You've got to clear it with her."

Trevor nodded.

She leaned back in her seat, twirling her spoon. "I'm pretty fast; I hope you can keep up."

He smiled. "That's okay. I kind of like chasing you."

Chapter Twelve

"Jenna?"

"Just a sec…" She was talking to the waitress who had stopped by again, probably ordering—oh, who the hell knows.

Trevor smiled. It had been a week since the funeral, and he sat in a booth across from Jenna in a dive coffee shop in the East Village—another place she'd recommended. The coffee shop was like the other places they'd been eating in recently—a real gritty place, with great food, torn menus, and waiters with attitudes. He wanted to bring up this morning, but he wasn't sure how to start. As she chatted on with the waitress, he fiddled with his water-spotted fork, tapping his foot against the sticky floor. He glanced about at the eclectic clientele—the young hipster guys stroking their beards, the designer-boot-wearing college students pretending to be struggling and not living off daddy's money, the photographers and models who flocked into these dive places after hours, and a homeless man huddled over a bowl of soup, sitting at the grimy counter. No one cared about Trevor or his celebrity in a place like this, and it was such a relief. This was his New York, and he loved it, and Jenna did, too.

Oh, Jenna. She was laughing with the waitress, about what? He didn't have a clue. He was lost in his own thoughts and in her beauty. The waitress walked away, and Jenna squared her shoulders toward him. Yes, he wanted to talk about their run this morning, but no, she probably didn't.

"Want to talk about this morning?"

She fiddled with her coffee cup. "Not really."

This morning, as they followed their usual running path and approached the reservoir, Jenna ran faster and faster until Trevor needed to push himself to keep up. She grimaced with every step she took, concentration and pain etched on her face, but still she ran faster. It was too much.

"Jenna..." He stopped her by reaching out and grabbing her hand.

She wheeled around, confused, her gaze landing on his. She planted her hands on her hips, panting hard. He reached out and wiped the perspiration off her brow, and she closed her eyes as his hand came to rest on her cheek.

His heart ached for her. "Baby, why are you always running from me?"

She shook her head, not speaking a word. Instead, she turned away and continued to run, leaving Trevor with an unshakable feeling of dread...

But tonight everything was back to normal, which meant, they were back to that freaking, civil, platonic relationship they were allowed to have.

"Jenna..." Damn. Frustration began in his jeans and worked its way up, swirling in his gut. What the hell was happening here? They were a week away from Valentine's Day and opening night—but also a week away from the date Maggie was expecting at the very least a promise from him, if not a flat out proposal. Thing was, he hadn't even considered moving forward with Maggie. How could he? If he wasn't worrying about Toby or rehearsing Hamlet, he spent all of his free brain space on thoughts of Jenna and why she would refuse to be with him even if he were uninvolved. There was no time to think about Maggie. Frankly, he never really thought about Maggie. Crap. What a lousy boyfriend he was. He hadn't spent the night with her in a month—and they hadn't had sex in nearly two. The last few times they did, it was less satisfying than a long run or a hot steam.

Trevor shifted in his seat, frustration burning a hole in his gut. Damn, these diners were hot, despite the frigid temperatures outside. Trevor yanked his sweater over his head, catching a glimpse of Jenna, ogling his arms in his short sleeve shirt. He smiled. Okay, maybe a change of tactic. "You know, it's only a week until Valentine's Day."

"Huh?" She tore her gaze off his arms.

He smirked. "Jen? Valentine's Day is in a week." He leaned forward, settling his eyes on hers.

"Yeah. Uh, are you nervous?"

"What?" Trevor cocked his head, the question catching him off guard.

Jenna blew on her cup of coffee. She took a sip and scrunched up her face.

"More sugar?" Trevor grabbed the packets.

"Yes, please."

"What are you up to now? Eight?"

"I think it's time I share with you, I have a serious addiction to sugar, Trevor."

"You don't say."

Jenna giggled as her enormous piece of pie à la mode arrived. "Yummy." She squiggled in her seat.

"Is that what you just ordered?"

"Yup. By the way, you didn't answer my question. Nervous?"

"Nah. You?"

"Not about the play."

Jenna smiled in a way that went straight to his core. She dove into her pie. "Mmm."

Trevor shifted in his seat as she moaned.

"It's cherry."

"Seriously?"

"Mm-hmmm…want some?" She held out her plate. Trevor shook his head.

"Okay, but you don't know what you're missing. I think they still use actual lard in the crust."

Trevor stared at her blankly as Jenna dug her spoon into the pie and ice cream. She pulled it up, licking the spoon.

Trevor adjusted his shirt, yanking the cotton away from his perspiring body. "I'm not sure I can watch you do this."

"Why not?" Jenna looked around. "Afraid of food poisoning? Don't worry about their seventy-one health rating. I've been eating here forever. Come on, try it."

Jenna lifted her spoon, holding out a big bite of pie for Trevor. He gobbled it, and she waited for his reaction.

"Mm…"

"See? Sublime, right?" She dug in again, repeating the action of licking her spoon.

Trevor adjusted in his seat, now convinced watching Jenna eat cherry pie with vanilla ice cream was the most erotic thing he'd ever seen.

"Want some more?"

"Sure."

"Order your own then, money bags." Jenna hunched over the table, wrapping her arm around her pie, protectively.

Trevor burst out laughing. "Really? You're going to eat all that?"

"Yup. Didn't you taste it? Why would I share?" She winked.

Trevor motioned for the waitress and ordered another. When she left with his order, Trevor turned to Jenna. "You don't diet, do you?"

"Nope. Not my thing."

"That's amazing." Trevor shook his head.

"Why?"

"Because the women I know, almost all of them are starving all the time."

"Women like Maggie?"

"Yes." Trevor looked away, uncomfortable and sorry he brought up Maggie.

"Listen." Jenna put down her spoon. "I would kill to spend a day in that body of hers. Just to know what it feels like. And she'd probably kill to spend a day with my metabolism. It's just the way life is. I'm a skinny kid, and she's a goddess. I get to eat pie with ice cream, and she gets to drink air." Jenna shrugged and picked up her spoon again. "Nothing really makes sense. So we do what we can with what we have."

"God, I love—" Trevor caught himself just before the word slipped out.

Now it was Jenna's turn to look uncomfortable. She dug into the ice cream again, her gaze glued to the table. She peeked up at him. "What about you? You ever wish for anything you can't have?"

Trevor's gaze locked on hers, his heart pounding.

"Oh." She blushed.

He smiled.

"Uh…anything else?"

"Sure." Trevor leaned back and twirled a spoon in his fingers. "I know I sound so spoiled, but I guess most of all I wish I were free to do what I wanted." He had never before admitted that to anyone—including himself. But the admission was freeing.

"What do you mean?" Jenna stopped eating and squinted at Trevor, trying to understand.

"To play the roles I want to play. To produce. To do more theatre—to take some risks."

She plopped down her spoon. "So do it, then."

Jenna looked deeply into Trevor's eyes, and his core tingled. There was such a connection between them, it was all he could do not to slide into the bench next to her and pull her into his arms.

"Trevor?"

"It's not that easy. I've got commitments. Obligations. You know that."

"Yes, but if you never take a chance, you'll never know what else you can do."

"But I know what I have now. And who relies on me. And what the hell am I complaining about, anyway? For God's sake, I'm Caspian Locke."

"No, you're not."

"Excuse me?"

"You're Trevor Hughes. An actor. And a damned good one. Caspian Locke is just another character you play. You're no more Caspian than you are Hamlet. You're you, Trevor. Go do a production of *Cat on a Hot Tin Roof*; you'd make a spectacular Brick."

"I would?" Excitement surged through his veins.

"Oh, good grief, yes. Go try it. Give yourself the chance to surprise you." She leveled her eyes on him, her voice soft and heartfelt. "I understand being stuck, Trevor. I really do." She raised her eyebrows, swallowing hard. "I know I haven't known you for very long, but I really believe there's more for you out there. Dare to—"

"Dream?"

"Yes." Jenna sat back, spinning her empty coffee cup.

Trevor sat quietly, her words running through his brain. No one had ever said anything like that to him. Before Jenna, no one had ever understood wanting more than Caspian Locke. Sometimes he felt so close to her he just wanted the rest of the world to disappear. He cleared his throat, regrouping. "By the way, I made some calls—I have a friend producing that new crime drama filming in New York—and anyway, I got Luis an audition. I think he'll be magnificent."

"Oh my gosh, Trevor. Thank you. He will be perfect." She beamed at him. "He must be so excited. And Kat, wow—she must be thrilled. Luis is a great guy, you know. Fought his way back from some dark stuff."

"He tells me you were a big part of his recovery."

Jenna waved him off. "Nah. I just gave him a place to crash when he needed it, and someone to talk to. It was so hard on him and Loretta. I'm so incredibly glad they made it. He's been a great friend to me. They both have. I hope I can be as good a friend to them."

"Sounds like you are."

Jenna shrugged.

"So what about you?" He nodded to her, smiling. "Have you always been serious, determined Jenna...? You ever do anything you shouldn't?"

Jenna rolled her eyes. Her whole face lit up as she laughed, turning away. She was stunningly beautiful. She covered her mouth with her hand and turned back. "I've never done anything I *should*, Trevor."

"What do you mean?" He sat forward, his elbows resting on the table, mesmerized.

"Where do I start? I had a full ride to four different colleges, good schools, but I chose to come to the city to be an actor."

"A full ride?"

"I had a perfect SAT score." Jenna shrugged noncommittally and looked down. Her cheeks flushed.

"Really?" He was more and more captivated by her.

"Really. But I gave it all up for this." She waved her hands around the coffee shop, smiling.

"I take it your mother—"

"Freaked. Yup. She's still angry with me."

"Is she coming to see you play Ophelia?"

Jenna leaned forward and rested her forehead in her hands. "It's complicated."

"I've got time, and I know the boss in case you're late for rehearsal tomorrow." He grinned.

"Oh ha, ha." She sighed. "My mom and I, we don't speak much, just a phone call here or there. She thinks if she comes to see me perform she'll be agreeing with my choices."

Anger welled inside Trevor, but he forced it down.

She focused on him, tearing at her napkin as she spoke. "Will Amanda be able to come?"

"That's the plan. She and Toby." His body shifted toward Jenna as he spoke. "I'm looking forward to introducing Toby to everyone. To you."

She smiled, but his thoughts darkened.

"That is, of course, assuming he's feeling well enough to take the trip into the city." His voice cracked the slightest bit, and his throat ached as he spoke.

Jenna leaned forward and took Trevor's hands in hers. She turned them over and let her thumbs caress the soft spot on the inside of his wrists. He closed his eyes and breathed deeply.

"He'll be fine, Trevor."

He opened his eyes, and she was smiling at him, her eyes glassy. He turned his wrists over, grasping her hands in his. She gasped.

"I'm so glad you're here, Jenna. This whole thing..." He tossed his head. "Don, the show, not knowing what's going on with Toby, I wouldn't want to have to face it all alone."

She cocked her head. "You're not alone, Trevor. You have a girlfriend. We...uh..." She pulled her hands away. "Your feelings are just misplaced, because we've been spending a lot of time together for the sake of the show. We're ready. You should probably go see Maggie. I'm sure she's feeling neglected."

Jenna grabbed her bag and coat and slid to the edge of the booth. She stood, and Trevor reached out, taking her hand.

"Trevor..." She pulled her hand away. "I'll see you at rehearsal tomorrow."

She rushed out of the coffee shop, and Trevor stood, watching her go.

****

Jenna knocked on his dressing room door. "Knock, knock. Can I come in?"

He wheeled around, and she caught her breath. In his black shirt and black pants tailored perfectly to him—good grief...he was so smart, and talented, and handsome. They'd only seen each other in rehearsals since her awkward exit from the coffee shop that night, but something deep in her belly told her she couldn't stay away any longer. She stepped inside his dressing room which looked very much like hers—large lighted mirror with two black leather chairs posed in front, clothing racks, and peeling paint on the windowsill. Although the theatre had been upgraded, they had never touched the dressing rooms during renovations. Most actors loved the feel of preparing in a room with so much history. On the far wall, a stack of posters advertising their show waited for his autograph.

"Uh, happy opening night." She waved a gift bag, with an opening night present tucked inside.

"Jenna..." He came toward her like a starving man set before an all-you-can-eat buffet.

She stepped back a tiny step just to keep steady and he looked her up and down.

"You look gorgeous."

"Yeah?" She appraised her full gold gown, complete with bustle and corset for a cinched waist. The bodice had a brocade overlay. "The gown is gorgeous. I wasn't sure I could do it justice."

"Oh, you can."

He smiled, and her fingertips tingled.

As he stood there before her, tall, strong, powerful, she fought for coherent thought. He wasn't saying a word, not moving a muscle, but his *presence* was crossing boundaries they had agreed wouldn't be crossed. "I uh, the makeup artist told me you wanted me to leave in my nose ring. Really?"

"Yeah, really." He stepped closer.

She gazed down at her gown again, struggling to keep calm. "Well, I like the mix of the traditional seventeenth century costumes with modern touches—like your costume. It's cool."

"Good." He was standing before her. "I like things that aren't overt."

"Um, yeah." Her stomach swirled with excitement. He was way too close. She gripped the gift bag tightly in her hand. "I…uh…" She tripped over her words.

Trevor lifted his fingers to her lips, quieting her, and slowly, he ran his fingers across her perfectly painted smile. Without meaning to, she let her head move with his touch, and the tip of his forefinger parted her lips, her mouth opening. He dragged his moist finger back over her pout, her chest heaving up and down. His eyes were fixed on her, his brow furrowed.

"Stop." Jenna pulled back, scooting past him, making her way to the window that was cracked open. "We're about to go onstage, and Maggie…"

"Oh, Maggie, Maggie, Maggie." He stormed about, pacing. "I am so damned sick and tired of hearing about Maggie."

"Trevor."

Jenna walked to him, and his frenetic action stopped. She placed her hand on his chest, settling his breathing. "What's going on with you? Are you nervous?"

"No." He scoffed and stepped back, settling by the window.

"Then what?" She followed. "Trevor, whatever's going on, you can talk to me. That's what friends do, right?"

"Friends, Jenna?" He raised his eyebrows. "I think you know I'd like you to be so much more than my friend." He grabbed her hand and pulled it to his chest.

She yanked her hand away. "Trevor. We can't possibly get into this now—we're minutes from going onstage…"

"What if I were free from Maggie?"

His words sat low, brewing in her gut. What if?

She dropped her voice to a whisper. "There is no 'what if' about that, Trevor. You know that. So there's no sense in asking. And you know that even if you were unattached, I still couldn't be involved with you."

"Why the hell not?" His voice was loud and demanding.

Jenna stood up taller. "I don't know if this is some fucked up Method stuff you're doing, but you're acting like a jerk. I'm going to leave because we both have a lot riding on this show, and I don't want to suck." She glanced at the gift bag she was clenching in her hands. "Oh, here." She pushed the bag against his chest. "Happy Opening-Night-slash-Valentine's Day."

He grasped the bag as she turned to leave.

"Jenna." He took her by the forearm, and gently spun her around. "I'm sorry." Trevor dropped his hand and leaned down to look at her. "I am nervous."

"The critics?" She pulled away, studying him.

He shook his head and grabbed his cell off his table, waving it. "I learned a lifetime ago not to care what people think of me. Critics don't matter. I haven't heard from Amanda. She texted me to say they were fine but not able to make it."

"You think something's wrong?"

"I know it." He stood up, running his hand through his perfectly messed up hair. "The expression, 'no news is good news' doesn't apply with them. No news means she's waiting to tell me bad news until after the show is over."

"She said they were fine. You don't know that."

"Don't I?" He raised his eyebrows.

Her stomach clenched in the way it did whenever she found out Olivia was working rather than studying.

"Trevor." Jenna placed her hand on his, holding it. "Whatever it is, you will handle it when the show is over. I'm certain of it. But right now, you need to focus on Hamlet."

"It seems so unimportant compared…"

"Of course it does. But you know she'd tell you if it were an emergency. So you've got to do this show. It's just a couple of hours and then you can get to Amanda and Toby. In the meantime, do it for Don. He would be so proud."

Trevor nodded. "When I went to talk to Don about *Hamlet*, he was incredibly supportive, told me it was 'high time' I got back on a stage."

"He was right." Jenna smiled.

"Maybe." Trevor looked off. "But now…tonight…especially since Don's passed…"

"You feel like if you mess up, you're dragging him down with you. Because you're the last of his legacy."

"Yes." Trevor nodded. "I have to be good—to honor Don."

"You are good." Jenna put both of her small warm hands on Trevor's wide chest. She fiddled nervously with the buttons of his black shirt. "Honestly, you're more than good. You're really wonderful."

He inhaled deeply as she continued.

"I understand, Trevor. I promised my dad, on his deathbed, I would be a success."

Trevor's gaze met Jenna's, steadily. "You are."

Jenna shook her head, looking down at her feet as she spoke. "I never told you my dad was an actor. But he gave it up when I came along." She looked up at him, her eyes softening. "He even had some speaking roles on a couple of New York soaps."

"Really?"

Jenna nodded. "I think all we can do is our very best. We focus on what we have to focus on first—the show. So we go out there and be there for each other just like Don told us to. And if we flop, we flop together. And we go do dinner theatre in some tiny town, somewhere."

Trevor laughed out loud. If felt so good to see the worry leave his face, even for a moment.

"Oh…speaking of dinner theatre, you should open that." She nodded to the gift bag still in his hand.

"I can't believe you got me a gift."

Her cheeks heated. "You'd better be careful opening it."

Trevor pulled a tiny plastic box from the bag and opened it carefully. He peeked inside, his head moving away when he caught the scent. "Sauerkraut? Really?"

A grin spread across her face. "I thought if you needed a boost tonight, you could come in and take a whiff and you'd be transported right back to our rehearsal theatre."

He reached out and placed his hand on her cheek,

stroking it gently. His gaze danced across hers.

"I, uh…" Her tummy rumbled with excitement.

"Thank you, Jenna. For all of it." He pulled back, letting his hand drop to his side. He walked to the clothing rack in the back of the room, dropped the sauerkraut, and dug a small pink box from his leather bag. "Here. I wanted it to be so much more but this just felt right."

Jenna took the box with trembling hands. She gave it a slight shake, listening to it rattle. "What is it?"

"Open it."

Jenna's heart raced as she tugged at the ribbon and lifted the top off the box. Inside were a hundred pink candy turtles—all stamped with the word "Dream."

She looked up at him, her eyes aching from tears. "How did you?"

"I know you'd want your father here tonight. And I know he'd want you to dream big, because that's what I want for you."

"Trevor, I…" Jenna threw her arms around his neck and held him, tightly, her gown bunching between them. When she broke away, she was inches from him.

"Perchance to dream, Jenna."

She smiled, biting the corner of her lip, exactly where his fingers had been only moments before. He reached up to touch her hair.

"Careful of the wig," she joked.

"And with that sugar addiction of yours, I figured Valentine's Day candy was a given."

"Oh, you know me so well, Mr. Hughes." Jenna fanned herself coquettishly.

He smiled. Trevor tossed the container aside and scooped Jenna into his arms. He held her tight.

"It feels like the nunnery scene." Jenna's voice was soft and breathy.

"Yes, but does this happen in the nunnery scene?" Trevor pulled her closer to him, and his lips nearly brushed against hers.

"Maybe it should?"

"Are you telling me…?" Trevor studied her, his gaze locked on hers. "You want me to—?"

The stage manager stuck his head through the door. "Hamlet? Ophelia? Places, please."

Her body ached as he released her.

"Damn it." Trevor shook his head, jumping up and down in place. He stopped and smiled at Jenna, taking her hand and kissing it, before letting go. "Here we go."

"Break a leg, Trevor." She smiled at him, adrenaline rushing through her.

"You too, Jenna."

She made her way to the door and turned back. "Trevor? Here's to not sucking and having to do dinner theatre in the middle of nowhere."

Chuckling, Trevor tossed his head back and Jenna scooted out the door.

Chapter Thirteen

"Hey, Trevor, nice job."

"Thanks, man." Trevor stood in the hallway of the dressing rooms, shaking hands with Guildenstern—quickly. "You too." He peered around his friend and into the men's dressing room to see a few more members of his cast. "Everyone, really nice job." He knocked against the door for luck and rushed past, hustling down the hallway to get to Jenna. He nearly knocked over poor Christina on his way. "Oh, Christina, I'm sorry." He held out his hands, steadying her.

She laughed. "Not a problem. Wonderful performance, Trevor." She embraced him.

"You, too." He let her go too soon, moving past her.

"Going somewhere in a hurry?" She raised her eyebrows, smiling at him.

Trevor waved, rushing onward to Jenna's dressing room. Even from a few yards away he could see her door was open. Yes. He jogged up to the door, knocking on the frame.

As soon as she saw him standing there, she ran to him and jumped into his arms. He lifted her off the ground and spun her around.

"You were awesome," he whispered, placing her down.

She smacked him on the shoulder, playfully. Her eyes sparkled and she was downright giddy.

"Me?"

"Yes, you. I saw your mad scenes. Holy crap. Nice job."

"You watched?"

Trevor shrugged. "When I could. When I wasn't otherwise engaged."

"With one of the largest speaking roles ever written?"

"Yeah, that."

"You were magic, Trevor. Really, honestly. I don't know how you do it." She beamed at him.

"Great look for you, by the way." Trevor nodded to Jenna's filthy, ripped gown and matted, tousled hair. How funny, for so long he had fantasized about ripping her clothes off of her and messing up her gorgeous, soft flowing hair. All it took to get her there was madness, and a crowd of a few hundred people.

"You like?" She ran her hand up over her wig. "I did just drown you know." Jenna began removing pins from her wig. "And I've got to say, you look pretty good for a guy who was just killed with a poisoned rapier."

"Thank you very much."

She yanked off her wig, letting her own beautiful hair fall free. Her brow furrowed, her expression growing serious. "Anything from Amanda?"

"Un-uh. I just texted her to tell her we were through."

"It'll be okay; I'm sure it's just—"

"Knock, knock." Larry rapped and entered. He turned to Trevor. "I thought I might find you here." He smirked. "Anyway, nice job you two." Larry hugged Trevor and Jenna. "Great work. First reviews are in."

"No," Jenna wailed, backing away.

"Don't want them, Larry." Trevor turned away as Christina and a few other cast members walked in, carrying glasses of champagne.

"So this is where the party is happening." Christina smiled and handed a glass to Jenna.

They toasted.

"You were amazing, Christina."

"You too, dear. You too." Christina put her arm around Jenna and drew Jenna tightly against her.

"Okay, guys." Larry put up his hand to get everyone's attention. "Trevor doesn't want to hear reviews. And I understand why. Many actors believe reviews, good or bad, hurt subsequent performances. They will be forever acting 'to' that review. I respect that—usually. But please, just indulge me on this one."

Trevor bowed and moved aside as Larry stepped up, holding a glass of champagne in one hand and a cell phone in the other.

"Uh-um." Larry cleared this throat and read off his phone. "Trevor Hughes was exquisite as Hamlet, far surpassing anything this reviewer could have imagined."

The cast burst out into applause, and Trevor held up his hand modestly, thanking them. The only thing he hated about theatre was the accolades—of course, the inverse was even worse. But still. Here he was, a thirty-two year old man, listening to what other people had to say about his art. Really, who cared? Christ. He was getting too old for this crap.

"Wait, wait. Let me finish." Larry read again. "But

equally thrilling was Ophelia, played by the young Jenna Joyce. Her mad scenes were heartbreaking, gripping, passionate, and emotional. A truly stand-out performance among a cast of excellent, seasoned professionals."

****

More roses and champagne bottles filled Jenna's dressing room as reviews came in. Trevor refused to listen to the reviews and he wouldn't let Jenna either, which was just fine by her. Trevor dealt with the producers and fans while Jenna laughed with her cast mates. She couldn't remember another time, in her whole life, when she had ever been this happy. She glanced at Trevor who was leaning down, speaking to one of his investors, and she knew he was the reason for her happiness. The moment would have been perfect if only he didn't look so worried. His face was drawn downward into a scowl as he turned away from the investor, checking his phone again. There still must have been no response from Amanda. Damn.

Kat Price made her way backstage with Luis and Loretta in tow.

"Jenna, you were amazing." Luis lifted Jenna into the air, hugging her.

Loretta planted a kiss on Jenna's cheek. Kat stood back, sniffling into a tissue.

"Is she crying because she's touched or because she thinks she's going to sell you to Hollywood and finally get that vacation home?" Luis whispered into Jenna's ear.

"You'll get her the house long before me." Jenna punched him playfully. "Mister, I-Have-an-Audition-for-the-Newest-Crime-Drama-to-be-Filmed-in-New-

York."

"You know about that?"

"Why wouldn't you tell me?"

"Because I found out this week, opening week for you. And you've been a little busy. Besides, you needed to focus on Ophelia. How'd you find out?"

"Trevor told me…" Her words fell away as Maggie sauntered into the dressing room.

Jenna's gaze ran up and down Maggie. Good grief, she was gorgeous. Her flowing blonde hair fell over her shoulders with loose curls hovering around her giant breasts. She wore a fitted red dress, hugging every freaking amazing curve God had blessed her with. Her long legs ended in a pair of nude pumps, and over her shoulders, cascading down, lay an opened red silk coat. Her soft gorgeous face was perfectly made up, emphasizing giant blue eyes and a shiny nude gloss accentuated her pouty lips. Like Trevor, it was too much beauty for real life.

Jenna's shoulders rounded forward. She felt incredibly self-conscious in her ripped gown and messy hair. But maybe it was better this way; even completely dressed up she could never compete with the likes of Maggie. Maggie inched her way over next to Trevor— the two of them looking like stunningly beautiful aliens among normal-looking humans. He leaned down and kissed her quickly, his gaze dashing up to Jenna. Jenna's face warmed, and her stomach clenched. Crap.

She turned to Luis. "I'm sorry Luis, just give me a sec."

Jenna moved away from Luis, closing her opened jaw. Maggie turned to her, and Jenna took a tiny step backward as Maggie walked over to her.

"Jenna."

Maggie held out her hand, and Jenna took it. They shook.

"Hi, Maggie."

Maggie smiled, exposing gorgeous white teeth. "That was an amazing performance. Honestly, when they first cast you, I didn't know you were that talented. I was pissed at him for not casting me. But now I see why."

"Oh. Uh, thanks." Jenna squeezed her champagne glass, nervously. "Um, Maggie, did you want to be Ophelia? Really?" The question slipped out before Jenna could think about what she was asking.

Maggie gave a half-smile. "Not really. I like being on TV. I know to some of you that's a weakness in me—that I don't love theatre, that I don't want to roll up my sleeves and dive in to the underbelly of my art or whatever…but it's where I'm comfortable."

"Then who cares what anyone else thinks? Fuck 'em." Jenna raised her glass in a toast.

Maggie giggled. "Yeah, well, that's the problem, isn't it? I do."

Jenna giggled along with her. She placed her glass down on the counter in front of her mirror. "Maggie. I'm sorry I was so rude to you that day at the theatre. It wasn't you. I was pissed and so confused…it's not an excuse, but I'm sorry."

Maggie nodded, smiling. "Thanks. See you, Jenna." She turned and walked over to Larry and a few of the other cast members. Within minutes was circled by a group of five or six men—some actors, some investors.

Jenna smiled, and out of the corner of her eye she

spied Trevor put his phone to his ear, rushing out of the dressing room. She found him in the hallway talking on his phone.

"Yes, yes. How long? Are they taking him in now?" Trevor rubbed his temple with his free hand. "I'll be right there." He clicked off his phone, shoving it into his pocket.

"What happened?" Jenna moved closer. "It's Toby?"

"Yes." Trevor jogged to his dressing room.

Jenna followed. "Trevor, tell me what I can do. Anything. Please."

"There's nothing to do but wait." He pulled on his gray parka, and threw his worn brown leather bag over his shoulder.

"Then let me wait with you."

He stopped moving to look at Jenna. "You don't have to do that."

"I want to. Let me just grab my coat and bag, and I'll let Maggie know so she can come too."

Trevor nodded as Jenna rushed to her dressing room. She spied Maggie laughing with a new group of men.

"Maggie."

Jenna tossed her head for Maggie to follow and Maggie stepped away from her group.

"Something is going on with Toby; we have to go." Jenna pulled on her army jacket and threw her messenger bag over her shoulder.

"Toby?" Maggie cocked her head.

"Trevor's nephew. The one who's sick. The one Trevor supports…?"

Maggie squinted.

"Look, Maggie, we don't have time for this now. Let's go."

"Jenna?" Luis and Loretta stepped up. "You okay?"

"I have to go. I'll text you the info from Trevor's phone."

Jenna grabbed Maggie's hand and pulled her into the hallway. They found Trevor and the three of them rushed from the theatre to Trevor's car.

****

Trevor sat on the hard white plastic chair and leaned his head back against the cold sterile wall of the emergency wing at the children's hospital on Long Island. Toby was having an emergency embolectomy to remove a blockage that was preventing circulation in his right leg. That's what Amanda hadn't shared, Toby was complaining about pain in his leg, and tonight they found he needed emergency surgery to prevent an amputation.

"Hey Trevor." Dr. Nars, one of the doctors doing rounds, walked up and shook Trevor's hand. "I heard you were here. I wanted to stop by to see if I could do anything for you."

"No, thanks." Trevor shook his head.

Dr. Nars sighed. "I wish I could say it was nice to see you. I'll let you know if I hear anything." He turned to Maggie who was sitting next to Trevor. "Hello."

"Hello."

She flushed a warm pink as Dr. Nars smiled. Trevor never before noticed that Dr. Nars was incredibly handsome in a very All-American, football-playing way. He was clean-shaven, at least six feet tall, with light brown hair combed just so and broad shoulders. Dr. Nars turned to Jenna to say hello and Trevor tensed like a dog about to fight. Thankfully, Jenna barely noticed the doctor. Trevor calmed a bit.

Damn, doctors were checking on him; he and Amanda, and especially Toby, were at the hospital much too often. Toby had gone through both of his open heart surgeries here, and here they were again. Trevor looked down the hallway—it was so freaking white. Why? Why couldn't it be blue? Or even pink? Why not some welcoming color? And the shiny floor with its "conservative tone" hopscotch-like pattern tile was damned annoying. Really? How many of these kids could go playing hopscotch down the hallway on their way into emergency surgery? And just how shiny does a floor have to be, anyway? He inhaled deeply, closing his eyes. And don't even get him started on the smell. Jenna was right, hospitals always smell the same— antiseptic and plastic. It was enough to make him want to puke. He opened his eyes and Jenna was smiling at him.

"The butterflies on the walls are really pretty. Probably make the kids happy on their way into surgery."

Butterflies? He'd never before noticed the large colorful butterflies stenciled into a border high on the wall. Trevor snapped his head down, leveling his eyes on Jenna. "Happy? You think any one of these kids is anything less than terrified?"

Her eyes widened as she sat back in her chair. "No, I didn't mean…" She looked away.

Maggie shifted in her seat. She hadn't spoken a word since they got there. "Jenna? Would you mind grabbing coffee for all of us?"

"Uh, sure." Jenna stood, her filthy torn costume dragging at her feet. She lifted it as she moved. "I saw the cafeteria on our way here. I'll just be a minute."

"Thanks." Maggie waited for Jenna to walk through another white double door before she turned to Trevor. "All right, Trevor. Stop being a jerk."

"Excuse me?" He sat forward in his seat, turning to Maggie. "Did you just call me a jerk?"

"Yes. I know you're worried but that girl is really trying and you're fucking it up."

"What?" Trevor fought to focus on Maggie's words. "Are you pimping me out?"

"Good grief, Trevor. I'm as sick of this as you are. We're good people but we're not right for each other, no matter how much my father wants us to be. And he only wants it, because it's good for ratings. I say, fuck the ratings. We need to live a little. Neither of us is getting younger." She tilted her head. "Look. This has been a long time coming. We're completely different and frankly, I'm tired of feeling like I'm not good enough because I don't enjoy the gritty artsy things you do."

"Maggie." Trevor sat up straight. "I'm sorry. I never meant to make you feel that way."

"I know that. Not directly, anyway. But I did. And you resented me at times. And frankly, no matter what people think of me, or what image I portray on TV, I'm a nice person. And a decent person. I'll be thirty years old in a couple of months, do you know that?"

"If I thought about it…"

"Oh, Trevor. I deserve a man who thinks the sun rises and sets on me."

"Yes, you do."

"That girl who came here with us tonight, she loves you."

"What?" He sat up, his heart racing.

"She gave up her Valentine's Day and her first opening night to come sit with you while you act like an asshole and just to be certain you were okay, she brought your soap-opera-star girlfriend along. Who else would do something like that except a woman who loves you?"

"I, uh…"

"Don't blow this. Let her in like you never let me in. I like you Trev, always have. I want to be your friend, but not your girlfriend and not your wife. Jesus." She shook her head. "I want some nice, normal, millionaire, middle-aged, pot-bellied guy who thanks God every day for the goddess he has lying in his bed. I want to grow old and fat in a mansion in Westchester with a whole brood of spoiled kids." She shrugged. "All those things that would make you cringe—I want them. And now is my time to get them."

"Okay." He looked deeply into her eyes. "After all this time together, you're really okay?"

"It's not like we were really together. Jesus, after nearly four years together the only things we left at each other's apartments were toothbrushes." She looked away and back again. "You know what does hurt? The thing that hurts is…you were afraid I would get my father to fire you, weren't you?"

Trevor didn't answer.

"That's what I thought. That's why you dragged this on and on. But come on, Trev. I like working with you. You're a great actor. And even if you weren't, give me a little credit. I have my dignity."

"I'm sorry. And yes, you certainly are dignified, Maggie."

"Thank you." She placed her hand on Trevor's arm and laid her head on his shoulder. "How come I never knew more about Toby?"

"The one time you met him you were completely disinterested."

"At that picnic?" She sat up, facing him. "If you remember that picnic, you'll remember my father was bugging me to meet some new investors who got drunk and tried to grope me. I was trying to survive that picnic. Not that you noticed. Sorry if I blew off Toby, I never meant to."

"Maggie." Trevor reached out and took her hands in his. He squeezed. A thousand pounds fell from his shoulders as he smiled at her. "I'm sorry I wasn't a better boyfriend. I should have seen that. I should have cared…about everything. About you."

"Yeah, you should have."

He smiled. "Is it weird this is the first time I've wanted to kiss you in a long time?"

She laughed, tossing her head back. "Well, don't. I want to go say hi to that doctor who walked by before…Dr. Nars, was it?"

"Yeah."

She smiled, opening her arms. Trevor embraced her. She was soft, and warm and beautiful but she felt all wrong. She broke their embrace, stood, and Trevor stood with her.

"I'm gonna take off."

"How are you getting home? You can take the car."

She planted her hands on her hips. "I make nearly

as much as you. I'll call a car service." She tightly tied the belt of her coat around herself. "Shoot me a text when he's out of surgery, please."

Trevor reached out and took her hand. "Thank you, Maggie. For all of it. I'm sorry I wasn't—"

She reached out and placed her hand on his lips. "It wasn't just you, Trev. I wasn't either. Anyway, Happy Valentines' Day."

"Happy Valentine's Day, Maggie."

She turned and sauntered away, and Trevor's shoulders collapsed with exhaustion and relief.

****

It wasn't exactly spying; it was just that when Jenna came back with three cups of coffee—two black, guessing Maggie wouldn't waste the calories on cream and sugar—she didn't expect to find them in an embrace. But what did she think would happen? Jenna peered through the crack she made with her foot wedged in the swinging double doors leading to the hallway of the ICU. She carefully balanced the coffee cups on their tray and peeked at Trevor and Maggie again. Damn, they were still hugging. The sight of them went straight to Jenna's core, swirling around like she had just eaten three-week-old Chinese food that had been left out in the hot sun. They stood, and Jenna backed up, letting the door close. The edge of her costume got caught in the door but she prayed no one would notice the piece of grayish silk sticking out between two stark white hospital doors. Crap. She really didn't need to see them kiss or whatever else they were doing. Besides, she had brought Maggie to help Trevor feel better, and if that's what it—

"Jenna?"

197

Maggie pushed open the door, interrupting Jenna's wild thoughts. Jenna's gown fell free. "I'm taking off. Thanks for bringing me here. It helped more than you could imagine."

"I uh…"

Maggie pointed to the coffee tray. "Is that for me?"

"Black." Jenna nodded.

Maggie removed the coffee. "Thanks." She held the cup for a moment, and then placed it back on the tray. "On second thought, I hate coffee." She shrugged. "Only ever drank it for him." She smiled. "Well, see ya around, Jenna."

Jenna watched her walk off. With her breath racing, she turned and pushed open the doors then slipped through. The coffee tray wobbled in her shaking hands. He stood there, all six-feet-two-inches of him, looking at her, his chest moving in time with his breath that was racing nearly as fast as hers.

What the hell would she do now?

****

"Mr. Hughes?"

A doctor he had never seen before charged through the opposite doors, moving like he pushed through water. Trevor held his breath as the doctor, dressed in green scrubs, removed his hat and untied his mask.

"He's out of surgery. We've saved his leg. Thank God your sister got him here as quickly as she did."

"He's okay?"

"He's resting. He needs to recover but the prognosis is good."

Air rushed from Trevor's lungs in relief. "Can we see him?"

"Your sister is asking for you." The doctor's gaze

fell on Jenna, taking in her costume as he pushed open the door. "Your wife will have to wait, only one visitor at a time."

His wife? Trevor stood up taller. For the first time ever, he didn't hate the sound of the word "wife."

"Oh, I'm not..." Jenna placed the tray of coffee on a seat as her words dropped off. She stepped up and slipped her hand in Trevor's. "You go ahead. I'll wait. Besides, I don't want to get too close and scare him. Between my filthy gown and white makeup, I don't want him to think I'm a ghost."

"He's not awake." The doctor smiled. "He won't even see—"

"Trevor!" Amanda rushed to Trevor, throwing herself into his arms.

He held on tightly as she sobbed against him. The doctor excused himself, disappearing through the doorway. They stood there for whole minutes until she pulled away.

"Damn you, Trevor Hughes. Not one single tear. I did not cry one single tear until I saw you and then—" The tears came harder again as she buried her face in his shirt, drenching it. She pulled back, wiping her eyes in the sleeve of her zip front sweatshirt. When she focused, her gaze went to Jenna, and Amanda started. "Hello." She wiped her hands in her jeans, reaching out for Jenna then shaking her hand. "I'm Amanda, Trevor's sister. You must be Jenna." She gently clamped her hands on Jenna's shoulders. "I'm glad to meet you, and really glad you're here—"

Sobs came again and Trevor pulled Amanda to him.

"Let it out, Amanda."

Amanda nodded, crying harder. "His leg, Trevor. All this time I have been so worried about his heart and now I've got to worry about fucking circulation on a goddamned leg. I mean, who would have thought? Fuck, fuck, fuck." She pounded her fist against his chest as she swore then turned to Jenna and sniffled. "I'm sorry about the cursing."

Jenna chuckled. "Oh, please. I curse more than that when I burn my toast in the morning. Curse away."

Amanda smiled. "It's just...I have to keep it together. Always. So when the relief comes, I just let go." She patted Trevor's chest. "Thank God he's there to catch me."

Jenna nodded, smiling. "Oh." She grabbed the tray of coffee. "Coffee?"

Amanda smiled. "I would love coffee. Thank you."

Jenna looked over the tray. "I have black or light with a hell of a lot of sugar."

Amanda clapped her hands. "Finally, someone who knows how to drink coffee. Light with a hell of a lot of sugar, please."

Smiling, Jenna handed her the coffee and Amanda slugged back a giant gulp.

"This is heaven, thank you." She chugged the rest of it and looked at the bottom of her empty cup. "Jesus, that was yours, wasn't it."

Jenna waved it off. "Oh, no worries. Really. I can drink black just fine. Do it all the time." She took a large sip of the black coffee and fought a grimace. "Well, maybe not all the time."

Trevor chuckled.

"Here. This is yours..." Jenna cleared her throat as she handed Trevor the other black coffee.

"You sure you don't want it?"

She glared at him and he beamed at her. Damn, she was spectacular.

"Tell you what." Amanda let out a giant sigh. "I need a walk and another one of those, so why don't Jenna and I go grab a few more coffees and you can go in to see Toby?"

Trevor nodded as Amanda put her arm around Jenna's shoulder, chatting as she led her off. Jenna peeked over her shoulder, smiling at Trevor, and in that instant, he knew.

Chapter Fourteen

As soon as he pushed open the doors leading to the hallway in ICU where she waited, energy and excitement shot through Jenna's body. He appeared relaxed and happy, and it was such a relief to see him this way. She smiled but he just nodded, as if he had made a decision—*the* decision—for the both of them. Longing brewed from deep in her core, traveling outward in heavy, molten bolts of energy making her growl with every breath. Warmth and pressure formed between her legs, and she squeezed them together, involuntarily. He lazily blinked his eyes. And the way he fixed his stare on her…she exhaled, her lips pursing, wanting him more than she ever thought possible. He gave her his hand, gently pulling her to her feet then leaned down so very close…his presence overpowering her.

"Baby…" He whispered into her ear.

Jenna closed her eyes, and for the moment, anyway, gave herself over.

****

"Penny for your thoughts."

They sat in the back of his car on the long drive back to the city. Jenna stared out the window, watching the Island race by. She was still in her costume, still covered in white makeup but when the lights of passing cars reflected off her skin, she was breathtaking. She looked at him and his breath hitched.

"You are so beautiful." Trevor whispered.

She smiled, but it was obvious her thoughts were millions of miles away.

"Do you think he saw us perform?"

"Don?"

She nodded.

"I think they all watched, Jen. All three of them."

Trevor squeezed her hand then took her by the shoulder, turning her slightly to face him. He reached up and stroked her hair.

"Mmm," she moaned, moving with his hand, closing her eyes. "That feels so good."

Too good, actually. Trevor pushed his breath out through clenched teeth. He pulled his hand away from her face, not sure if he could contain himself much longer.

She reached out and took his hand, placing it back on the side of her face. "Trevor." Her voice was soft. "Remember the night you asked me if I've ever done anything I shouldn't?"

"Yes." Trevor kept his hand on her, his breath quickening.

"Have you ever done something you knew was wrong but you did it anyway?"

"Of course. I'm sorry to say about a million times." His thumb caressed her cheek.

She looked up at him with that incredibly hungry look in her eyes. "How about something that might hurt someone you care about…very, very much?"

"I guess that would depend on what it was, and who it was. I can't think of anything I would ever want to do if it meant hurting you."

Jenna leaned forward, resting her hands on the tan leather seat between them. She was so close, his skin tingled from her warm breath.

"We're actors, Trevor."

"Yes." He cocked his head.

"We're both really good at playing pretend."

"I'm confused."

"Can we just go pretend for a while?"

"What do you want to pretend?"

"That our lives are our own."

"They are, Jenna."

She shook her head. "Mine isn't."

"What are you trying to tell me?"

"I want to spend the night with you."

"Jenna." His voice deepened. "Are you asking me to spend another night on your floor?"

"No floor..." Jenna's gaze dropped to the seat. "I—I want to be with you."

Trevor grabbed Jenna's hands so quickly her eyes widened.

"Jenna..."

She looked away.

"Jenna, look at me." He waited until her gaze drifted back to his. "Of course, yes—yes in every way I want this to happen. Yes, yes, yes. But I want you to be sure. You keep telling me there's some reason we can't be together."

"There is a reason, so if we do this, you have to understand it's only for tonight."

"Jen, I can't make that promise."

"You have to." Her voice was soft. "If we can't pretend to be in different circumstances, just for tonight, I can't do this."

"We can say and do anything you want, baby." Trevor placed his hand back on her cheek. "But it doesn't change what's real. That's why we're good actors. Because we know fiction from reality."

"But we can slide back and forth in and out of each."

He inhaled, deeply. "Look, Jenna." He took her by both hands again and tightly held them. "I want this more than I have ever wanted anything. But I want you. I don't want to play some theatre game; I don't want to pretend to be anyone else."

Her head dropped forward. "Me either." Her voice was weak. "But I don't want to think about tomorrow. Or a week from now. I only want to live for tonight. To live in the moment—just like we do onstage."

Trevor nodded. If he wasn't so sure, he would stop this. But he knew no matter what her reasons were for keeping her distance, they could work them out. This one night she planned was just the beginning of forever for him.

"So it's us, then?" She looked up at him, her lip trembling.

"It's us, Jenna."

"And no talk of tomorrows?"

He inhaled sharply. If denying tomorrow was what it took to begin his life with Jenna, then that would be what he would do.

"No talk of tomorrows. As long as you understand this will never be a one-night stand for me. I am invested here, Jenna. And I am certain no matter what, if you let me, I will be here for all of my tomorrows."

Jenna sighed and he gently placed his hand back on her cheek.

****

After stopping at her apartment so she could shower and change her clothes, it was dawn when they arrived at his penthouse. Heat and energy vibrated out of her fingers as he kept his wrapped tightly around hers. He let go only to open the door to his apartment, a feeling of contentment washing over him. They stepped into his living room as the sun just broke over Manhattan, softly filtering into his apartment like it was designed by Blanche DuBois herself for a scene from *A Streetcar Named Desire*.

Jenna moved to the windows, staring out, mesmerized. "I guess Valentine's Day is over."

He walked to her and turned her toward him. "It doesn't have to be."

She looked up at him and her expression very nearly broke his heart.

"Jenna." He stepped back from her. "We're not doing anything unless you want to."

"I do, Trevor. I really, really do. If you knew how excited I am, I'm just…nervous."

Her admission made his heart swell. All he wanted was for her to be happy and feel good. She had no reason to be nervous.

"Why?"

"Really?" She looked up at him. "I mean, look at you…and look at me. You're used to women who look like Maggie. Who, by the way…it's, uh, really over between you two?"

"Yes. Really."

"And she's not angry?"

"If anything she's relieved. Seems she was only staying with me to keep her father happy."

"Oh, Trevor. I'm sorry."

He chuckled. "It's fine. I promise. Honestly, that means nothing to me. You, on the other hand..." He slipped his arm around her waist and held her tightly. He leaned down close to her as he spoke. "And as far as what you said before, about being used to women who look like Maggie...Jenna, I don't think you have any idea how beautiful you are." He leaned back, smiling. "Especially right now—in your old faded jeans, with your face scrubbed clean...besides, this is not a performance. I just want to be with you. However it happens, it happens."

Her body relaxed, and he pulled her closer, wanting...everything with her. One night would never be enough for what he was planning. He pulled her even closer, inhaling the magical scent of her shampoo, excited and ready for her. But he had no intention of rushing this. This was finally his night with Jenna and he was intending to use it, fully. What the hell was this hold she had on him? He couldn't explain it. He had known hundreds of beautiful women in his life. And he had slept with many of them. But there was something about her. She looked up at him and he saw the answer in her eyes, so smart and intense. "The first day I saw you I felt like a raven had swooped in watching everything, seeing everything, understanding way more than I ever could."

"Trevor..."

"Shh." He placed one hand under her chin and tilted her head upward. He gazed at her mouth; he had fantasized about those pouty lips for what seemed like an endless amount of time. He had never before waited so long for any woman. But he didn't mind if he had to wait forever, as long as he could finally be with her.

Easing his hands to her face, he held her, softly. Having her there, it was everything he could do to move slowly. He tilted her head back as he leaned down and kissed Jenna softly on the lips. Her kiss...her lips were soft, and her mouth, warm. She tasted like cinnamon. He gazed at her, his breath racing, the morning sun reflecting off her black hair. Jenna pulled back from him, and he let go, waiting for a cue she wanted more. She closed her eyes and leaned forward. That was all he needed.

In a flash, Trevor embraced Jenna's face with his two hands again, holding her as he kissed her softly, over and over. She kissed back, hungrily. Damn. She felt so warm, and soft, and...right. Now that he had started, he may very well never stop kissing her. With his hands still on her face, he pushed her back to the wall beside the windows. She hit with more force than he had intended, releasing a tiny gasp.

"Jenna." He growled her name. She was smaller that he was, so he would have to be careful.

Trevor pulled back from her, looking at her pouty mouth, already red and swollen from kissing. Their size difference gave him pause for a moment but as she closed her eyes and whispered, "More," he dove back into the kiss, planting his two hands on the wall beside her head. He would just move slowly and carefully and if he hurt her, he would stop immediately. He could do this. He could maintain some semblance of control.

Trevor nudged his body against hers. Sure she was smaller but when she lifted onto her toes and he leaned down, his hips pressed against her hips, and her breasts rested against his abdomen. She moaned into his mouth in response, and Trevor leaned in harder against her. Every push solicited a moan from Jenna, making him grow and swell in response.

Damn, damn, damn…he wanted to move slowly, but what could he do when she felt so freaking incredible? He sucked in a gulp of air, trying yogic breathing, anything to pace himself. Feeling her warm soft body against his was too much. He pulled back from her only to reach up and tear off his t-shirt then resumed his position, cocooning her against the wall. She touched him tentatively, placing her hands on his bare chest and Trevor shuddered in response. He kissed her more and more forcefully, scared he may not know when to stop…

He unlatched from her mouth and made his way down her neck. She craned her head upward, giving him direct access, panting heavily. Her nipples poked through her t-shirt, grazing his abdomen. It was too much. He needed her to be his, once and for all. Standing upright, he found his way to her mouth again, his tongue strong and forceful. He pressed her to the wall, grabbing her legs, lifting her easily so she straddled his waist. He held her tightly, one hand around her waist, the other, supporting her bottom. She clamped her mouth back onto his, and carefully, still kissing her, he walked them to the stairs leading to his bedroom.

"Wait." She lifted her head from their kiss. "Can we go to the music room?"

"You're sure? There's no bed…" His words were choppy.

"Yes. Please."

Trevor placed his mouth on hers again and carried

her to the music room. He laid Jenna down on the couch, lowered himself over her, then took her soft hands and placed them on his chest. He closed his eyes, inhaling, feeling the magic of her warm touch. Slowly, she traced the outline of his tattoo, her fingers brushing against his nipples. He opened his eyes, smiling at her.

****

He leaned down, covering her, his weight resting on his elbows, his strong hands stroking her hair. Jenna nuzzled against him as he opened his mouth to speak.

"No—" Jenna flattened her hands on his chest, shaking her head. "Please, Trevor. Please don't say anything." One ill-timed word, and she would have no choice but to leave. Forever. Eyes wide open was the only option.

His eyes flashed with sadness. "I was only going to ask about birth control." He held himself above her. His wavy messy hair fell forward; his gorgeous gaze fixed on her.

"I—I'm sorry." She squeezed her eyes shut, trying to regroup. She looked up at him again. "I'm...uh...on the pill."

"Really?" He tilted his head, squinting.

Crap. She'd need to explain. "Yes. Not for long, but long enough, I think. Six weeks."

"That's long enough."

His reassurance was so sexy, her already moist jeans dampened. The fact that he was experienced, and he knew and liked women—it was all a complete turn-on. He squinted again, and she was sure he was doing the math in his head.

"I didn't go on it for sex." Why was this conversation so difficult? "Obviously."

"Why obviously?"

He leaned down on her, his weight heavy on top of her. He pressed against her, and her thoughts jumbled. She wiggled beneath him.

"I wasn't planning a relationship."

"And yet here you are."

"Trevor…" She tried to move, but he held her still.

"Shh…" He leaned down and kissed her. "Jenna." He shook his head.

She sighed and relaxed into him.

He smiled, his eyelids lazily closing and opening. "When we get there, do you still want me to wear a condom? I've been tested. I'm clear, but would you feel safer?"

Jenna looked up at him knowing this feeling of closeness and excitement she was experiencing was a feeling she may never encounter again. This one moment, this perfect mixture of him, Valentine's night, and opening night; it was the happiest she had ever been. And she was certain she would never experience it again. She shook her head. "I have never felt safer in my life than when I'm with you."

****

Hell, yeah. The fact that Jenna felt safe with him made him more excited than he could possibly imagine. So not only would he blow her mind but he would do it in a way that made her feel even more secure and protected. She wiggled beneath him and he just couldn't wait any longer. "Jenna…" Trevor whispered, sliding over to her side. His hand cruised down to her stomach and grabbed onto the belt loop of her faded jeans. The jeans were so old and worn they were nearly as soft as her skin…okay, maybe not that soft. "Jenna, look at me."

Her eyes opened. His hand lingered on the top button of her jeans. He wanted to yank the buttons and tear her jeans off of her but he wouldn't. His breath raced as he stared into her eyes. His chest moved forcefully as he popped open her top button.

Her breath hitched. "Trevor..." Her word was a moan.

Trevor breathed deeply, overcome. Nothing had ever felt quite like this before and as she grew more excited, he was certain he belonged with her, and she belonged with him. "Jenna. Baby..." His voice was a deep whisper. "Look at me."

She rolled her head toward him. Trevor smiled. He had never before taken this long with a woman; he'd never waited this long or fought so hard against his desire. Not only did he want her physically, he wanted her emotionally. He wanted her as his and he never wanted her to leave...ever.

No. He shook his head. He had to stay in control. He had to let her feel what she needed to feel, and they needed to make it through this show. Then he could fight for her.

Trevor calmed his racing thoughts. Good God, yes, he wanted her but he also wanted to make sure their encounter was unforgettable for her. He slid his hand up, under her soft bra, and held her, his experienced fingers making their way to her nipple. She felt so good, so soft and so responsive...she moaned as he squeezed gently. She turned her mouth to him and he kissed her, just once, then pulled away. With her eyes shut she opened her mouth, her tongue licking her lips, leaving a moist trail behind.

"Jenna…" Trevor moaned as she licked her lips again. Slipping his fingers from her bra, he slid his hand upward. Slowly, one by one, he ran his fingers across her mouth. She kissed in response and his thumb parted her soft red lips. Her tongue darted out, and he slid his thumb in…her eyes opened halfway as she licked and bit and sucked his thumb. He closed his eyes and dropped his head backward. Uhhh…he wanted to be in her, now. Damn, her jaw was tight. And the way she handled his thumb…Trevor shook his head, sweat clinging to his back. He needed to stop this. He freed his thumb from her ever tightening jaw and her eyes widened as he pulled away. Moving faster now, he pulled off her t-shirt then reaching around behind her with one hand and lifting her slightly, he unhooked her bra, sliding it off. She lifted her arm across her chest; maybe she was self-conscious? She looked away.

"Jenna…" He shook his head and gently guided her arm away from her breasts. Damn, she was beautiful. Her breasts were fuller than he imagined, the shape of large teardrops, sitting high and tight to her body.

She squirmed, her face flushing. "I've never known what to do with these things." Jenna giggled, covering her mouth with her hand.

"Lucky for you"—Trevor moved on top of her—"I know exactly what to do with them."

He winked at her and she grinned. Trevor kissed her again and made his way to her collarbone, planting kisses as he went. Finally, he moved down and took her into his mouth.

****

The warmth of his mouth on her breast was almost

more than she could handle. Her body was taking over now, acting in ways she never anticipated. She sucked in a deep breath, her back arching off the couch. She wanted him so much, there wasn't anything she wouldn't do…well, for tonight, anyway. She reached up, placing her hands around his neck, pulling him tighter to her, but Trevor held his weight on his elbows. The way he used his tongue—flicking, licking, sucking—made her cry out, and as soon as she opened her mouth, his was back, latched onto hers. She leaned up, kissing him so completely…feeling somehow, if she let him, he could restore her soul.

****

Good God…how was he going to keep this under control? Her mouth was so warm and open. Trevor's breath came in short little gasps as he devoured her. He pulled back to see her mouth, wet and puffy. "Jenna…" he growled.

She wrapped her arms around his shoulders with so much need, Trevor was certain the only thing that made sense in this entire crazy life was being inside her. Balancing his weight on one elbow, Trevor reached down between them and tore through her button fly jeans. They slid easily over her slim hips, the soft denim like butter in his hand. Pink lace framed her protruding hipbones and Trevor stayed on top of her, balancing his weight on his elbow, while his free hand cruised down her stomach and made its way to her panties.

"Huh." Jenna's eyes flew open as his fingers slid into the top of her panties, the soft lace brushing the back of his hand. She gripped his shoulders hard as he moved his fingers downward. "God, Jenna…"

She panted her response, her soft breasts nuzzling against his chest with every sharp inhale. Her head rolled back, and her eyes closed as he ran his fingers up and down.

Trevor whispered her name, placing his forehead against hers, before leaning up to gaze at her beautiful face. "Jenna, look at me."

Her eyes opened, settling on his. Moving next to her, he slid off her panties and tossed them aside. Then he moved his fingers to settle on that spot that would make her—

"Trevor..." she moaned.

Trevor sucked in a gasp of air, overcome. Quickly, he slid his finger down, pushing its way in. Moist and tight, her muscles clenched around him as her head rolled back. He pushed his finger farther, sweat dotting his forehead. Nothing had ever felt quite like this before, and as she grew more excited, he became more and more possessive. There was no way, no way in hell, he would let her leave without a fight. No matter what. He belonged with her, and she belonged with him—he was certain of that. "Jenna?"

"Mmmm?" The sound was guttural and animalistic.

"Why are you always running from me?" He pushed his finger farther, and she arched upward again.

She clung to his arms, holding his finger deep inside her. "I'm not running now."

That was it. Faster than before, he slid in a second finger, and she rolled to her side, her body shivering beneath him. "Jenna, baby..." His voice was a deep whisper.

She turned her head toward him, making the

sexiest little throaty noises that drove him crazy. She gasped as he pushed farther, feeling the dampness and swelling that were right now, all his. Damn, damn, damn. The crotch of his jeans stretched, nearly bursting from pressure. With her gaze locked on his, he pushed farther still, feeling the strong suction he had fantasized about since the day he met her.

She moaned, closing her eyes, rolling toward him. With his fingers sliding in and out carefully, he found her mouth again, securing his lips to hers. She shuddered, a chill passing over her. He let his fingers slide out of her and come to rest higher, planning to have them work their magic until she couldn't think straight. It only took another moment until she grabbed his hand.

"Trevor I—"

He knew what was happening. He kept his pressure steady as he wrapped his free arm around her and opened her mouth with his. She moaned into him, her body rising off the couch, her arms pulling him closer. She broke their kiss to catch her breath and Trevor seized the opportunity to slide off his own jeans. He wanted inside her. Now.

****

My…God…Jenna fell back against the couch, panting and aching to have him inside. She clamped her legs shut tight and squeezed, trying to alleviate at least some of the pressure. He hovered over her, and took her hand in his, guiding it to his boxer briefs. She wrapped her hand around him, inhaling deeply.

He closed his eyes. "Oh, God, Jenna…"

She explored the length of him, running her finger across the tip, and suddenly he reached out and grabbed her wrist.

"Huh!"

He opened his eyes, his breath rushing in and out of his wide chest as he held her hand still. She clamped her legs together tighter as she realized he was completely in control. The power was all his. He was so much stronger and bigger and older, there was no way she could break free even if she wanted to. He moved her hand inside his boxer briefs. She inhaled sharply as she ran her hand up and down the length of him. And damn, he was big.

He must have read her mind because he smiled sweetly. He leaned down and whispered into her ear. "I won't hurt you. Trust me?"

She nodded, his words a pure turn-on. He kissed her gently, easing out of his boxer briefs. He pressed against her, slowly running the tip up and down the length of her, until he came to rest at her opening. He pushed softly at first, and then with more force, as she finally, body and mind, let him in.

****

Holy crap. In all the years Trevor had been with women, he had never before experienced anything like this. She was so smooth and so very very tight. They fit together like—like she was made for him and he was made for her. He still moved slowly, somehow managing to convince himself he could stop if he needed to, although it would be…tough. Her body moved upward, trying to accommodate him. He was so hard now he could have penetrated steel.

She turned her head to the side, and her fingers wrapped around his waist. Making his way in farther, he lowered himself to his elbows, and with one final careful push, he was inside, as far as she could take him.

"Trevor…" Jenna growled, and her eyes closed as she grabbed his hips.

Trevor inhaled deeply, moving slowly, in and out, wanting to experience every bit of her. With every push, she grunted a tiny bit in response. It was so, so freaking sexy. He could move her into any position now, she was more than willing, but he didn't want to. This position—ironically, male superior—was all he wanted and needed. Of course he never, not once, felt superior to her but he did feel stronger and incredibly protective of her. As he continued to move, slowly and carefully, he swore to himself he would take care of her, in all ways, forever.

He smiled as she panted beneath him. Her breathing quickened; she was close again. Damn, she was responsive. He leaned forward, resting his weight against her in just the right way. Jenna's eyes flew open, and her body pushed hard against his.

"God…" she whispered, her breathy voice making him harder and harder. She pressed against him, her upper body lifting off the couch.

He wrapped her body with his arms and pulled her up, tucking her legs around him. On his knees, he supported her easily.

"Trevor," she murmured, her hot breath caressing his ear.

"I've got you." He held her tighter, driving harder into her, still careful not to hurt her, but needing more of her…now.

Trevor laid her back down, leaving her legs tucked tightly around his waist. As she turned her head into the couch pillow, he watched her every move. She was there, he could feel it, and he timed his rhythm to match hers.

"Trevor, I can't…anymore."

That was all Trevor needed to know. The tightness around him throbbed and he finally, completely let himself go.

Chapter Fifteen

Trevor collapsed on top of her, holding his weight up on his elbows so not to suffocate her. He took a moment to catch his breath. He didn't want to move, somehow terrified if he did, everything would suddenly change.

"Trevor?" Jenna's soft, raspy voice stunned him back to reality and alleviated the fear inside him, at least somewhat.

"Yeah, baby?" Trevor lifted himself up and looked at Jenna; his breath caught at the sight of her. She looked so soft and gorgeous with her swollen lips, pink cheeks, and hair falling back across his couch. He lay down next to her and let his hand come to rest on her naked belly. "You okay?"

A smile crept across her lips. She blushed and nodded.

"I'll take that as a yes?" Trevor chuckled.

"Yes." Suddenly her eyes glassed over.

"Jenna? What is it?" Trevor wondered everything at once—had he hurt her? Was she disappointed? He knew enough to know he had made her happy. Twice. So why this reaction?

She only shrugged.

"Jenna? Is something wrong? Did I hurt you?"

Jenna shook her head. "No. I—I'm sorry."

Her gaze dropped down, and Trevor placed his

finger under her chin, lifting it upward.

"It was incredible, Trevor." She smiled at him. "Happy Valentine's Day."

Trevor ran his hands over her tight, small curves, wondering if he and Jenna, together and apart, were doomed to a life of make-believe. "Happy Valentine's Day, Jen."

****

She shivered.

"Are you cold?"

"A little." She shrugged.

"Hold on." Trevor jumped up, pulled on his boxer briefs then went to a tall armoire on one side of the music room.

Jenna propped herself up onto her elbows and watched him. He grabbed a t-shirt and tossed it to her. The soft cotton t-shirt fell gently on her lap. She slipped it over her head. He held out his hands and pulled her to her feet, the t-shirt dropping down almost to her knees. The t-shirt felt like an extension of him, and it felt…good to be covered by Trevor Hughes. Too good.

Trevor smiled. "That looks incredible on you. You look…so sexy." His eyes were fixed on her as he pulled her to him, wrapping his arms around her.

Jenna molded herself tightly to him. She knew in every cell of her body this was wrong but it also made her so happy. The fact that they were playing a dangerous game she forced out of her mind. Right now, she felt only happy and lucky. It was easy to feel pure bliss in the arms of Trevor Hughes. She inhaled his incredibly masculine scent. She turned her cheek and rested it against his chest, and he leaned down and kissed her on the head.

"You are so beautiful."

Jenna closed her eyes, enjoying her time in this fantasy world. He lifted her chin and kissed her gently. She looked into his eyes that were sultry and confident and so incredibly sexy.

"You know what we need now?"

"There's more?"

Trevor chuckled. "Ice cream."

Jenna smiled. "Trevor Hughes, I think you may very well be the perfect man."

Trevor took her hand.

"Oh, uh, just a sec…" Jenna stopped and slipped on her pink panties that Trevor had tossed aside.

He smiled, took her hand again, and led her out of his music room and into his kitchen.

****

"Coffee, mocha chip, chocolate fudge, or mint chocolate chip?"

"Yes, please." Jenna was perched on Trevor's counter, the long t-shirt tucked under her legs.

"All of them?"

Jenna nodded.

"You got it." He laughed. "I've never met someone who likes ice cream as much as me."

"Love it."

Trevor glanced at her quickly, struck by those two little words. Jenna looked away. Who could blame her? Damn, what was he doing? In all his years as a bachelor, sleeping with some the most beautiful women in the world, he had never—not once—contemplated love. So what was going on here? Focusing on anything that may cool his feelings for Jenna, Trevor opened his sub-zero freezer and brought out four pints of ice cream. Jenna clapped.

"Let me just grab some bowls." Trevor spoke as he rummaged for two spoons.

"Trevor…" Jenna put her hands on her hips, her legs swaying back and forth against the counter. "After what we just did, I think we can eat our ice cream straight from the containers."

Watching Jenna sit there in his oversized t-shirt, ready to dive into pints of ice cream with him, Trevor couldn't imagine being any happier. Ever. He knew he should count his lucky stars and enjoy every moment with her but there was something in the way she said these words that worried him. She shimmied herself off the counter and onto one of his bar stools then leaned across the giant island, digging into the mint chocolate chip.

"Jen." He looked down at the pint of ice cream, took a deep breath and faced her again. "I hope you don't think I do this all the time."

"Eat four pints at once?" She looked up at him with her big hazel eyes. There was no sarcasm in her tone. "'Cause I sure would if the ice cream tasted like this. What is this?" She dug in again.

"Technically, it's gelato."

"How did I not know about this?"

She licked her spoon and a grin spread across his face.

He shrugged. "There's a great gelato place not far from here. That's where these come from. We should go one night."

He expected her to freeze; to run screaming from the kitchen at the thought of spending more time with him. But she didn't. Instead, she smiled and dove in again. Trevor ran his hand up through his hair. "What I meant was…what I mean is…" Jenna diving into the mocha chip sidetracked him.

She moaned. "This is heaven."

"Okay." Trevor reached across the counter and took her hands in his. "Now I'm starting to get a complex. I think you're enjoying that gelato more than you enjoyed…" He tossed his head in the direction of his music room.

"Are you kidding me, Trevor?" She let her spoon drop onto the counter, making a splattery mess. She looked at him and he let go of her hands. "The only reason this gelato tastes like heaven is because of you."

Trevor smiled, seizing the moment. His heart raced. Why was he tripping over his words? He was the older, more experienced one. What was going on? "That's what I was trying to say. I hope you understand I don't do this…" Trevor twirled his spoon. "Not the gelato." He tossed his head toward the music room, again. "I mean the couch…"

Jenna stared up at him blankly.

"Or the gelato. A lot." A drop of sweat slid down Trevor's neck, and he reached up to wipe it away. Why was he so invested in this?

"Of course you do." Jenna reached across the counter and squeezed his hands. Then she grabbed her spoon and shoveled another bite of gelato into her mouth.

"What?" Trevor laughed off her response. He waited for her to laugh but she didn't. Her stoicism created fear in him, a fear that overtook his heart. This was the last thing he would ever want her to think—that she was a one night or one show, stand. "Jenna…"

"Wait." She put down her ice cream and stabbed her spoon into the container. She looked Trevor straight in the eye.

Jenna had so much confidence, it was unnerving. He stood up taller, bracing himself.

"I think you have had a great deal of experience. And that's cool. You're a single guy." She reached out and touched his hands in the way that calmed him. "And you're not altogether horrible looking."

Trevor chuckled, his eyes on her as she continued.

"You're fairly successful."

He laughed some more.

"If it weren't for this dump you live in, you'd probably get laid a lot more often."

"All right, all right." Trevor smiled, feeling that certain emotion he had never experienced before Jenna. "Do you have a point?"

"Look, Trevor." Her gaze dropped then returned to him. "I'm not one of those girls who's immune to sex. The ones who do it as a performance, because that's what's expected of them."

Trevor nodded, understanding completely.

"I feel sorry for those girls. I think society has pushed them into that position." She smiled. "No pun intended. But I was never that girl. Sex means a lot to me. And from the way you just had sex with me, despite the amount of experience you may have, I think it means a lot to you, too." Jenna grinned and tilted her head, looking so much older and wiser.

"Jenna." Trevor moved around the island to get to her. He spun her stool so she faced him then leaned down, his hands resting on the high back of her stool. His body enveloped her. He wanted so much from her but he needed to be careful not to push. "I didn't have sex with you; I made love to you."

Jenna sighed, her body leaning toward his.

He knew she was terrified, but he wanted her to know this. "I've had sex...this wasn't just sex. This was more."

"Trevor—"

"Yes, I know there's some mysterious reason you think we can't be together, but I'm telling you, Jenna, it won't happen."

Jenna placed her small warm hands on his chest. Trevor inhaled sharply.

"Trevor, have you ever wondered why you're an actor?"

"Because it was my calling, I guess." He crossed his arms.

"Yes. And you know why? Because we have gypsy blood in us. All actors do. We're nomads by choice. We don't stay in one place very long—or with someone else very long—we're incapable of it, somehow." Her eyes glassed over as she smiled.

"Lots of great actors have life partners. Don and Evelyn for example."

"Yeah." Jenna nodded. "Except Evelyn gave up her career to support his. Someone always, in some way, has to give. What about you?"

"What about me?"

"You're thirty-two years old. What happens when you decide you're ready to settle down? What happens to your partner? You buy her a McMansion in Jersey or Westchester, which should make her happy, right? And then the car takes you to work every day while she's stuck home with unfulfilled dreams and crying children.

While you play Caspian or Hamlet or Brick, she goes to PTA meetings and fights off suburban mothers who watch your show and dig at her with questions about what you're like in bed."

Trevor stepped back. "That's exactly the reason Maggie didn't want to be with me anymore. Because she wanted those things and knew I never would. It doesn't have to be that way, Jenna. What makes you think I would ever be so selfish?"

"You won't realize you're being selfish. That's the whole thing. Don't you get it?" Jenna shook her head. "As much as I like being with you, I'm not prepared to give it all up before I even get started. Are you?"

Trevor clenched his jaw.

"So this has to be it, tonight. Only tonight. Because you'll want to move on. You're burned out, Trevor. I can see it. You're so sick of playing Caspian your soul aches. That's the reason we just connected the way we did. Honestly, before me, when was the last time Trevor Hughes, not Caspian Locke, made love to a woman?"

"I don't know." His voice was low and filled with anguish.

She tilted her head and nodded, wiping a tear. "I understand, Trevor, I really do. But I will never leave this city, or this business, ever, and if we push this any further, it will ruin our show. And neither of us can afford to have that happen." She stood and touched his cheek.

He closed his eyes, holding her hand then dropped it and stepped back. "This is bullshit. Sorry, Jenna. But you're wrong. If people want to be together they make it work. So tell me, right now, what's the real reason you won't give this a try?"

"I have obligations elsewhere."

"What? An arranged marriage?"

"Of course not. I just—I can't tell you, Trevor."

Anger and hurt welled up inside him. Heat flashed through his body, his ego taking a punch to the gut. He backed away from her. Damn. Exactly what hurdle did she imagine could stop him? He could buy and sell most obstacles and he could hold his own against any man, physically or mentally. So what?

"No more ice cream?" She tilted her head.

Trevor stared at her. His heart felt...sore for the first time. He rubbed away a pain in his chest. In his life, if he worked hard enough he could always get what he wanted. That's how life worked. But Jenna—smart, talented, beautiful, break-the-rules Jenna—there's no way she would conform to his model of success. Even if he worked harder, would he get her? He shook his head. No, he didn't want more ice cream.

"Kaaayyyyy..." Jenna plopped down off the stool then closed containers and tucked them into the freezer. She cleaned up the splatter and placed their spoons in the sink. She looked around uneasily. "I guess I should..." Then her gaze met his.

Trevor stood perfectly still, unsure for the first time ever, of what to do next. Jenna inhaled deeply then took his hand and gently pulled him toward the music room.

****

Her hand entwined in his and pulling him forward, Jenna backed into the music room. She folded herself onto the couch, tucking a blanket beside her. "Can I stay?" She looked up at him and her heart raced. Yes, he liked her and liked spending time with her, but at what point would he decide she just wasn't worth the

228

hassle? She was nothing special. Nothing at all. He didn't move. Looking into his icy blue eyes, now warming with desire, Jenna understood he was hurting. Damn it. That was the last thing she wanted.

He glanced at her legs poking out of his t-shirt. Slowly she rubbed them together and took a long breath, finding it hard to make eye contact. "Just a few hours ago was Valentine's night. I really don't want to be alone—" Before she could finish her thought, Trevor's mouth was on hers.

He stopped for a moment, pushing her hair back from her face, tucking it gently behind her ear. "Would you rather go to the bedroom?"

She shook her head. "I like it here. Okay?"

He nodded and she opened her arms to him. He caught her in his embrace and lay with her—facing her, their hands intertwined. Unspoken words crowded Jenna's mind, but she couldn't free a single one…it wouldn't be fair. Instead, she turned her back to him, and he draped his heavy arm across her. She loved it. Jenna ran her fingers up and down the length of Trevor's long, strong arm. She traced the sinews of his muscles, from fingertip to elbow. His breath escaped in bursts, warming her neck, as her touch elicited goose bumps on his arm. She subtly leaned back against him, feeling for his reaction.

He shifted closer to her so she fit her bottom up against his waist and his arm tightened around her. He buried his nose in her hair. She grabbed onto his forearm with both of her hands, and moved her head to kiss him. His grasp tightened and she reached down, sliding off her panties. He was ready, pressing into the small of her back and she moved closer in response, waiting, wanting, needing.

"Jenna, baby," he whispered. "Stay with me." His voice was nearly as erotic as his actions. He repeated his words as he entered her.

Jenna gasped as Trevor tightened his hold on her. This time when she let him in, she wasn't sure she would be strong enough to let him go.

Chapter Sixteen

Jenna shivered as she bent down to relace her running shoes. Damn, February 15 had to be the coldest loneliest day in New York City. She stood on the corner, looking at the bodega next to her. Half-frozen flowers hung out of display containers and others lay trampled on the road, victims of last evening's rush to romance. People shuffled their feet as they pushed by her on their way to grab dirt water dogs from a nearby vendor. An old card shop across the street displayed a "Half-Off Valentine's Day" sign and a gym next door advertised: "Get Better Buns, for Better Luck Next Year."

There were so many lonely people in the world. So many people who would give years of their lives to experience what Jenna had with Trevor and yet here she was, alone the day after Valentine's Day.

She wasn't proud of her actions, but the man was playing Hamlet again later that day. And leaving him a note was certainly the polite thing to do. She had to go and let him get some rest. That's why she had sneaked out of his penthouse like the unpopular girl at school running from the "in" crowd. Which, ironically, was exactly what she was. The complicated elevator gate was far less complicated for this, her second escape. Unfortunately, the same wasn't true of her feelings. "He needs his sleep," she muttered as she left his building and went into the bitter cold of New York. One step out onto the brutally frigid street, and the wind had slapped her face, deservedly.

What a coward. She should have at least *told* him she was leaving.

Jenna trudged on. A note? She left a freaking note? How would she feel if he had walked out on her? Shaking the horrid thoughts away, Jenna began jogging again, moving faster and faster until she broke out into a run. She pounded her way up the avenue, hoping her steps would bring her clarity. Instead, they brought a throbbing headache. Up ahead was the entrance to the park. Should she take it?

Like an old horse who knew the trail, her body instinctively swerved toward the usual running route. Her fingers tingled…she wanted so badly to take it. She wanted him to wake up, notice her missing, read the note, and come running after her. Jenna forced her chin down, concentrating on the ground before her. Life wasn't a soap opera, even if your life was intertwined with a soap star. She pushed harder, passing the entrance, her heart aching more than her body.

****

"Ow!" Jenna grabbed her thigh then plopped down on the next step. She used the handrail to drag herself upward. After hours of running, her legs were rubber and climbing the stairs to her apartment was torture.

Jenna used one hand to support the other as she fought her fatigued trembling arm muscles. Finally, the last lock of the four locks clicked open and she threw herself inside. She slumped down on the floor by the door, not sure she would ever be able to move again. Her tummy grumbled so she craned her neck to peek into her near-empty kitchen cabinets. Great. Freaking peanut butter. Forget it. What she needed was a hot shower to loosen her aching muscles. After all, he wasn't the only one performing in a few hours.

The warmish water ran down her body, but thanks to her lousy water pressure, the gentle stream felt more like a caress than a cleansing. Damn it. She didn't need to be caressed, she didn't need anything that would remind her of Trevor, not that he was ever out of her thoughts, anyway.

Closing her eyes, Jenna leaned against the shower wall, her fingers making their way to her lips, thinking of every detail of their time together…no. Enough. It was one night only. That's all it could be. She opened her eyes and scowled at a smiling Papa Smurf.

****

"What the hell?" Jenna clamped the top of her robe closed as she stared at Trevor and Luis standing in her living room. She shuffled from foot to foot, conscious that, in her white robe with the white towel wrapped around her hair, she looked like a mini marshmallow. "Wait…is Toby okay?"

"Yes. He's fine. Recovering well."

"Thank God." Relief washed over her, as she balanced the towel on her head with her hand. "Then what the hell are you two doing in my living room?" Jenna glowered at the two men. This time they had really overstepped boundaries.

"We came to make sure you were all right." Trevor's voice was low and measured. His chest heaved as he spoke, a worried look etched on his face.

Jenna narrowed her eyes. "What do you mean if I'm all right? And how dare you barge in like this? I—I was naked in the shower."

"I'm not interested." Luis stepped back.

"And I've seen it all before," Trevor said sharply.

Jenna gasped, glaring at Trevor. He gazed back at her—his eyes alive with fire. He moved closer, his aura filling the tiny room. He was so tall, and smart, and gorgeous, and the way he looked at her...hell no. She needed to focus.

Trevor scratched the scruff on his chin. "I am so relieved but so angry right now, I don't know if I should hug you or put you over my knee."

"Huh!" Jenna's mouth dropped open and she released her grasp on her towel. Heat rose in her cheeks, and her heart raced from embarrassment and desire. A misplaced smirk threatened to make an appearance, but she couldn't let it happen. She needed to stay strong and regroup.

He grabbed her by the elbow and pulled her closer. Her body fell forward. A warm, prickly sensation flushed over her. Her nipples hardened, a sharp ache forming between her legs. She looked up at him, her body flooded with desire and excitement. He pulled her closer still, her breath moving in time with his. Finally, he shook his head and released his hold on her. He turned away. Droplets of water dripped down her neck. She exhaled, audibly.

"Jenna." Luis stepped forward. "I let him in. The man called me, really upset."

"Why were you upset?" Jenna turned to Trevor who looked at her in that same unnerving way.

"Because you left a note saying you were going running. And when I went to catch up with you, you were nowhere on our running path. So I went back to my place to wait for you. But you never showed," Trevor said through clenched teeth.

"I went a different way." Frustration swirled in Jenna's chest. "I don't have to explain myself."

"No?" He raised his eyebrows. "You have no cell phone. What if something happened to you?" he asked sharply.

Drip, drip, drip...droplets of water trickled from the sides of the turbaned towel in her hair, annoying her. She fought with the towel, finally letting it drop to the floor. Her wet hair hung down over her shoulders.

Something flickered in Trevor's eyes then, a different kind of passion. His voice softened. "It's a big, bad city, Jen."

"Oh geez." Luis whistled, moving away.

"Oh no, you don't." Anger poured forth out of every cell in Jenna's body. Her fists closed into balls and she squeezed them tightly.

"What?" Trevor scoffed, looking at Luis and back again. "No one's allowed to say anything bad about New York?"

Jenna stepped toward Trevor, taking a deep breath, checking her anger. "People who hate the city try to get other people to leave it."

"What?" Trevor's eyes narrowed. "Why would I want you to leave the city? I want you here. With me. I just want to take care of you."

"I'm not a responsibility." Jenna spoke slowly. "And I'm certainly not your responsibility, Trevor."

"But what if I want you to be?"

Jenna rocked back on her heels, tears forming in her eyes where anger danced only moments before. "I am a person, Trevor. Not a responsibility. I can take care of myself."

"Jenna…" Trevor's shoulders dropped a bit. "I know that. But part of being a man is taking care of the people we l—"

Jenna's heart pounded and perspiration dotted her forehead.

"I want to take care of you, Jenna. I want to be with you. Why won't you let me?"

"Because it's not possible, Trevor." She saw the ache in his eyes. Damn it. She hated that she caused it.

"Why not?" Trevor stroked her cheek.

Jenna swayed into him, almost giving over. "I—I can't tell you."

"Fine." Trevor dropped his hand.

"Oh, just tell him, Jenna," Luis said from the other side of the room.

Jenna wheeled around to face Luis. "Luis, I shared that with you and Loretta one night in confidence. And I was drunk. You said you'd never bring it up. I love you like a brother, but this is none of your business."

"No, Jen, it's all of my business, because I have been the one who's been here for you. Time and again. And I have a family now. Besides, life is made for couples, not groups. There will be things you need—big support, and you should have someone for that."

"That's exactly the reason I can't, Luis…you know that."

"Jenna, this guy is a good guy."

"I know that." Jenna's gaze dropped to the floor as she collected her thoughts. "But why are you pushing me?"

"Because you need more than a friend. You deserve it."

She was losing the battle with her tears.

"I think you're making a mistake, Jen. Don't shut him out. He's the best thing that's ever happened to you."

Jenna bit the inside of her cheek, her breath shallower. She looked back and forth, from man to man—she was cornered, trapped like prey. A bitter taste formed in her mouth. Hateful words swirled in her brain—she knew they were poisonous, but she couldn't help herself. "And tell me something, Luis. Isn't there just a tiny part of you that thinks he's the best thing to happen to you as well?" Jenna raised an eyebrow.

"Excuse me?"

"The audition. The new show Trevor's friend just happens to be producing."

"That's it." Trevor moved forward. "I'm not going to allow my unrequited feelings for you to hurt Luis or your relationship with him."

"No, man." Luis put up his hand. "It's cool. Yeah, well, Jenna. Now I know what you really think of our friendship." Luis fished Jenna's keys out of his pocket and dropped them onto her small kitchen table. He stared at Jenna for a long moment. "Later, man." Luis pulled open the apartment door and left.

"Shit." Jenna bowed her head. "I didn't mean to hurt him." With her damp robe wrapped around her, she shivered in her chilly apartment.

"You know…" Trevor clamped his hand to the back of his neck. His head dropped backward and he exhaled audibly. "You don't seem to understand, Jenna. To have people in your life you love, it means they get to love you, too."

Jenna's head snapped up. She gazed at Trevor,

knowing this may be the very last time she would ever see him offstage. "No, Trevor." Jenna's voice was soft. "That is exactly what it doesn't mean."

****

Before he left, Trevor handed Jenna an extra Valentine's Day gift.

"A smart phone?" She held the cell in her hand like it was a bomb about to detonate. "I can't afford this, Trevor. But thank you."

"It's paid for."

"No way." Jenna gave the phone back to Trevor. "There is no way I can take this."

"I'm not asking, Jenna." He pried her fist open and stuffed the phone back into her hand.

Her body tingled at his touch.

"It's for work. As your *boss* I insist you have it. In case I need to inform you about…something… anything. And that means answering the damned phone when I call. Understood?" He raised his eyebrows, no doubt waiting for her to disagree.

Her heart raced again, her body warming with the strength and power of his voice. "Fine."

"Fine." Trevor nodded. "And before you get all angry at me for not knowing who you are and all that— listen." Trevor pushed a button playing a ringtone that sounded like an antique phone. "And yes, I understand you're not a cell phone type of girl, but I don't give a crap."

"What?"

"These things keep you safe. And I don't care what your deep, dark secret is, Jenna. There's no way I'm going to let you walk around without a cell."

He turned to leave, and her stomach cramped.

He whirled back. "And one more thing."

Jenna looked up at him, swallowing hard.

"I'd like you to accompany me to a charity dinner in two weeks."

"Trevor, I don't think it's a good idea." Her voice cracked.

"I was just being polite. It's not a request."

Jenna gasped at the demand in Trevor's voice. Her body warmed with a definite pull toward him. She narrowed her eyes.

"It's for business." He rubbed his unshaven chin. "Kat has the details. They asked for Hamlet and Ophelia."

"I don't...I don't have anything to wear." Her cheeks reddened.

"I'll take you shopping."

"No." Jenna put up her hand, stopping him. "No. I'll...I'll handle it."

"It's black tie."

"Crap." Jenna dropped down on the chair in her kitchen.

"Let me help you, Jenna."

Looking at Trevor standing there in running pants and a sweatshirt, all Jenna wanted to do was to say yes. To everything he was offering. Instead, she shook her head.

"Fine." He looked away and then back to her. His eyes softened. "Honestly, even if you wear that same damned blue dress again, you'll look stunning. But you don't have to." Trevor's gaze stayed on hers. "I'll buy you whatever you want, Jenna."

"I know."

"I'm free of at least some of my obligations now,

and I was really hoping we could still spend these next couple of weeks getting to know each other...even if it is as friends..." He moved closer to her and leaned down. "Jenna, I don't know what suddenly scared you off. If we went too far—"

"No. It was perfect."

"Then why?"

Jenna shook her head, unable to look at him.

"Yeah, well...okay." Trevor stood up, reaching to rub one shoulder. His hand dropped. "We have a show in a few hours. I'm going to get ready."

Trevor opened the door but it was all too final. Jenna jumped from her seat, and burst forward.

"Trevor?"

He turned quickly. "Yes?"

The way he looked at her, so strong and protective, all she wanted was to throw herself against his chest and hold him while he held her.

"I'm...I'm sorry."

"I'm not." He walked out the door.

****

Performing with Jenna every night was the only thing Trevor looked forward to. Thankfully, the tension between them didn't spoil their performances. If anything, it heightened the stakes even more. But he would have given that up in a minute if it meant they could go back to their dinners of cherry pie at dive bars.

Each night at the theatre Trevor stole glances at Jenna, and every time he looked at her, she was even more beautiful and talented. The only problem was she also looked sad...very, very sad. Not at all *Jenna*. He wanted so badly to hold her and make all the hurt go away but she wouldn't let him. At least he had the nunnery scene when he could hold her. His acting had never before been quite so alive and in the moment. Don would have been proud. But unfortunately, all of this would be over soon. Long before he was ready, their limited engagement would end…and Jenna would walk out of his life forever.

He couldn't let that happen.

****

Performing opposite Trevor every night was the only thing that kept Jenna going. She would spend all day, every day, thinking of nothing but him. She lived to get out onto that stage with him. Every night in their opening scenes she would smile at him, real smiles onstage, allowing Ophelia to live the life Jenna wished she could. Every night her heart would race when Trevor held her closely in the nunnery scene, hoping and praying he would break protocol and kiss her…and every night her heart would break when Hamlet abandoned Ophelia. Ophelia had been driven mad over her love for Hamlet, and Jenna now understood Ophelia completely.

After the final curtain call of every performance, Jenna moped through the hallways on her way to her dressing room, fighting her tears. Some nights she'd walk past his dressing room when his door was opened, and she'd peer in to see him still wearing Hamlet's customary black, his demeanor every bit as melancholy as the Prince of Denmark himself. And why wouldn't it be? He was falling for her, just as she was falling for him. Damn it.

She couldn't let that happen.

Chapter Seventeen

On the way to Jenna's apartment to pick her up for the charity event, Trevor's knee bounced like a jackhammer as he sat in the back of the limo. Holy crap, how could he possibly be this nervous over a date? He'd been dating since he was fifteen, and all of his adult romantic life was documented in the trash magazines, killing even the most remote chance of privacy, so why was he so nervous now? He watched out the window at Manhattan whizzing by, rethinking his decision, or rather, demand. What if she was still angry with him? What if the whole evening was nothing but awkward? But no, after the night they had shared a few weeks earlier, there was something real between them. He knew it.

Trevor fiddled with the small, black, rectangular, velvet box he held in his hands, and as the limo turned onto her street, he caught sight of Jenna standing there, waiting. What the hell? He sat forward, livid. Why wasn't she upstairs? Why was he the only one concerned for her safety? He would have gone up to meet her at her apartment door. There was no reason for her to be out here, freezing and unsafe.

As the car pulled closer, his furrowed brow relaxed, and his anger was replaced by awe. "Jenna." Trevor bounded out of the limo before it had stopped completely. "Jenna, you look..." He gazed up and down her body. "Gorgeous."

Jenna blushed, smiling the first real smile she had given him offstage in—he couldn't remember how long. He smiled back, so incredibly happy to see it. He was happy to see the rest of her as well, the beautiful, long black lace dress that fit her body perfectly, the soft black wrap thrown over, her gorgeous hair pinned up messily, her eyes smoldering. Trevor fought to take a breath. "Jenna, you are..." He shook his head, speechless.

Jenna smiled and looked away. "Thanks. How's Toby?"

"He's okay. Recovery is going well, and there's no reason to think it was anything more than an isolated occurrence."

"Thank God." A gust of wind blew by and she shivered.

"Come on." Trevor led her to the opened door of the limo and climbed in next to her as the driver shut the door behind them. "You really are stunning."

"Thank you." She adjusted her gown, letting her small shiny clutch rest on the seat between them. "But I can't take the credit. It was all Loretta. Except the gown. I found that at a vintage shop downtown. Is it okay?"

She looked up at him with eyes filled with so much vulnerability, all he wanted was to take her in his arms and prove how right it all was.

"Jenna, it's perfect," he whispered, his voice cracking slightly.

She sat back, turning her head to look out the window, her wrap falling off of her shoulders. Trevor glimpsed her breasts, looking incredibly full in her gown. He inhaled deeply. Hell, yes. They should get dressed up more often.

She faced him again. "The rest Loretta created from her makeup kit. And the pearls"—Jenna played with her earlobe delicately—"are hers."

"Luis has great taste."

He leaned over and touched Jenna's earlobe, lightly. She closed her eyes, swaying toward him but Trevor backed off immediately, keeping his hands on his side of the limo. There was no way he would push her; he had already scared her off once; it wouldn't happen again. The re-wooing of Jenna Joyce had to be done carefully. He shrugged off a cold chill, hating anything so calculated. He would never play games with her, but he had to be careful. He placed the black velvet box on the seat between them, sliding it to her. "I was wondering if you might want to wear these."

Her eyes widened and he silently prayed she wouldn't push them back at him because it was too much, too soon.

****

Jenna's heart pounded. The idea of Trevor giving her a gift after this much time had passed was so…unexpected. She ran her fingers over the soft velvet of the box, desperately wanting to see inside. But how unfair would it be for her to accept this? It would only be leading him on. "Trevor, I can't."

"Go ahead." He nodded gently.

Jenna grasped the box in her shaking hand and opened it carefully. Nestled in a black satin interior were the most beautiful golden sapphire and diamond earrings, shaped like tiny sea turtles.

"Trevor, I…"

"Do you like them?"

"They're amazing."

"Like you."

Jenna looked up at him. "I can't keep them." She closed the box and pushed it back toward Trevor.

His eyes hardened. "Well, that might be a problem, seeing I had them made for you."

"You did?" Never in her life had someone thought about Jenna so completely. "That was so incredibly thoughtful."

"Aside from the obvious connection..." Trevor patted his chest above his heart as he spoke. "I had them use deep golden sapphires to match your eyes and diamonds...well, because."

Jenna froze at the word "diamond."

"Want to try them on?"

Although her brain screamed, "No," her head nodded.

Trevor leaned over, tucking a loose tendril of hair behind her ear, and Jenna closed her eyes, breathing him in. He smelled incredible, like light spice and clean laundry. She wished they could stay there all night, in the back of the limo, so close they were nearly touching. Trevor lingered with his hand at her ear. He touched her hair gently, and traced his finger down her cheek until it came to rest under her chin.

Jenna glanced up at him, certain he was going to kiss her. Her body leaned forward, feeling that undeniable pull toward him. She lifted her chin. But there was no kiss. Instead, he smiled, and the limo driver said, "We're here, Mr. Hughes."

Jenna cleared her throat, quickly removing her pearls and tucking them into her clutch, replacing them with her new stunning earrings.

$$****$$

They stepped out of the limo, and Jenna turned toward the museum hosting the benefit, reading the sign hanging over the museum's rotunda. "It's a benefit for an animal charity." Jenna turned to Trevor and playfully slapped him on the shoulder with her clutch. Giddy inside, she fought back a giggle. She took a deep breath of the cold night air and it rushed into her lungs. She hadn't felt this free since…the last time she saw him.

"Oh, look at that." Trevor feigned surprise.

Jenna squeezed his hand. There was a spark from his touch and she quickly broke away.

He leaned down to whisper in her ear. "Jenna. Just for tonight, let's just be happy. Wherever that takes us, it takes us."

Jenna tried to speak but he gently placed his finger to her lips.

"And wherever it doesn't take us, it doesn't."

"But Trevor…" Jenna looked down. "I don't want to be unfair to you."

He placed his finger under her chin and lifted it. "Hey."

He smiled, and her defenses slipped away.

"I promise I heard your warning. I'm a big boy."

"Oh…" Jenna giggled, covering her mouth with her hand. "I know."

Trevor chuckled, his broad shoulders shaking with his laugh. He took Jenna's hand, slipping it in the crook of his arm. He tightened his muscles and Jenna immediately felt safe and relieved, but unfinished.

"Trevor?"

"Yeah, Jen?" He looked at her with eyes that for the first time in weeks were filled with happiness rather than sorrow.

"I—I'm sorry."

He nodded.

She searched for her words. "If you had run out on me after we had spent that time together, I would have been devastated. And instead, you came to find me and brought me an incredibly thoughtful gift." She paused for a moment, collecting her thoughts. "There's really no excuse. I—I just panicked, because I didn't want to hurt you, and yet that's exactly what I did."

"I understand."

"Really?" Jenna looked up at him. He was so strong and smart and mature. She felt like a teenager in comparison. But she wasn't just a kid; she was a woman, a woman who was involved with Trevor Hughes…in one way or another.

"Yes."

Trevor led her forward a few steps, but Jenna hesitated. She drew a deep breath. "And I'm not…"

He slipped her hand out of the crook of his arm and lifted it to his lips. He kissed her hand, gently. "I just want you here, Jenna. With me."

She reached up with her free hand and played with her earring, delicately. She smiled at him and he led her inside.

****

"Wow." Jenna took one step into the event room of the museum and stopped short. "Oh my goodness…" Her words fell away as she took in her surroundings: the high ceiling draped in millions of tiny white lights; dozens of large round tables covered in white tablecloths with white cloth-covered chairs flanking them; long birch branches climbing up the museum pillars, shimmering with sparkling lights; and large framed photos of animals everywhere along the sides of the room. A long bar with high white leather stools and at least a half dozen bartenders was before them, and a staff of dozens of waiters, dressed in black tuxedos, walked through the event room, carrying hors d'oeuvres on shiny silver platters. The room was warm and smelled like burnt sugar and vanilla. Hundreds of people milled about. "Trevor, this is…" Jenna walked closer to a photo of a dog with only one eye and a lopsided ear. "This photo—it's incredible. Looks like a professional photographer did it."

"It was a professional. Professionals photographed all the animals, hoping they'll have a better chance at being adopted." He tossed his head. "Come on, let's get our seats."

"Caspian…?" Before they could take a step toward the table, a woman in her mid-thirties wearing a long, black, sleeveless, satin dress and fire engine red lipstick stepped up to Trevor. Incredibly tanned, toned arm muscles flexed as she stood on her toes and kissed him on both cheeks. She didn't even glance at Jenna. "Gloria. Remember? I work with the turtle charity."

"Yes, hello." He took Jenna's hand, pulling her closer. "It's Trevor, actually. And this is Jenna."

"I know your name, but to me you'll always be Caspian. So it's true? You and Maggie?" Gloria looked Jenna up and down.

Trevor nodded. "Yes, she decided it was time to part ways."

"She decided, huh?" The woman raised her

248

overarched brows. "Well anyway, I'm hooked up with the photographer Henri and we're using celebrities in the next series of pics. I'd love to use you..." She smiled, patting his bicep with her hand, trying to wedge herself between Trevor and Jenna. "I've heard the rumor that there's a turtle tattooed on that wide chest of yours"—she made circles in the air around his heart— "but you're super private about it. Why not give me a peek, and I can let Henri know it's for real. It'll be perfect with the underwater series we've got planned." She nodded toward one of the doorways. "We can have some privacy over there. Behind coat check. Why not give me a look?" She licked her lips.

Trevor cleared his throat, standing up taller. "It's very flattering that you'd like to use me for your photos, thank you. Why not give me Henri's contact, and I'll have my agent be in touch." Smiling and winking at Jenna, Trevor took Jenna's arm, leading her away from the woman and over to the bar.

"That's nerve," Jenna said over the soft band music as Trevor took two glasses of champagne from the bartender and handed one to Jenna.

"What's that?"

"Asking you to disrobe in the middle of a black tie dinner?"

Trevor laughed it off like it was nothing. "Oh, I've been asked at the grocery store...Central Park...the middle of Saks."

Jenna's heart ached. "That's not very cool."

"You get used to it." Trevor shrugged.

"But could you imagine if a man asked that of a woman? It would be scandalous. Not to mention incredibly tacky."

"I guess." He smiled, but his jaw jutted forward, his muscles clenched. "But what can I do? An occupational hazard, right? I mean, I do walk around shirtless nearly every day. I can't expect people to look at me as more than bare-chested Caspian Locke if that's what I show them." He tipped back his champagne flute, swallowing hard.

Jenna took the empty glass from his hand and set it down on the bar. "Trevor, you do know how incredible you are, right?"

He snickered, rolling his eyes. "How much champagne have you had?"

Jenna put her hands on her hips. "Don't laugh this off. Yes, you're incredibly handsome, and yes, you are awe-inspiring shirtless…"

He scoffed, but Jenna went on. "But more importantly, you are a wonderful person, and you are so talented."

"I sold out, Jen."

"Caspian?"

Trevor nodded. "Sure."

"But you're playing Hamlet, now."

"And it has been the most rewarding experience…" He reached out and touched a loose tendril of her hair. "In so many ways. But it's too little, too late."

"What about Brick? Like we talked about?"

"Jen, you know as well as I do, roles don't just happen."

Jenna nodded, understanding completely. "But there are ways, Trevor. You don't have to play Caspian Locke forever."

"Jenna, you know my situation. Amanda and Toby rely on me; how can I make that income anywhere else?

Who will take a chance on a soap opera bad guy? What else would I do?"

"Why not produce, like you told Luis you'd like to do? You've got an eye for spotting talent. You cast me." Jenna prodded Trevor playfully, trying to lighten the mood.

"That's true, I did." He grinned.

"And you got Luis an audition for the new show, and you and I both know he is a fabulous actor. He deserves that role, no matter what lousy things I said to him. And while you're at it, why not take over for Don?"

Trevor threw his head back, laughing uncomfortably. "Jen, you know the only students I would get would be wannabe soap actors. And I'm not sure I'd want to do that."

"Then what? What would you like to do?"

"Honestly?" His eyes sparkled. "I'd love to start my own theatre company."

Jenna nodded. A wave of excitement crossed her chest and shot down her arms but her belly filled with lead. "Then do it." Her voice cracked.

He gave her the smallest, saddest smile.

"But you don't want to do it in the city, do you?"

"No. I don't know if I really want to deal with the crap it takes to start a theatre company in New York City."

"I get it. As much as I love the city, I would imagine it would be incredible to start a theatre company somewhere upstate. Buy an old barn. Lots of land. House the actors. Do real, important theatre all summer long. Be part of a working community."

Trevor smiled.

"Lots of greats started on soaps, Trevor. You're not that show. And it's not you."

"I don't know."

He looked away, but she reached out and touched his cheek. Gently, she turned him toward her. She stroked his scruffy beard. "I know."

****

When they made it to their seats, Luis and Loretta were sitting there, engrossed in conversation. Luis stopped talking when Jenna walked up and stood close to them.

"I didn't know you two were here. I'm so, so happy to see you." Jenna fought the tears in her eyes as Loretta stood and hugged her. Jenna stepped back, taking in Loretta's full-length peach gown. "You look gorgeous. Why didn't you tell me you were coming?"

"Trevor set it all up. Wanted you and Luis to get a chance to talk." Loretta patted her husband on the shoulder. "It was my job to force him into his wedding suit and make him come."

Jenna smiled. "Well you look great, Luis."

"Thanks." Luis sipped soda, watching as the first few couples made their way to the dance floor.

"Luis," Jenna implored, moving closer to him. "Please, please forgive me. What I said, it was awful."

Luis avoided eye contact.

Trevor whisked around behind them and took Loretta by the hand. "Loretta? Could I have this dance?"

"Absolutely." She leaned down to whisper in Luis's ear. "She's sorry. We all do and say stupid things. *All* of us."

Luis watched Loretta as she waltzed off with

Trevor.

"Guess they really want us to get a chance to talk." Jenna sat next to Luis. She tossed her clutch onto the table and leaned back, ready to take whatever horrible things Luis had to say to her.

"Guess so." Luis picked up his soft drink and sipped it, watching the dancers as they twirled their way around the floor.

"Luis." Jenna put her hand on Luis's. "Please, please tell me what I can say to make this better."

Luis shook his head and turned to her. Her hand fell away. "You and I…Jen, we've been through a lot."

"Yes." Jenna bit the inside of her cheek.

"Aside from Loretta, you've been my best friend for a long time now." His gaze flashed to the table and back to Jenna.

"And you've been mine."

"I still remember the first time I saw you. I had just been cast as Othello, big surprise, for my exam plays at school, and they told me they had a fabulous Desdemona for me, and in walks your first-year skinny ass." Luis shook his head, laughing. "I kept thinking, 'These are my exam plays and they're giving me some first year kid who hadn't even gone to get a BFA yet?'"

"That was when we met Don. He came to watch you."

"And he snapped up both of us." Luis looked at Jenna. "But they were right, Don and the school; you were a fabulous Desdemona. You're a great actor, Jen, but you're an even better friend. You've seen me at my lowest points. You've never judged me. You've given me pep talks after I've blown auditions. You let me puke in your bathroom when Loretta wouldn't let me come home. So I guess"—he sighed heavily—"what I'm trying to say is, I forgive you for what you said to me." His gaze darted up to hers. "But it hurt, and I hope to hell you didn't mean it."

"I didn't. I swear, Luis."

Luis nodded. "I know that. You've had a lot thrown at you lately. And I know you're not feeling like yourself. I think it was just passion talking."

Jenna threw her arms around Luis's neck and hugged him tightly.

Luis pulled back, chuckling. "But Jenna, as your friend, I'm telling you, he's a good guy. And guys like that don't come along very often."

Jenna turned to see Trevor twirling Loretta on the dance floor. They were both laughing. Jenna's shoulders slumped forward. "I know, Luis."

"Don't make him wait forever."

"You waited for Loretta."

Luis pointed at Trevor. "You can't compare us. I mean, sure we both have rugged good looks..." He chuckled, and Jenna laughed with him. "But I was a screw-up, Jen. You know that. Until I kicked my habit, I did a lot of things I'm not proud of. And a lot of what I did hurt Loretta. I waited for Loretta to say yes to marrying me because I had to prove myself. And why she waited for me..." He gazed at Loretta. "I don't know. I'm just incredibly lucky, I guess."

"Yes," Jenna whispered.

"But what does he have to prove?"

Jenna swallowed hard. "Nothing." She shook her head. "But you know I'll never be able to make this donation if he's in my life. If I think there's even a chance, Luis...and what if, by some miracle, we make it? He's so sick of being Caspian. He's done. He'll want out. And I haven't even started yet. I can't end up like my dad, my dreams tossed aside, because it's time to be a parent."

"You're not your dad, Jen. And Trevor's certainly not your mom."

"I know, but what about—? Luis, he has obligations. He already takes care of people in his life. I can't add to that. I can't bring my crazy mother and my commitment to my sister to him. He'll want to help, I know it, and it's just too much. There are so many reasons why we can't work."

"And one big reason you can. Take a gamble, Jenna. Just like the rest of us."

"But what if I lose?"

Luis leaned forward and took Jenna's hand. He smiled. " 'And if we should fail? We fail. But screw your courage to the sticking-place, and we'll not fail.' "

Jenna smirked. "You doing a *Macbeth* I don't know about? Perchance?"

Luis shook his head. "Nah, I'm afraid there's no theatre for me for awhile."

"No theatre?" Jenna frowned, trying to understand. "Luis, that's like having no air to breathe."

"I got the show, Jen."

Jenna sat forward, her heart racing. "The new crime drama?"

"The audition Trevor got me, yeah." Luis nodded. "Kat called me earlier today. I almost can't believe it myself. Just over two years ago I was a mess…and today…?"

Luis raised his glass and Jenna grabbed a nearby water goblet, toasting back. They placed their drinks on the table.

Jenna hugged Luis tightly. "Congratulations, Luis."

He pulled back from her. "Jenna, you're amazing as Ophelia in an Off-Broadway show. You've got a guy, a handsome, smart, talented guy who's crazy about you. This should be the best time of your life."

"I know." Jenna looked at Trevor as he spun Loretta around the dance floor. "I know."

****

The band began a slow, classic, love song and suddenly Trevor was there. At his intent gaze, Jenna's stomach flip-flopped, like she had opening night jitters. His hair was perfectly disheveled and his scruff tamed. The way he moved—in control and confident—he was so incredibly sexy. He put out his hand and lifted her to her feet. Without a word, he led her to the dance floor and wrapped his arm around her waist. He took her other hand in his and held it tightly between them. As the band sang lyrics of a man professing his love, Trevor hummed along. He leaned down, moving her body with his.

For two minutes, it was utter bliss. Jenna knew it would have to end, but for now…she breathed deeply as Trevor held her tighter. She gave over to him, completely, his strong hand on her lower back moving her in time with his body. Together, they swayed slowly, barely moving from their one spot on the dance floor. She warmed at the feel of their two bodies, tight together.

His hand spread wider on her back, claiming her as his own. She sucked in a choppy breath, an undeniable ache forming at the thought of belonging to Trevor. He pulled her closer, and she clung to him, knowing she was safe, protected, and wanted. He leaned down and breathed her in, and for a moment, Jenna felt such a responsibility toward him—she wanted to protect him from anything and anyone that may hurt him—including her.

She squeezed her eyes shut, holding on tighter as she whispered, "Trevor."

****

That one little word—his name—whispered in her soft, breathy voice, was all Trevor needed to throw caution and his plan of playing it cool, to the wind. Desire burned like a raging fire in his gut; before Jenna, he had never felt these feelings—these feelings of protectiveness and peace and happiness and possibility and strength—and love. And tonight the feelings were too strong to deny any longer. Trevor pulled her closer; they were no longer dancing, they were morphing into one. The only time he had ever felt this close to another person was when he made love to her, all those weeks ago.

"Jenna..." He needed her to understand he was here for her, and always would be. Thankfully, the song ended at just the perfect moment, and he sang the final words of the song into her ear. "I'm in love with you..." Trevor waited for her to push away from him, but she didn't. Instead, she looked up at him with her beautiful eyes, glowing. Trevor took her by the hand, protectively. "We're leaving now."

She nodded. She understood. This was his time. Tonight, he would win Jenna Joyce, once and for all. He held her hand firmly as they made their way around the room, saying their goodbyes.

Loretta smiled brightly at Jenna. "Not staying for

dinner?"

"I guess not."

"It's vegan, anyway." Luis sighed, leaning forward against the table. "Go grab yourselves some burgers."

A woman at another table shot Luis a dirty look.

Luis cleared his throat. "Tofu, of course."

Trevor said goodbye, shaking Luis's hand and kissing Loretta on the cheek. Texting his driver, he led Jenna to coat check, but Jenna still hadn't uttered a word. Quickly, he laid her wrap over her shoulders and guided her out onto the cold streets of New York. She bounced on her toes in response to the bitterness, and Trevor wrapped his arm around her to keep her warm as he escorted her into the waiting limo. Settling in, he gave the driver directions. Finally, he turned to Jenna. Flushed, beautiful, Jenna. Every time he looked at her, he needed a beat to pass, just to reclaim his senses. He reached out and rested his hand on her shoulder. "We're grabbing something to eat."

Jenna nodded.

"And then, finally, we're going to talk this thing through."

There really was no option. He wouldn't bully her or coerce her into anything she wasn't ready for but frankly, it was time she was ready. She was a beautiful, talented young woman who was in a beast of a business, and that meant there would be people at every turn trying to take advantage of her. He had seen it so many times. But Trevor knew in his heart he belonged with her, that it was his job to protect her and watch her become a star, rising higher than she ever imagined. This was only the beginning for her…and for them.

The only real problem he faced tonight was the

unknown, her secret, and more importantly, her reaction to her secret. That was the one variable he couldn't control, and despite his confidence, this one little worry was eating away at him. Their show was ending soon and if he couldn't get to the bottom of this now, he may very well lose her forever. He shifted in his seat. Losing her for any amount of time was out of the question— losing her forever was unthinkable.

Chapter Eighteen

Jenna followed Trevor down a few concrete steps to a small restaurant on the Lower East Side, nestled in the outskirts of a trendy neighborhood. The restaurant was situated in the bottom of an old brownstone that sat back from the street, hidden from view. She'd never heard about this place, and there wasn't even a street sign marking it. Jenna glanced up at Trevor as he held the door for her and her heart pounded from nerves.

The warmth of the restaurant enveloped her as she walked through the door. She shook off her chill, breathing in the smell of candle wax, burgers, and fries. Without stopping for a hostess, Trevor led them to a small table near the very back of the restaurant. The table was covered in a black linen cloth, the woven texture matching the black textured wallpaper. Plush chairs, also covered in black linen, were pushed up tightly to the table. Trevor held her chair for her, and she slid forward as he sat across from her. His gaze was heavy on hers. In the dim candlelight, he was so handsome it was too much to handle. She picked up a stack of sugar packets from the white porcelain sugar dish, fiddling with them nervously.

He pointed to the packets. "Coffee?"

Jenna nodded, her teeth chattering too much to form words. Despite the warmth, she pulled her wrap tightly around her shoulders and blew into her hands, trying to shake off the last of her chill.

Although the place was nearly empty, a waitress all dressed in black and carrying a pot of coffee, took her time ambling over. She picked up her pace when she spotted Trevor in his tux.

"Hey, Trevor." The waitress smiled at both of them. "Burgers—medium rare—and extra salty fries?"

Trevor turned to Jenna. "That okay for you?"

"Yes, thank you."

Trevor reached out and took Jenna's trembling hands in his as the waitress poured coffee into large, white, square-topped, porcelain mugs. He smiled as the waitress walked off.

Jenna wrapped her hands around the mug, warming her hands. "The coffee smells incredible. Come here a lot I'm guessing?"

He nodded, fixing her coffee with sugar and cream. "It's an escape for me. I know with the darkness and candles it looks like a date place, but I come here alone to read…with a book light…" He chuckled, running his hand through his hair. "And just to escape Caspian sometimes. No one gives a damn about some stupid soap character in this part of the Village, and I love it. Actually"—he shifted in his seat as he spoke—"I've never before brought anyone here. Ever."

"Then why bring me?"

He raised his eyebrows. "Really, Jen? You really don't know?"

"Trevor…" Crap. This would be even harder than she anticipated.

"Drink up." Trevor lifted his chin toward her mug. "I think it's going to be a long night."

Jenna nodded, lifting her mug to her lips, blowing

on the coffee. How was she ever going to get through this? She shifted in her seat, but before she could utter a word, their burgers arrived. Trevor dug into his, but Jenna's stomach was all tied up.

"You're not hungry?"

"Not really." She fiddled with her fork.

Trevor raised his eyebrows in disbelief. "I don't think I've ever seen you pass on food. Okay." He swallowed his bite and sighed as he pushed his plate aside. He leaned across the table and pushed hers away, too. He took her hands. "I want to be with you, Jenna. I—as cliché as this sounds—I was lost, and you showed me the man I wanted to be. I'm a better actor because of you, and a better person. I'm not talking about wanting some quickie romance, I'm talking about a commitment."

Jenna leaned back in her seat. "Oh, crap."

He chuckled. "Not exactly the response I wanted." He smiled. "I know you like me…or am I wrong?"

"Of course you're not wrong. I want to be with you more than anything. But it wouldn't be fair to you, and I just…can't."

"But that's what I don't understand. I've given this a lot of thought. Okay, so you're worried we'll leave the city. I promise Jenna, no matter where life takes us, I will keep an apartment here. Always. And I don't expect you to give up your career; you are incredibly talented. As a matter of fact, you're a better actor than I am."

"Trevor—"

"It's true. All I want to do is to be with you and help you shoot to the stars."

"You're not making this any easier."

"That's my goal." He smiled. "Jenna, no matter what you tell me, it won't matter. By now my mind has imagined everything. I've guessed you belong to a devil-worshipping cult, from which I am prepared to save you." He grinned. "You've already told me there's no husband and no arranged marriage. I know you are not, nor have you ever been, a man." He raised his eyebrows.

"Ha, ha."

He shifted in his seat and leaned closer to her. "So as you can see, I've thought of everything."

"Not everything." Jenna gazed at the table.

"Jen, Jenna. Look at me."

Jenna forced her gaze off her plate and onto Trevor.

"That's better." Trevor brushed a stray hair away from her face.

His touch made her dizzy.

His hand lingered. "Just tell me, Jen. Whatever it is. In case you didn't notice, I just went all out back there. I told you how I feel about you, and nothing will change that. Nothing."

Jenna swallowed hard, gathering her courage. "Trevor, I don't know how to begin."

"Just tell me."

"My mother blamed me for having to leave the city. If I had never been born, maybe my dad would have had an acting career, and she could have stayed. I owe her." Jenna leaned forward, resting her forearms on the table. "What you don't know is, like you, I support my sister. Not to the extent you do but I send my mother and my sister money every chance I can. I pay the salary for an extra employee, someone who does the job my mother thinks I should be doing. My plan is to keep my sister in school and not working at the laundry my mother owns." She looked up at Trevor. "She—my sister, Olivia—she's really incredibly smart. Wants to be a scientist. I want her to go to the best school she can."

Trevor nodded.

Jenna sighed. "I'm an egg donor, Trevor."

"A what?"

"I'm scheduled to donate my eggs to an infertile couple so they can make a baby."

"Oh. I—uh…" Trevor sat back.

"Weren't expecting that one, right?"

"I'm not quite sure I understand. When are you scheduled?"

"My retrieval is right after the show closes. That's why I was on the pill, to regulate my cycle. I already started the hormones, which is why my body is changing. I saw you staring at my breasts in the car tonight."

"Jenna, I think this happens all the time, right? I'm not sure I understand why you think this would keep us apart."

"Because that's only half of it. What Luis and Loretta know, it's only part of it. The truth is, I've already donated. Twice. This would be my third time." She swallowed hard.

"Third?"

"Yes." She nodded. "That means there is already the potential that what could have been two of my children are right now either being born, or growing inside the belly of a very different mommy." Jenna tucked a stray piece of hair behind her ear, composing herself. "I was okay with it when I knew I'd never be able to give my child what someone else could: riding lessons or theatre classes or family dates on Friday nights at paint-your-own-pottery places. But if I were with you—" She shook her head. "I don't care what those psychologists try to tell me every freaking time. It *is* like giving up a child for adoption."

Trevor shifted in his seat.

"I don't expect you to know what to say. I don't know what to say. Jesus." She put her head in her hand and pressed her cool palm against her forehead. "Gotta love science, right?"

"Jenna—"

"So Trevor, if I were ever to someday get married and have a child, and that child wanted to marry someone here in the city, they'd better be damned sure to get a DNA test so they're not marrying their half-sibling." Slumping, she leaned back in her seat. "It gets even better, since I don't want to leave New York and my eggs have been donated here, well, the chances go way up that my teenager could date his sibling. One hell of a prom night, right? With me screaming at my son not to do anything romantic, because unknowingly, he could be dating his sister…?" She shuddered, finally making eye contact with him. "Now do you understand? Do you see now why I can't have a relationship that could ever become more? Now do you see that if I had a relationship with someone as wonderful as you, every day of my life I would regret having given away what could have been our child…? It sucks and I hate it." Jenna drew in a large gulp of air. "Now do you see why there can never be an 'us?' "

"I…"

The look in his eyes told her what she needed to know. He dropped his head.

"I told you, you didn't want to know this." Jenna pushed her chair back from the table and made her way to the door.

Dropping money onto the table, Trevor ran after her. "Jenna!"

****

It was too late. The cold New York air smacked against him as she hailed a passing cab and climbed inside. Trevor watched in disbelief as the only woman he ever loved sped away.

Chapter Nineteen

Of course she shouldn't drink. Drinking was the absolute last thing she should do, but it was also the only thing that made any sense right now. As Jenna sat in the cab, her cell rang, over and over. Her stomach ached. She hated ignoring his calls but she had nothing left to say to Trevor. He was a great guy, and he deserved a woman who could give him the life he wanted, a woman who wasn't answering to a mother and a ghost.

The damned cell rang again, so she clicked it off, jumping out of the cab at a random address somewhere far from Trevor's place and hers. Stumbling up the street, Jenna entered the first noisy bar she could find, hoping the sound of bad karaoke would drown out her sadness.

The place was dark and dingy, with dark wood paneling on the walls and a low tin ceiling. Dart boards covered the walls. One long bar made of wood sat near the opposite wall. People singing karaoke stood on a low rickety-looking platform stage.

Jenna maneuvered through the crowd, throwing herself against the bar. She ordered a shot of bourbon, and after flashing her ID, ordered another. She dropped her clutch onto the bar and quickly downed the shots. Staring at the empty glasses, she yanked her arm away from a man at her side, whose arm touched hers.

"What are you drinking?"

Jenna didn't bother to respond. Why would she? She'd just walked away from *Trevor Hughes*, the sexiest, strongest, smartest, most gorgeous man on the planet.

"Bitch." The man stormed off.

Jenna pulled herself onto a high bar stool, balancing on the round, brown leather seat as she ordered and drank another and another, until finally, the room grew fuzzy. With her stomach burning, she pushed back from the bar. Her gaze settled on the blurry stage where a band began warming up as even more bad karaoke assaulted her ears. Finally, she had a lucid thought: she had just done the stupidest thing any woman in New York City could do; she was all alone and out of control.

Panic shot through Jenna, sobering her up the tiniest bit, and she glanced around the room. Bodies, smashed up against each other, swayed to an off-key karaoke love ballad. All of these lonely souls, just trying to make a connection. Jenna raised her hand, signaling for the bartender. She drowned her fear in another shot. Would this be her, a lonely soul with no hope for a life?

There was only one answer: drink more. Jenna ordered another round, and by her sixth—seventh?— shot of bourbon, standing was a challenge. She clung to the bar, trying to steady herself then gestured for the bartender who made his way over.

"No way." The bartender shook his head. "You're cut off, kid."

Giant tears gathered in Jenna's eyes before spilling down her cheeks. She threw her arms onto the bar, and ignoring the odor of stagnant water and stale beer, she placed her sweaty forehead against the cold wood. While the music pounded through her head, she sobbed.

"Hey, kid." The bartender was back. "You're all dressed up. You alone?"

Jenna nodded without lifting her head. "Yes." She finally made unsteady eye contact and banged a fist against the bar. "Ow." Even her moan was pathetic. She shook the pain away. "Very alone."

"Look, we've all been there, kid. A broken heart sucks."

"Yes," Jenna whispered, desperately wanting another drink. "So how 'bout another?"

"No way." The bartender wiped the bar in front of her.

Jenna nodded, straightening herself up. She slid off the stool and tried to stand, tottering. She fell against a man standing next to her, bracing herself as she bumped against his arm. He helped her upright before turning back to his date.

The bartender crossed his arms. "I can't let you leave like this. Who can I call?"

"No one." Jenna shook her hands and breathed deeply, trying to regain composure. She swiveled her head to the door and the room spun. Damn, that door was so, so far away. Hoisting up her fitted lace dress, she jumped onto the stool again, as the floor rose up. She balanced herself, just in time.

The bartender handed a beer to a customer and said to her, "There's got to be someone."

"I'm alone. Always have been and always will be." A tear fell again. What was that expression about happy drunks? It sure wasn't her. The more alcohol she consumed, the more miserable she was.

The bartender grabbed her clutch and pulled out the cell. Before Jenna could make sense of what he was doing, he pushed a button and gave the bar's address.

"Oh, crap." Jenna put her head down again.

"Yeah, I called your, 'In Case of Emergency' number. Hold on." The bartender dashed off then returned, holding a mug of black coffee. "Here."

"Black?" Jenna turned up her nose, the smell making her nauseated.

"Drink it, kid. Ever been drunk before?"

"Once." Jenna nodded as her stomach flipped. "But not like this."

"Fun, huh?"

"No…"

"No. And the guy I just called, he didn't sound very happy to find you're drunk and alone at a bar."

"Crap." Jenna blew on the coffee and sipped. It was so bitter she scrunched up her face. How did Trevor drink this?

The bartender popped open beer tops and handed the beers across the bar. "Most people who come in here to get drunk because they're heartbroken; no one cares enough about them to be mad at them."

"Lucky me." Jenna moaned into her sleeve.

"Yeah, lucky you. I'd give up my studio in Brooklyn for a house in Jersey if it meant someone cared that much about me."

Jenna made unsteady eye contact with the bartender, his words resonating through her fuzzy brain. Before she could make sense of them, someone shoved the karaoke mic into her hand. The mic was cold, but her body began to warm as she swayed along with the intro of a slow dirge, a classic rock song she knew and loved.

Holding her breath, Jenna hopped off the barstool, landing hard on her feet. She giggled, staggering her way to the stage, a snickering crowd parting as she wobbled past. Missing the first step, Jenna finally made it up onto the riser as the intro ended, and the music played. Still swaying, she began to sing, clearly and in a higher key than the song, but in perfect pitch. After a few more measures the band, which had been warming up, joined her, the drummer first and then the guitar players. They played along, their heads bobbing with the music. The saxophone player was the last to join.

By the time Jenna reached the third verse, Trevor had walked in. Her heart thumped, sweat dripping down her back. Tears filled her eyes as he gazed at her, but still, she kept singing. He made his way to the base of the stage, only a few feet away from her. Almost all of the women in the bar turned to him, some obviously recognizing him, others simply in awe of this gorgeous man in a tux who just walked into a dive bar. Woman after woman pushed to stand closer to him, but Trevor's gaze never swayed.

Jenna finished her song and the crowd applauded, thickening around the stage as they waited for the band. The band members went to shake her hand, but she just stood there, completely still, lost and confused...staring at Trevor. Someone squeezed her waist. She wheeled around to see the sax player by her side, his arm draped around her.

Jenna gasped as he pulled her closer, and she stumbled into him. "No." She pulled away from him but he held tight. He leaned down, his breath reeking of cigarettes, hot on her face. "I said, no." Jenna fought to wedge her hands between them, but before she could pull away, Trevor was there. He pushed the sax player off Jenna, and she threw her arms around Trevor's neck. "Trevor..." she whispered softly.

****

Thank God she was okay. Thank God he arrived when he did. Trevor wrapped his arms around Jenna's tiny waist and held her as the crowd disappeared around them. But that sax player...Trevor shook his head, exhaling loudly. He turned to the musician. "Are we going to have a problem?"

The sax player put up his hand. "No, man." He skulked away.

God damn it. Trevor breathed deeply again, fighting to keep his anger in check. That sax player was an asshole but he needed to focus on Jenna, not some random guy at a bar. Keeping his arm tight around her middle, he led her to the bar to settle up. "What does she owe you?" he said through clenched teeth.

"It's cool." The bartender nodded to Trevor. "She's pretty heartbroken and I think it's the first time she's ever been this drunk."

"No, it's not cool." Trevor's chest heaved in anger. "She stood at your bar and you let her get drunk. Here." He dropped a hundred dollar bill on the counter. "I have to think that will cover anything she had to drink. It couldn't take much to get her drunk."

"You don't have to be such an asshole, man. I didn't have to call you." The bartender picked up the money. Muttering, he wandered off.

Trevor sighed heavily, clamping his free hand to the back of his neck. Damn it. The man was right.

"Hey." Trevor signaled for the bartender who approached. "I appreciate you calling me. Really." Trevor dug into his pocket and pulled out another hundred. He handed it to the bartender.

"Thanks, man." The bartender pocketed the hundred. "I see a lot of drunks. But she's just a kid. Thinks she's all alone. I'm glad you came for her."

Trevor looked down at Jenna, her hair fallen loose, her hands gripping his arm, and he knew right then and there, no matter how infuriated he was with her, he never wanted her to be alone, ever again. But that may not be his decision to make. He wrapped his arm around her waist and led Jenna out of the bar.

Outside, he stood her against the wall. It wouldn't take long for the cold New York air to sober her up. Why would she do this? Damn it, damn it, damn it. Anger coursed through his veins, bubbling up inside him. He needed to release it somewhere, somehow, but she could never withstand the battery of words he would unleash to express the fury he felt.

Trevor paced back and forth, running his hand through his hair, trying to calm down. He needed to get hold of himself. He counted to one hundred forward and backward. He sucked in a deep breath and another, fighting for rational thought. How dare she put herself in this much danger? What if he wasn't able to get there in time? What if someone like that sax player had taken advantage of the situation and hurt her?

"Ugh." Trevor wheeled around and faced her. The thought of something bad happening to her made his gut ache. He wanted her home—at his place—where he could watch out for her and protect her. He contemplated locking her away and never letting her go. Her actions were those of a child. Maybe that's what she needed, to be treated like one. Damn it. He wasn't thinking clearly. "One one thousand, two one thousand..." He paced, fighting against the cold Manhattan wind, as he counted again. He took another deep breath, cooling his temper, finally able to approach her.

She stood exactly where he had put her, her teeth chattering, her nose red. Her eyes, like two bright shining spotlights, followed his every move. Trevor's shoulders slumped and his tight muscles unclenched slightly. There was no way he could stay mad at her, but still, that didn't change the fact her actions had been childish and dangerous. He would tell her all of this when they talked everything out but it would be later, not while she was freezing on a New York City street corner.

He inhaled sharply, the cold biting his lungs. Looking deep into Jenna's glassy eyes, he searched for the answer—would there be a later? "Come on." Trevor took Jenna by the hand and led her to his limo.

****

Jenna woke up the next morning achy and confused. She sat up quickly, grabbing the soft, familiar bed sheet and pulling it up, tucked it around her. She looked down to see she was wearing one of her t-shirts. Rubbing her blurry eyes, she struggled to make out her surroundings. Dirty laundry pile, magazines on the floor, sink filled with dishes. She was home, in her apartment, without him. Jenna's face fell, and she swallowed hard, pulling her knees up to her body. She was alone.

"Trevor?" she called tentatively but there was no

answer. He wasn't there. He had taken her home and left. She reached out and found her cell phone on the bottom of her bed. With shaking fingers, she called one of the few numbers programmed into the cell.

"Hey, this is Trevor, please leave me a message."

Jenna cleared her throat. "Uh. Hi, Trevor. It's…Jenna. Anyway, um, thank you for—well, all of it. I was hoping we could talk. But uh, well, thanks again. Bye." Her throat aching, Jenna clicked off her phone and sat perfectly still on her bed, staring out her tiny window.

An hour passed, and Trevor still hadn't called.

Jenna climbed out of bed, her body achy from her hard mattress. Then it dawned on her, he would never leave her alone with her door unlocked. She raced to her front door, but the locks were bolted. He must have used Luis and Loretta's keys.

Jenna sighed and stumbled to her fridge, hoping for a miracle. Pulling open the door, she found one. There, in the otherwise bare refrigerator was a bottle of orange juice, a bag of bagels, and a tub of cream cheese.

"Huh." Jenna stood up, a tiny smile cracking her glum expression. She grabbed the juice then noticed a bottle of painkillers on the table. Opening the bottle and dropping two tablets onto her palm, Jenna sighed. Swallowing back the pills, she rubbed an ache in her chest, the ache telling her she had really blown it this time.

****

He didn't come to her dressing room before the show. Actually, the first time all day she saw him was onstage. He was there, fully present and magic to play off, but when the show ended, he disappeared.

Panic swirled inside Jenna as she stripped out of her Ophelia costume and hurried into her street clothes. Faster and faster she rushed, terrified she would miss him and he would be gone. Unreachable. Ungettable. Leaving on her stage makeup, she sprinted to his dressing room. His door was open and he stood inside with his back to her. Jenna sighed with relief, lingering outside his door. His gaze caught hers in the mirror.

"Hello, Jenna."

"Hi, Trevor." She rolled her shoulder forward, leaning against the doorway, her body aching to be with him. "I was, uh, hoping…could we talk?"

"What about?" He turned to her, his voice cold.

"About last night." She pushed off the doorway and shuffled from foot to foot. "Um, can I come in?"

Trevor shrugged. "Of course."

As she entered his dressing room, her heart raced. She had never before felt quite this invested. She wiped her clammy hands on her jeans, as he slowly unbuttoned his shirt. Yanking it off his body, he fixed his gaze on her. Her breath hitched at the sight of him, so strong and powerful. She looked at his tattoo and her fingers tingled, aching to touch it. Aching to touch him.

Trevor mopped up his sweat with the shirt. "So? Let's talk." Tossing it aside, he stood there bare-chested.

"I uh…"

Cast members walked by Trevor's dressing room, but her focus never veered from him. She cleared her throat. "Could we go talk somewhere? Maybe? I just got paid. Buy you some cherry pie?" She bit her lip, praying her banter might work.

"No, thank you." Trevor crossed his arms in front

of his chest and leaned back against the shelf of the dressing mirror.

She nodded. "Oh, uh, okay. Well, first off, I want to say thank you. You took care of me last night, and although I don't remember all of it, I know you brought me home. And got me painkillers and food. Thank you."

"You're welcome." He didn't move from his spot.

"Trevor." Jenna looked up at him, her eyes pleading. "Please. Please tell me how to fix this."

"How to fix what, Jenna?"

"Us." Her breathing grew faster and faster as she fought back tears.

"Is there an 'us'? Because last night, you very clearly told me there was no hope for anything."

"I know." Jenna nodded, looking down at her feet. "But Trevor..." She gazed up at him. "Today, thinking you were gone, the thought of being without you..." Her words fell away.

Trevor sighed deeply. He pulled a chair from his dressing table and placed it next to her, nodding at it. She sat. He resumed his spot, leaning against the shelf. "Jenna, more than anything, I want there to be a you and me. But I'm not sure there can be."

She gasped, covering her mouth with her hand. "I told you, you wouldn't like it when you learned the truth. I knew you would hate the fact that I was a donor."

"No, that's not it at all. I just wasn't expecting it. But that doesn't bother me, unless you feel forced into it."

"Of course I'm forced into it. Why else would I do it? But if that's not it, then what? Is it because I

277

screwed up last night? Getting drunk?"

"Of course not. Everyone makes mistakes. The only thing I'm worried about is your safety."

She swallowed hard.

"But Jenna, I've never done anything halfway in my life, and I sure as hell don't plan to start with you. I want to be with you, but if we're together, we do it for real. And that means there are rules to follow."

Jenna's heart thumped so hard she felt it in her ears. "Rules?"

"Yes, rules. I can't play games. But I understand you're twenty-two, so maybe, as much as I want you to be, you're just not ready."

"Trevor, I am ready. I—I don't know how to do it, but I want to be with you. Last night, without you…waking up today, thinking I lost you…please, Trevor. Let's try to fix this."

He nodded. "Then we need groundwork. And the first rule is, we talk. Always. I know you're young and I know you're passionate. I would never want to change that. And I'm certain there's a lifetime of arguments ahead of us, but no more running away. Ever. We talk like two adults and we work through our problems. Understood?"

She nodded.

"Good. Next, when it comes to your safety, I win. Every time. All the time."

"I—"

"Jenna?"

He moved closer to her, and her breath hitched.

"Yes."

"Next time you want to go on a drunken karaoke binge, I come along." He raised his eyebrows. "Got it?"

She nodded. "Yes. But there won't be any drinking for me for a while."

"Damn right there won't be."

Jenna opened her lips but no words came out. Heat overtook her cheeks as she closed her mouth, her eyes wide. He reached out, took her arm and gently pulled her to her feet, backing her against the wall. Her chest heaved in time with her breath as he towered over her, shirtless, and so incredibly sexy.

"Jenna, just as I don't want to change you, you can't change me. I am a man. And I'm not entirely sure you know what that means. But I am stronger, and more successful, and if we do this, we do it for real. You cannot ask me to stand by while you donate your eggs to get money, or starve, or put yourself in harm's way. I won't do it. If we do this, we make a life together. My money is yours, and we make smart, educated decisions, together."

"Trevor, I—"

"I'm not done. You never risk your health, either. Without mentioning your name, I called the clinic."

"What?" Jenna rocked forward, his energy holding her against the wall. "How did you find the right one?"

"Loretta went back to your apartment last night. She still had keys, thankfully. She found the fertility drugs and we got the name of the doctor. Anyway, although I'm not thrilled you went on a drinking binge last night,"—Trevor raised his eyebrows—"you will be fine. But Jenna, I'm going to tell you this right now, if we are together, I won't let you donate."

He leaned forward, and heat radiated between them.

"So you need to decide now. Jenna, do you want to

leave me?"

Her breathing grew shallower, her body warming. A vein pulsed in his temple. "No, Trevor. Of course I don't want to leave you. But I need the money. I still have to make sure my mother and sister have enough. I don't want my sister working in the laundry business."

"Didn't you hear what I just said? My money is yours."

"But you take care of Amanda and Toby, and there's no way I'll let that be affected by me. No way, Trevor."

"I appreciate you worrying about them and I promise it won't. Jenna. You will have more money than you'll ever need."

She shook her head. "But you're sick of being Caspian. I can't let you keep going—"

He closed his eyes then slowly opened them. "There isn't a choice here, baby. I'll do what I need to do, and who knows, maybe in a few years you'll be established, and I can produce or run my theatre. But for right now, I'll take care of everything."

"But—"

"Everything, Jenna."

She closed her eyes and leaned toward him. Opening them, she swallowed, her voice a whisper. "But what I've done…"

"Donating? You haven't done anything wrong, Jenna. On the contrary, what you did was to give someone else a chance at a life they couldn't have otherwise. But how you feel about it, that's what we can work on. We'll get you someone to talk to if that's what you need. And we'll handle worrying about our kids when we get there."

She smiled, her insides warming.

"But you can't plan to spend the rest of your life alone because you were an egg donor. It's not reasonable."

"I know."

"And it's an incredibly lonely existence."

"Yes."

"So no more 'friend' talk, and this can't be some casual fling. If you're with me, you're with me—for real. As my girlfriend." He reached out and stroked her hair. "Jenna, on the day I met you, something changed in me. I remembered what it was like to be an actor, not just some shiny character on TV. You made me want more for myself."

"Trevor—"

"Shh. Please. Let me finish." He smiled. "Then I realized it was way more than that. You reminded me what it was like to be alive and have passion. My feelings toward you grow more and more, every minute we're together. And I ache those times we're apart. Then I realized it wasn't about me or my feelings, at all. All those things you did for me, they're great, but what really mattered to me was you. I wanted you to be happy. And then last night, when you disappeared and I thought…" He ran a hand through his hair. "I thought something bad had happened to you…Jenna, your dad…"

"My dad?" Jenna cocked her head, fighting to understand.

"Did your dad ever tell you he gave up on his dream?"

"No, but—"

"No 'buts.' Did he ever say he gave up his dream

because of you?"

"No." Jenna shook her head. "But Trevor, no one moves from New York City to a hick town upstate by choice. No one gives up an acting career to open a laundry business, because they want to."

"That's the funny thing about dreams, Jen. They change. Believe me." He smiled, reaching out to stroke her hair. "I don't think your dad gave up on his dream. I think you were his dream come true. All I want is to be with you and make all your dreams come true." His hand came to rest on her cheek. She closed her eyes. "But you have to trust me, Jenna."

"I do."

He smiled, and his hands dropped down to her waist. He pushed her tighter against the wall. "Jenna, I don't think you understand the depth of my feelings for you." He slipped his hands into her t-shirt, resting them on the warm skin of her back. She shivered with his touch. He leaned forward, kissing her lightly on the lips, and pulled back. "You're still in trouble for last night." A grin spread across his face. "But we'll handle that when we get home."

"Home?" She tilted her head.

"Yes, home. To my place. I just have to figure out how to get you moved in, considering your complete aversion to money."

"What?"

Trevor leaned forward again and touched his forehead to hers. "You heard me." His voice was low and breathy. "You can paint, redecorate, whatever you want. But be with me. And if I still haven't convinced you we can live your grunge lifestyle with money, well then, we'll move into your place."

She giggled.

"So what do you say?" He looked into her eyes as he leaned against her.

Jenna couldn't contain her smile. "Let me think…" She tapped her finger against her chin. "What's the word you so eloquently used all that time ago? At my audition? Oh, yes, I think that would be 'awesome.' "

"Oh, you little brat."

Jenna slipped out from his grasp and bounced away.

"You'd better hope I don't catch you."

It only took a few steps for him to grab Jenna. She squealed as he pinned her to the wall again. He rested his forearms along the wall, framing her body. She rocked back and forth in the protective nest his arms and torso made for her. "I want you…" His voice was hot against the nape of her neck. "So much. Right now." Stooping, Trevor pressed against her, his bare chest hard against her breasts. Her eyes half closed. He planted a soft kiss on her neck, and she moaned.

"Trevor?"

"Yes, baby?" He pulled back.

"Do you think I'll be letting someone down? Someone who was waiting for me to be a donor?"

"I knew you'd be worried about that so I did some quick research and it seems it happens all the time. Someone else will donate in your place if you say no. Unless, of course…you want to do it?"

She shook her head. "No, Trevor. I never did."

"Then it's settled."

She flushed, smiling at him.

"My God, you are so beautiful and so talented." He kissed her on the nose.

"Mmm…"

"And so smart." He kissed her gently on the lips.

"And so lucky," she added. "I am incredibly lucky to be with you, Trevor. And not just because you're gorgeous and successful, but because you're a really great guy. Thank you."

He smiled. "You're one other thing, too."

"What's that?"

"Loved. I'm in love with you, Jenna Joyce. I have never said 'I love you' to another living soul. And I've wanted to tell you that for a long time. I love you."

He leaned down and kissed her full on the mouth.

"I love you too, Trevor." Jenna placed her hands on his chest. "So we're really going to give this a try?"

"No." Trevor pushed himself back, his finger tracing her cheek. "We're not going to try, Jenna; we're going to do. This isn't an improv. I wrote the script and I like it so we're going to follow it. It just took me longer than I planned to get you to act two."

"What's act two?"

"When you're finally my girlfriend." He softly kissed her again and leaned against her in just the right way. "And then, when you're ready, we'll take some even bigger steps together. Okay?"

"Okay." She closed her eyes. "Trevor?"

"Mm, baby?" He eased his hands up inside her t-shirt.

"What's act three, then?" She gasped as he pulled her closer.

His hands drifted downward, wrapping around her. "They lived happily ever after, of course."

Epilogue

Four years later

The grass tickled Jenna's legs as she sat on the hillside, looking out over the mountains of upstate New York. She held the baby close, nuzzling him, his full, black, curly hair tickling her chin. She bounced him in her lap but he wouldn't stop crying.

Trevor joined them. "Want me to try?"

"Be my guest." She handed the baby to Trevor. His arms flexed as he took the baby. Wow. As good as he always looked, he looked even better holding a baby. Jenna shook her head. "Loretta said he had her up most of the night. Teething."

Trevor held the baby from him, bouncing him as he spoke. "Hey, little man. Hey, Luis Jr."

The baby shrieked louder, and Trevor frowned.

Jenna giggled. "I think he wants Loretta or his dad. Is Luis in rehearsal?"

"Yeah." Trevor moved the baby into a different position but he continued to cry. "I don't want to disturb Luis. He opens in a week. And poor Loretta's getting a much needed nap."

"We'll handle it, then."

Luis Jr. calmed a bit as Trevor drew the baby to his chest. Jenna smiled, understanding the baby's reaction. She leaned back, tilting her head and looked lovingly at

Trevor. "Ever look at us and wonder how we got here?"

"I know how we got here." Trevor held the baby up and made a funny face at him. "I chased you until you gave in."

"Ha." Jenna clicked her tongue and looked away. "But just a few years ago everything was so different. And now we've been married for three years and you left Caspian and produce full time. We run a thriving summer theatre in upstate New York. Olivia's away at a good school and my mom is happier, and thank God, Amanda and Toby are okay—I mean, it's everything I've ever wanted. And more."

Trevor looked at her. "How many times do I have to tell you, Jen? If you just give me a chance, I will make your every dream come true." He took her hand and kissed it.

"Well there's one more wish I've been thinking about."

"A new role?" Trevor raised his eyebrows.

"Yup." Jenna bit her lip, playfully.

Trevor bounced the baby. "Well, Luis has the house sold out for the rest of the summer. I'm thinking we should extend him main stage. Oh, and has Kat given you dates yet on the sci-fi sequel? Who knew my little theatre geek would become a bona fide movie star?"

"I'd hardly call me a star."

"I would. So do you have dates?"

"Kind of...we're not going into production until next year."

"Really?" Trevor pulled his attention away from Luis Jr. and looked at Jenna.

"She has an indie for me. I want you to read the

script of course, but we'd start filming in LA immediately and Kat said I'll be done in two months."

"Nice. We'll leave for LA next week? Once Luis is set?" The baby fussed, and Trevor rocked him again.

"That's fine." Jenna gazed out over the mountains. "Although I hate leaving here. There is something just magical about this place."

"Yes." Trevor gazed at her.

"So I was thinking..." Jenna drew her legs up under her, running her hands along the grass.

"The role?" Trevor lifted the baby, making him laugh. "That's you, Jen, trying to schedule a show before you take off to film another movie. So what are you thinking?"

"I was thinking, maybe...Stella?"

"Really?" Trevor turned to her, wrinkling his brow. "*Streetcar*?"

"Feel like playing Stanley? You'd be spectacular."

She took the baby back and rocked him. Trevor smiled at her and Jenna's heart melted.

"You think you're ready for Stella?"

Trevor ran his hand up through his hair and Jenna recognized that look of serious concentration.

"I think I'd better be."

"Okay, but we'll need—"

Jenna took Trevor's hand to quiet him. "I'm ready now."

Trevor looked at her sideways. He shifted on the grass, balancing his arms on his knees, and sucked in a huge breath of the fresh upstate air. "I'm not sure I understand, Jen. I get the distinct feeling you're not just talking about a show."

She nodded. "I think *Streetcar* would be a good

choice because Stella and I have something in common." She looked directly into Trevor's eyes. "I skipped this month, Trevor."

"Skipped what?"

Luis Jr.'s hand captured Trevor's finger. Trevor shook it and the baby giggled.

Jenna waited for Trevor to look at her again. When he did, she raised her eyebrows.

He repeated his question. "Skipped what, babe?"

She smiled again.

Carefully shaking free of the baby, Trevor quickly stood up. Jenna clutched Luis Jr. and stood too.

"What?" Trevor's eyes grew wide, and he leaned over, running his hands through her hair until they came to rest, cupping her chin. "Are you sure?"

"I've never skipped before, so I took a test this morning and well…"

"You're pregnant?" Trevor tilted his head.

"Seems so."

"Oh, Jen."

Trevor embraced her with Luis Jr. squeezed between them, and Luis Jr. giggled in response. Trevor pulled back, making sure he hadn't squished the baby. Jenna moved Luis Jr. to her hip, and Trevor reached out to touch her belly. "Jen, I just can't believe…"

"Believe, Trevor. You're going to be a daddy."

Trevor smiled at Jenna so completely, it warmed her core. He wrapped his arm around her from behind, his hand resting on her tummy, holding them both protectively. Luis Jr. grabbed a piece of Jenna's hair and chewed it while they looked out over the mountains.

"You hungry?" Trevor laughed.

"No." Jenna leaned into him. "Just happy. For all these years Trevor, you've wanted to make my every wish come true, and you have."

"And you've made mine come true as well, Jen. Marrying me and now this...this is more than I ever could have asked for. I can't believe you're having my baby."

She turned and stood on her tip-toes as he leaned down and kissed her.

Smiling, Trevor broke away and placed his hand back onto her abdomen for a few moments longer. Then he whispered into Jenna's ear. "Joy."

"What's 'Joy'?"

"The baby's name. What do you think?"

"I love it...unless it's a boy."

"It's not. She's going to be a little spitfire like her mom."

"Mom. I like that word." Jenna looked up at Trevor. "Why Joy?"

"Well, she'll be my joy. Like her mom." Trevor smiled.

Jenna beamed at him.

"And also to honor your dad—it'll almost carry on your family name, Joyce, since you changed your name to Hughes."

Tears welled in Jenna's eyes. Careful of Luis Jr., she threw her free arm around Trevor's neck. He pulled her close. "You can't hurt the baby, you know. She's well protected in there."

"I know that." Trevor held her at arms' length. "I know she has the best mom in the world, a mom who was worried about her long before she ever came to be."

Jenna smiled at him as he stroked her face.

His brow knitted. "But it's my job to take care of you both. And I will."

"Oh, I know."

Jenna laughed as her handsome, successful, wonderful, protective husband wrapped his arm around her and pulled her close. He kissed her so completely, there was no doubt, their life was absolutely meant to be.

A word from the author...

To Be or Not To Be: The Actors, has a special place in my heart, as I began my career in NYC, sometimes working in decrepit theatres just like Jenna's theatre…in the basement of ancient churches, with no plumbing and puddles the size of ponds backstage.

I am very excited to bring you *To Be or Not To Be: The Actors*, the next book in The New York Artists series, standalone novels about strong, artistic men, and the smart, unexpected women they fall for. If you like sexy, tortured rock stars, I hope you read and enjoy Book 1 in the series, *Summer of Irreverence: The Rock Star!*

I am a bestselling author. I write "gritty romance," and I'm also the author of *The Letting* and *The Coupling*, books 1 and 2 of The Letting series. I began my career as an award-winning playwright, and I am a proud member of RWA, PAN. I have my BA in English and my MA in Theatre.

The loves in and of my life include: Luna Bars, decaf coffee, yoga, Hemingway, Bukowski, family and friends, and above all, my husband and my two young girls.

To find out more about the New York Artists series, The Letting series, and what's coming soon, please visit: www.CathrineGoldstein.com

Thanks so much, and I hope you enjoy!